Blood Sports

Blood Sports

EDEN ROBINSON

McCLELLAND & STEWART

Library and Archives Canada Cataloguing in Publication

Robinson, Eden
Blood sports / Eden Robinson.

ISBN 13: 978-0-7710-7604-6
ISBN 10: 0-7710-7604-5

I. Title.

PS8585.035143B56 2006   C813'.54   C2005-905384-4

We acknowledge the financial support of the Government of Canada through the
Book Publishing Industry Development Program and that of the Government of
Ontario through the Ontario Media Development Corporation's Ontario Book
Initiative. We further acknowledge the support of the Canada Council for the Arts
and the Ontario Arts Council for our publishing program.

The epigraph on page v is taken from "Burn Man on a Texas Porch,"
a story in the collection *19 Knives* by Mark Anthony Jarman.
Copyright © Mark Anthony Jarman. Used by permission of
House of Anansi Press, 110 Spadina Ave., Suite 801, Toronto, ON, M5V 2K4.

The lyrics on page 216 are from "Sunshine On My Shoulders." Words by John Denver
Music by John Denver, Mike Taylor and Dick Kniss
Copyright © 1971; Renewed 1999 Cherry Lane Music Publishing Company, Inc.
(ASCAP), Dimensional Music Of 1091 (ASCAP), Anna Kate Deutschendorf,
Zachary Deutschendorf and Jesse Belle Denver for the U.S.A.
All Rights for Dimensional Music Of 1091, Anna Kate Deutschendorf and Zachary
Deutschendorf Administered by Cherry Lane Music Publishing Company, Inc. (ASCAP)
All Rights for Jesse Belle Denver Administered by WB Music Corp. (ASCAP)
International Copyright Secured   All Rights Reserved

Typeset in Janson by M&S, Toronto
Printed and bound in Canada

This book is printed on acid-free paper that is
100% ancient-forest friendly (40% post-consumer recycled).

McClelland & Stewart Ltd.
75 Sherbourne Street
Toronto, Ontario
M5A 2P9
www.mcclelland.com

1 2 3 4 5   10 09 08 07 06

Hate is everything they said it would be and it waits for you like an airbag.

– Mark Anthony Jarman,

from *19 Knives*

CONTENTS

AURA

Hi Mel,

If you're not eighteen yet, I want you to put this letter down right now. Okay? There's a whole bunch of shit you don't need to deal with until you're ready. Your mom (I call her Paulie, even though she hates it. Try it, and you'll get her Popeye squint) and I talked it over. We agreed not to put the heavy on you because we're trying not to fuck your head up too bad.

You probably won't be Melody when you read this. I'm wondering what Paulie will change your name to. Paulie was stuck on Anastasia, after the princess, but I thought no one would be able to spell it and you'd get tagged with Stacy or Staz or anything but your real name. My top choice was Sarah, but Paulie thought that was going to bite you in the ass in school when you met up with the hundred other Sarahs in your class. We went through a whole bunch of baby-name books, and couldn't agree on a single name. Paulie's picks were too fancy and she thought mine were dull. Her words in the operating room: "If you fucking stick my girl with *Jennifer* while I'm under, I will rip your nuts off."

Paulie wanted an all-natural birth at home. Her friends here are into hippie shit like giving birth in wading pools and eating the placenta. Besides, she hates hospitals, doesn't think they're clean enough and hated the thought of you in a germ-factory. I'm not a big fan of hospitals myself, so we were all set to have you enter the world at home (no pool or placenta though). But things got hairy, and Ella, the midwife, called an ambulance. Paulie kept saying she'd spent enough of her life wasted and didn't want any shit, but she ended up having every drug in the book. I'm sure when she's mad she tells you what a pain you were to deliver.

Paulie exploded when they put the tent around her belly because she wanted to watch you coming, even if they were going to cut you out. Is your mom all ladylike now? Ha. I bet she is. You wouldn't believe the things that came out of her mouth, but they put the tent up anyway and she asked me to videotape everything so she could watch it later. I saw the first incision and said, "Can't do it, Paulie."

The midwife wouldn't videotape, but she said she'd describe everything to Paulie. Ella is this tiny fireball, a Filipina in her mid-forties, and she had to hop to peek over. I went and found her a stool and then waited in the hallway because there was no way I could listen to that. I walked down to the vending machine and got a coffee. So I missed your grand entrance. But we have a tape of everything up to that point, even the ambulance ride. I'm sure Paulie's made you watch it by now. I stapled Ella's business card to the back of this page, so you can look her up if you want.

I could hear you crying. You were loud as an opera singer. I could hear you all the way down the hall. Sad fact: Your dad is a big old weenie. I got a head rush and had to sit down. When I finally got my rear in gear, the nurse and midwife were checking you out, cleaning you up and swaddling you in the corner. The surgeon was finishing up your mom. She was pretty wiped. We'd been awake for three days by then.

When Paulie asked Ella if she should nurse, Ella laid you on her and you latched just like that. No problemo. All the shit going down and you took it in stride. Your mom's smile, all proud of you.

"Come around here, you've got to see this," Paulie said. "It's like she's mainlining."

The nurse beside her stiffened. We'd had to disclose about Paulie being in Narcotics Anonymous. I think we freaked some of the staff. The whole week we were in the hospital, they acted like we were going to break out the rigs and turn our room into a shooting gallery.

I never got the deal with newborns. You were bald but hairy, red and wrinkled like any other newborn, and I'm sorry, Mel, but man, that is not a good look on you. You were sucking at Paulina's boob like there was no tomorrow, your eyes screwed tight in ecstasy.

Before she left, Ella made sure we had a six-pack of supplement. She showed me how to pour it into this plastic cup about the size of those ketchup cups they have at McDonald's. You were sleeping, and Ella said I was going to have to feed you and change your diapers because Paulie was against the wall.

When you have kids, you'll know what that first night is like. You were intense, babe. Jonesing for the boob-juice, as Paulie would say. I tried to tilt the cup slowly into your mouth but it got all over your face and down your neck. A nurse came running when you started freaking out. Once you were screaming, I dumped the formula down your throat and you choked it back.

Oh boy, were you mad. You had this "Fuck you, you cunt" look that your mom gets when she's in a pissy mood. I guess I was pretty punchy, because I started laughing. You were just too cute. You and your fuck-you look. Only a couple hours in the world, and you were already giving it attitude.

Paulie phoned her family to ask them to come check you out, but they were like, yeah, whatever. When Paulie was eight months pregnant, we realized we didn't have enough money for all the shit we needed. She dressed up all careful, and I dressed up all careful and we tried to go to them, and they were like, give it up. Let some nice couple adopt your kid. Junkies shouldn't raise kids. A whole bunch of shit like that, but with swearing and screaming. Paulie thought that once they saw we were serious, once they saw how cute you were, they'd come around.

Your mom's parents hated my guts from the get-go, so I can't say I was surprised or disappointed. If you go and talk to them, they're going to bad-mouth your mom. I know it. I've listened to enough of their crap. Let me tell you something: there's no one more sanctimonious than a dry drunk. It wasn't like they were saints, you know? But Paulie was their first addict, and they thought she was lower than them because they were just alcoholics.

The first time Paulie relapsed, her dad was like: "I knew you wouldn't last, you slutty piece of shit."

That's when your mom and I got together, after she got out of rehab. She wanted to make amends, admit to another human being.

How much has Paulie told you? I wish I knew. It's hard to write it down because it's all grown-up shit. You've been gone a few days now. Your mom and I decided that this was the best way to deal with things. Maybe it isn't, you know? We can't think of any-thing else to do, Mel.

I respect your mom. Yeah, she'd relapsed a couple of times, but that's the way it goes, you know? In the movies, everyone who goes straight stays straight. It's all "Oh, I will never touch that evil stuff again" and then whatever actor is playing a junkie will look all soppy and pleased, and end credits, happily ever after. But it takes time to realize how deep the hooks go. You never believe how hard they've sunk in until you try pulling them out. The first time you clean up, you feel immortal, untouchable. You get cocky. You want to test it out, ride that dragon one last time. Or you realize that your life is still in the crapper anyway and clean-ing up hasn't done fuck all. You hate yourself and everyone agrees that you are worth hating.

I don't know where your other Gran and Granpa are these days. Eugene and Chrissy Bauer, if you want to look them up. Eugene went MIA when I was two. Chrissy phones it in. You're going to have to do the heavy lifting to keep a relationship with her going. I'm not trying to discourage you from meeting them, but be warned they're big talkers. Their promises are sugar-covered shit.

I don't want you to think I'm not around because I don't care, Mel. Okay? Lots of things happened that had nothing to do with you. Daddy's knee-deep in a mess and has to dig himself out. Paulie and I agreed that it would be safer if you guys went away. Wherever you are, I'm thinking of you.

Bad news on the genetic front: my side of the family has never swum in the cool gene pool. I don't think they've even dipped their toes in it. Have you ever seen that televangelist who wears silver lamé muumuus on late-night TV? You know, the one who believes that God is an alien who will ride a comet to earth to kick-start the Apocalypse? He's a great-uncle of yours, sweetie, and our only claim to fame.

Your eczema is from our side of the family. Two of your aunts and a couple of your cousins have adult onset diabetes. The uncles mostly get Alzheimer's in their late sixties. I'm the only one with epilepsy, so the doctors don't think it's genetic, but that's their best guess.

It's not that scary, though. I don't even think about it most days. I'll run you through it. Put your palms on your temples. Okay? Cover the tops of your ears with your thumbs and your index fingers. Cup your head with your fingers. Your temporal lobes are patches of squiggly grey matter underneath your hands. Daddy has what they used to call temporal-lobe epilepsy, but now they call my type of epilepsy partial seizures secondarily generalized. They'll probably call it something else by the time you read this. They change the name every time they find out something new.

When Daddy freezes up, that first seizure is called an aura. Not the New-Age you-must-be-angry-because-you-have-a-lot-of-red-in-your-halo aura, but a sensory seizure. When it starts, I feel it in my stomach, like I'm seasick. Then it changes. You know that feeling you get after you've watched a scary movie late at night, alone, and you know no one's in the house with you. It's just your imagination but you can't stop being scared anyway. That's how that seizure feels.

The second seizure starts right after the first one, but I'm not awake for it. When you think of an epileptic attack, I'm sure you think of people falling down and convulsing. It's over in a few minutes, and Daddy wakes up tired, sore, and confused.

For a while, Daddy was self-medicating with pot. All those NA meetings rub off on you though, and Daddy realized he'd been over-medicating, and got himself down to two hoots, twice a day. Don't go overboard when you're trying pot, Mel. It's right up there with watching too much TV: a whole whack of your life passes you by, and you don't realize it until you stop. You get stuck in this zone not quite in the real world.

Your mom and I were always careful. Condoms and spermicide. Condoms every single time. You must have really wanted to be born, Mel. Paulie almost had a heart attack when she learned she was pregnant, and we started going to every NA meeting East Van had to offer. That was our life for two weeks: eat, shit, NA, eat, shit, NA, sleep. Wake up, eat, shit, NA. If there wasn't a NA meeting open, we went to AA. Paulie wasn't using when you were conceived, but she was shaky. She was at that point when she could have slipped over. And by then we both knew how easy it was to slip.

Jazz was Paulie's sponsor. They talked long and hard. Paulie just didn't say, fuck it, I'll have this kid. She thought about you. Everyone on The Drive who ever went to NA knew about you when you were the size of a cocktail shrimp because she'd fucking talk to everyone.

When Paulie makes up her mind, then it is game over. She took out every book in the library that said anything about being a mom. She badgered her way into parenting courses with waiting lists the length of your arm. She'd corner these new parents and quiz them until they got this glazed look, filled with the fear of God because this woman would not let go.

We were both scared shitless because we didn't think we were good enough for you, Mel. But we wanted you. You were the biggest risk we ever took. You were the only good thing to come out of a lot of bad.

The waiting room of Wal-Mart's photography studio had all the charm of a bus depot. Tom held Melody in his lap. The other parents were uniformly grubby, but their children sported starched name brands as they tore through the sticky selection of toys. Melody squirmed as she watched the children, lifting the hem of her dress to gum the lace. Tom brushed her hair to the side. Soft and white blond, it sprouted from her head like dandelion fluff.

Paulina wandered back with the promised McDonald's fries and, alas, the dreaded paint swatches.

Mel bounced excitedly at the sight of the fries. "Uh! Uh! Uh!"

"Just one," Paulie said, handing her a crisp, dark one, Mel's favourite kind of fry.

Paulie sat in the orange plastic chair one over from Tom, spreading the swatches out on the chair between them. Today's Sesame Street will be brought to you by the colour yellow, Tom thought, and every frigging shade of it imaginable. Mel slouched against him, her hair tickling his stubble. She gnawed contentedly.

"I'm leaning toward Lemon Zing," Paulie said. "With a Washday White trim. What do you think?"

"Which one's Lemon Zing?"

Paulie set it apart from the others. "I know it's a little darker than," shuffle, shuffle, "Prairie Snow, but the living room is so bright, maybe we should go with," shuffle, shuffle, "Summer Wheat."

"Uh! Uh! Uh!"

Paulie absently handed Mel another fry before Mel went ballistic.

"Lemon Zing reminds me of those Easter egg–shaped cookies my mom used to get half price."

Paulie stopped playing with the swatches to eyeball him, making sure he wasn't poking fun.

"You know," Tom said. "The ones with the crunchy icing. You only get them at Easter."

"Do you like the colour or don't you?"

"I like it."

"Hmm." Paulie scowled. "If we go with Lemon Zing in the living room and the hallway –" And she was off. He watched her mouth moving, her lips chapped and red. She used to wear cotton-candy-pink lipstick, or, when she was feeling dangerous, dark, dark red.

Looking around the room, Tom realized they looked as time-warped as the other parents. His plaid shirt with the grey thermal underwear poking through the holes, his shaggy hair, and ragged sneakers all screamed grunge, a look that had died four years ago with Kurt Cobain. Paulie dressed like she did in high school. Biker chick. Tight black jeans tucked into knee-high shit kickers and a low-cut Metallica tank top. She hadn't dyed her hair since she got pregnant, so from her ears down, her hair was frazzled strawberry blond. Her roots were light brown.

"Look at Paulina's real hair," his mother had said before their big blow out. "Yours is just as dark. Now look at Mel's. Tell me who she took after."

Mute with frustration, he hadn't said anything, hadn't been able to drag out Paulie's baby pictures in defence.

"And then look at her last boyfriend's hair. You can't tell me you've never wondered."

"Tom?" Paulie said. "I'd appreciate it if you actually fucking listened to me." When Paulie was seriously mad, her blue eyes went so dark they looked black. They narrowed, beady.

"Sorry," Tom mumbled.

"This is important to me."

"You're just hot, Paulie. Sometimes I get floored looking at you. You're so hot sometimes I can't think."

"You *asshole*," Paulie said, but her eyes lightened.

"Sorry."

Mel yawned.

Paulie gathered up the swatches and jammed them in her purse.

"Seventy-six," the assistant called out. "Number seventy-six."

"That's us," Paulie said, picking up Mel.

Tom reached beside the chair for the diaper bag. The middle-aged couple across from him grinned. The man touched the rim of his baseball cap. *Nice save*, he mouthed.

▮▮▮

Paulie dozed on the floor, letting Mel crawl over her. The phone rang and Tom picked up, expecting Jazz to ask for Paulie for their nightly catch-up. The line hummed in silence.

"Hello?" Tom said. He waited, and then sighed and hung up. He marked the time on the calendar. His mom was averaging three calls a week. They'd traced the numbers back to pay phones in the skids.

"She's still trying, which is more than my parents are doing," Paulie said. "Cut her some slack."

"I'm detaching," Tom said.

"Detach with love," Paulie said.

"If she keeps this up," Tom said. "I'm detaching with a restraining order."

"Tom," Paulie said.

"You know what gets me? She doesn't say anything. She's just waiting for me to break and pretend –" Tom shut his mouth. He didn't want to spend the rest of the night analyzing what was probably a drunken grand gesture on his mother's part.

Tom scooped up Mel and took a whiff of her diaper. He stood her in front of him. She reached for his hands, ready to be finger-walked around the room.

"You're choosing to hold this grudge," Paulie said. "And the only one it's hurting is you."

"Write that down," Tom said. "I'll read it back to you after Thanksgiving dinner at your parents' place."

Paulie threw her pillow at him. "You can be such a dink."

▐▐▐

"You are the son of a gambler and a whore," his Aunt Faith had told him when he was almost five. She'd reached down to stroke his hair as if this was a reassurance. The Greyhound had pulled into the station. VANCOUVER spelled in dull white letters on the bus's chrome forehead. His mother was inside buying their tickets, last minute. Her love of drama precluded planning. Aunt Faith guarded him and their luggage as they waited.

His mother burst through the doors, unmistakable with her mane of big bar-hair. She ran awkwardly in her laced-up granny boots, in the tight skirt with ruffles, pastel blue with matching pantyhose overlaid with ruffled socks, a popular look in the early eighties, ZZ Top–inspired fashion.

"It would have been better if they'd given you up for adoption or not had you." Aunt Faith so serious and scrubbed, grey sweater set and slacks under a tailored coat, pearls but no makeup, her skin under the fluorescent lights the colour of bread dough. In the winter air, her breath frosted over her head as she spoke. "Some people are not meant to be parents."

The bus had a sickly sweet smell of cheap strawberry air freshener and stale cigarette smoke. Tom knelt in his seat and rested his forehead against the window. His mother dozed beside him. The window was cold, but the heater beneath it blasted hot air. Tom's cheeks felt sunburnt if he stayed that way too long.

They'd scored the front seats by the door, overlooking the driver and the road ahead. The lights from passing cars and trucks and semis kept him awake, and now, in the pre-dawn, the view was the same as it had been yesterday: long stretches of highway dusted with blowing snow, rolling hills dotted with the occasional horse or cow herd. They'd had lunch in Calgary, his mother leaving their coats on the seats so no one would steal them.

"Do you want to play a video game?" his mother had asked. "Look, they have Pac Man."

"No."

"Do you want a chocolate bar?"

"No."

"Now I know there's something wrong," she said. "My sweet tooth never says no to candy." She felt his forehead. "How about a comic?"

She bought an *Archie & Jughead*. She pointed to the pictures and read the bubbles as the bus swayed.

"You're not laughing," she said. "What's wrong?"

Tom shook his head. "Nothing."

"Are you scared?"

"No."

"Are you sad about leaving your auntie? We can go out for Christmas once we're settled."

"I don't want to. She's mean."

His mother closed the comic. "What happened?"

"Nothing."

"Oh, Lord," his mother said. "Oh, honey, come here."

"No, no, I'm a big boy."

She pulled Tom into her lap. "She's not trying to be mean, you know. Do you remember when we talked about her being blunt? That's what she is. She likes you, Tommy."

"No, she doesn't."

"She does. She wouldn't have let us stay so long if she didn't like you."

"I'm tired."

"Whatever she said, she meant it in the best way. She thinks she's just being honest, but she doesn't know how she hurts people, and she doesn't understand why they don't like her any more. She's very, very lonely – Tommy, look!"

Mountains like crooked teeth glittered in the distance.

"Don't be sad, Tommy. The sun is shining and the whole world's opening up for us."

███

Paulie's favourite TV show repeated at 3 a.m. They found this out when Mel started teething. Mel had been sleeping through the night for two months, and they'd been smug because all the other parents in their parenting group were having problems getting their kids down. They'd even got Mel in her crib in her own room. Then her cheeks became red and chapped, her gums swelled, her weaning stopped, and her schedule went to crap. Mel was back in their bed, snuggled into Paulina. They temporarily moved the TV into the bedroom. The pert host of *DIY Live!* bounced around the set with starched bangs and a ponytail that bobbed with each excited flick of her head.

"I think she's on speed," Tom said.

"Who?" Paulie said.

"Ponytail, there."

"No, she's not."

"She's been fucking going on about *curtains* for an hour. She's got to be cranked, man."

"Window treatments, dummy. Shh. We're coming up to the blinds."

"If you know it already, why are we watching it again?"

Paulina reached over to the nightstand and handed him the remote.

"No, that's okay," Tom said.

"Watch what you want."

"I don't care about the curtains, Paulie. I don't care about the paint or the furniture. We got a nice place."

19

She sighed. "We've got a shit hole."

"Says who?"

"Mom. Dad. Everyone who's visited."

"Your parents were here?"

"Resentfully, yeah. Just to shut me up about how they 'forgot' to visit us at the hospital."

"When?"

"First week after Mel was born."

"Weren't impressed, huh?"

"Oh, ecstatic. Mom wouldn't sit on the furniture and Dad counted the condoms and needles in the alley."

This was the height of irony coming from the people who drank themselves stupid in their basement so they wouldn't break their antiques when they went haywire on each other. "So? Mel's happy. That's all that counts."

Paulie squeezed her eyes shut. "Go to sleep, Tommy."

Tom shut the TV off. "Don't listen to them, Paulie."

"Maybe they're right."

"You're a good mom," Tom said.

Paulie went quiet. He thought she'd fallen asleep, was drifting himself when she touched his hair, brushed it from his face.

The 20 Downtown bus crawled along Commercial Drive. Tom pushed his way to the back, dropping his knapsack to the floor between his legs. The sharp, musty tang of sweat hung in the air. Tom wished he had a car. Any car. Even a bike would do.

At the bottom of Commercial Drive, the waterfront turned industrial, with rundown stores, boxy warehouses, and old factories. The bus turned west on Hastings Street and then picked up speed as the stops came wider apart. The number of boarded-up stores began to outnumber the stores still open. Wrought-iron bars appeared on windows. The old brownstone hotels with their grand names and neon lights took over from the modern buildings. The deeper into the skids the bus travelled, the more churches and detox centres started popping up.

Tom automatically scanned for his mother. He felt bad about not wanting to see her. But he'd spent so much of his life wandering in and out of bars looking for her, waiting for her, worrying about her, that he didn't want to do it any more. Assuming she was drinking again. Maybe she wasn't. Maybe she lived down here on one of the more respectable residential streets and she had a good guy in her life and she had the garden she'd always wanted. Even if she was on a tear, she was a big girl. She could handle herself.

He worried, though. You heard so many rumours. People disappeared down here all the time. Besides the obvious OD's and muggings gone wrong, you could die for the dumbest reasons. Go to the wrong party. Stand under the wrong window. Have the wrong colour hair. He jerked awake, realizing he'd missed his stop.

The Regina still had ornate signs over separate entrances to a now-defunct bar for Ladies and Gentlemen. Tom had lived there for two months when he first moved to Vancouver with his mother, way back before the carpet was ripped up in favour of the original concrete. His mom had hooked up with a bull bucker named Frank who was passing the off-season in Vancouver. When his mom told him Frank was a logger, Tom had been disappointed. In the picture books, loggers were brawny, square-jawed men who wore plaid and big boots, and carried axes. Frank was a heavy-set, balding, and bearded man who looked more like Santa. He would sneak Tom jelly beans and jujubes and chocolates.

The Regina had been respectable then, and the owner, a retired fisherman, had actually lived in the hotel. But then he'd died, and The Regina had been sold to a number of indifferent owners until the current ones took over, overseas investors who'd decided heat and hot water were unnecessary luxuries. The Regina held the record for the most emergency calls in a day.

The lobby door had been kicked in again, so Tom walked into The Regina without having to buzz his friend Willy. The metal door, off-kilter, whined as it scraped shut. The lobby had once boasted a front desk with a uniformed clerk and a bellhop, but now it was abandoned. After the searing afternoon sunshine and the honking sprawl of late-afternoon traffic, the quiet of the dark, close lobby made him uneasy.

Tom took the stairs two at a time. Willy lived on the third floor, in a corner room. A dark-haired man on the second floor blocked his way. They were the same height, but the man was probably the ideal weight of a socialite. He shook like a cold dog. "Weed? Powder? Rock?"

"I'm good," Tom said.

The man nodded absently and wandered down the hallway, knocking on doors.

Tom slung his knapsack forward and searched for the flashlight he carried when he visited Willy. The lights between the second and third floors had been burnt out for years and never replaced. He snapped the flashlight on and started up the stairs. The acrid, sweet reek of piss intensified. On the middle landing, glossy cockroaches swarmed a hardened coil of shit. Tom felt a bump and heard a crisp crunch as he stepped on a roach. He lifted his foot and knocked it off with the flashlight.

Double pinpoints of red light bobbed and weaved ahead of him. Rats slid past, squealing away from the watery yellow light as if it burned. Near the top of the stairs, parts of the wall were sprayed with chunky vomit, other parts with fine arches of blackened blood.

▐▌

"Penny bets will get you penny wins," his cousin Jeremy had liked to say. But Tom was not a high roller. Management did not offer him VIP suites with free mini-bars, stretch limos, or accommodating hostesses. Tom was perfectly happy nursing his free drink, diddling with the quarter slots, pull tabs.

"Come on, Big Spender," Jeremy said, pulling him away from a one-armed bandit. Jeremy pressed a five-thousand-dollar chip into his hand. Tom tucked it into his wallet. He knew he'd need it later.

"No, no, no," Jeremy said. "Watch and learn, Tommy."

Jeremy rolled and rolled and his chips were fruitful and multiplied. Maybe it was the free drink, maybe it was the boozy bonhomie of the crowd around the crap table, maybe it was Jeremy blowing smoke up his ass: "Life is a limited-time offer, Bauer. Grab some *cajones*. Risk something. We were born to take risks. That's what life is, isn't it?"

They cheered when he rolled, and the temporary attention made him feel ten feet tall and bulletproof. It was all very exciting until the people around the table booed.

"Snake eyes," the stickperson said.

"What happened?" Tom said.

"You crapped out," Jer said. "Don't worry about it. That was chump change.".

Tom stared at him, finally realizing he'd lost.

"You didn't know the numbers, that's all. Once you know the numbers, everything falls into place."

⦚

The third floor had ten rooms on either side of the hallway. The doors were shut, the hallway filled with the tinny echo of classic rock from a slightly out-of-tune radio station. Willy's room was the first door to the left, distinctive because he'd spray-painted eyes on his door and the surrounding walls. One of his less lucid states, he'd explained when Tom asked about the eyes that stared, shocked wide and dull.

Tom passed Willy's room. He walked to the end of the hallway. The communal bath was in the room on the left side, and the toilet was separate, on the right. The window was boarded up to prevent frequent flyers. He flicked the switch. A bulb in a cage lit a room overwhelmed by the rusting, claw-foot bathtub. Tom turned and shut the door, locked it behind him. As an extra precaution, he took three plastic wedges from his knapsack and jammed them under the door.

He unrolled a threadbare towel in the yellowed tub. In the towel, he'd stashed a utility knife, a roll of joint tape, a small can of antiquing wash, a sponge brush, a paint scraper, and a mini-tub of putty. He held the knife in one hand. Stepping up, he balanced himself by straddling the wide rims of the tub. Under the dim light, the walls were the colour of old piss. He ran his fingertips along the wall until he felt a raspy line, and he brought the knife up and sank it in, cutting a square. He eased the piece down, leaning it against the tub's wall. A fat hook gleamed from one of the wooden struts. He pulled on the thin, silver chain attached to the hook until he brought up a black metal briefcase. He shook off the roaches, and sat on the edge of the tub, resting the briefcase in his lap. He spun the combination locks until the snaps cracked open. The case was filled with money and three keys of coke.

He kept a mental tab of the money he'd "borrowed" the last few years. In all the excitement, Tom wondered if his cousin even remembered the briefcase. He'd never mentioned it. Tom could probably blow all the money and it wouldn't matter, meaning his precautions – keeping it out of their apartment, hiding it in the wall instead of a safety deposit box – were pathetic, like a loser convinced the government was after him, because it made him feel important. Jer used to wad hundred-dollar bills in his pockets and give them out at strip clubs. Tom was rationalizing. Jer didn't particularly care for skimmers.

He had meant to tell Paulie about the briefcase, but he was afraid she'd burn the money when she found out it was Jer's. And they needed a cash cushion. He didn't dip much. A couple hundred here or there when his paycheque didn't stretch. Three thousand for Mel's baby stuff and the apartment. He wouldn't dip now, but he wanted Paulie to have something nice to celebrate three years of sobriety. A couple of cans of paint, some money for a haircut. Little things that made the grind bearable. Given the choice of crawling to their parents for crumbs, or having Jer break his leg, Tom would go with the broken leg any day. He could also be inviting trouble back into their lives.

That's your problem, Jeremy had told him, knocking his knuckles against Tom's forehead. You overthink things. That's why deer get run over. They aren't dazzled by the headlights. They're weighing their options – should I go back, no, I should keep going, shit, is that the right thing to do? And then their time runs out and, WHAM, Bambi burgers for dinner.

"Willy," Tom said, knocking on the door. "It's Tom. Willy?"

He wouldn't be surprised if Willy didn't answer. Tom could hear him moving around, the squeak of the springs on the bed, the rustle of clothes.

"Are you up for company?"

Shuffling footsteps grew louder. The door cracked open. Willy grimaced, his lips thinning as he scratched his chin, then stepped back and swung the door wide.

Willy's redecorating had extended to his room. Tom hated being here at night, when the spray-painted eyes on the walls, the ceiling, and the floor seemed to move with the flash of the head-lights from passing cars. Willy said they were a comfort.

Makes people think twice before fucking with you, Willy had said. People leave you alone if they think you're more fucked up than they are.

"Hey," Willy said. His expression was flat, more from the side effects of his schizophrenia medication than from anti-social tendencies.

"Hey," Tom said.

Willy shuffled back to his bed, sat down, and picked up a smoke burning in the ashtray. The window was open, but it didn't make the room less stifling. Tom wiped his forehead with the back of his sleeve.

"Are you up for dinner?" Tom said.

"Already ate," Willy said.

"Fair enough," Tom said. He walked over to the window and stared down at the street. Deranged Jesus, a homeless man in blue shorts and red headband, dragged a twelve-foot plywood cross to the corner, and waited for the light to change. Tom turned his back to the window and leaned against the sill.

"Working tonight?" Willy said.

"Yeah."

"Huh. Did you bring my meds?"

"Yeah." Tom rummaged around in his knapsack and pulled out a paper bag with the pharmacy's logo bright and primary.

"Thanks," Willy said. "TV?"

Tom nodded.

Willy reached over and snapped on the black-and-white TV, tuned permanently to the CBC, the only free channel that had a decent reception in Willy's room. Tom sat beside him on the bed. Willy chain-smoked through the evening news, the red and green dragon tattoo on his neck rippling when he inhaled or exhaled. Their visits often were nothing more than watching TV together, but Tom usually came once a week. Paulie thought it was guilt.

"You've made amends," Paulie had said many, many times. "Let him go, Tom."

When the time came to leave, he stood up and Willy followed him to the door and shut it behind him without saying goodbye. Tom started down the stairs, trying not to think about what he'd taken from the almost seventy thousand dollars in small, unmarked bills and the three keys of coke still hidden in the bathroom wall.

▌▌▌

He heard strange voices in the apartment, arguing. He realized it wasn't his mother coming home. She would never bring home two men. He rolled off the bed, crouching down low. They were in the hallway, looking out the peephole at something or someone. They whispered to each other in furious tones: I saw someone, I saw someone – we're being followed. Fuck, stop being paranoid. No one's there. Check the apartment. Make sure no one's home.

▌▌▌

"Shh," Paulie said, "it's okay. It's okay, Tom."

She patted his head absently, barely awake. He felt Mel's foot in his ribs, the sheets tangled in his legs. His breathing steadied. He got up and checked the apartment, every room, every closet, every window, every door. Even though he knew it was stupid, he couldn't stop himself. He thought he was being quiet, but Paulie sat on the edge of the bed, hugging herself.

"I don't like it when you visit him," Paulie said. "It brings back too much."

28

"Did you get the laundry, Tom?" Paulie shouted from the bedroom.

"No, I'm making the bottles."

"We're late, we're late, we're late," Paulie chanted as she hopped by on one foot, slipping a black cowboy boot on her other foot. She grabbed the laundry basket from beside the door and sprinted out.

Mel scooted under her high chair. She dug around and picked up a linty hunk of teething biscuit and jammed it in her mouth, grinning, pleased with herself.

"Gross, babe," Tom said. He bent over and fished around her mouth.

She clenched her jaw when he pulled the biscuit out.

"No floor food. Look, fresh biscuit. Mmm. Nice and clean. See?"

Voicing her displeasure at a decibel level equalled only by planes taking off, Mel threw the new biscuit down, pointed to the linty piece on the kitchen table, and kicked her feet, her face flushing. She kept screaming while Tom screwed the bottles shut and put them in the lunch box. In the beginning, they'd meticulously labelled everything, neat printing on masking tape. Diapers in one section with Zincofax, baby wipes, change pad. Clean clothes, sunscreen, and first-aid kit in another section. Now they threw everything in the bottom of the stroller, and they were getting out the door later each morning.

He wanted Paulie to skip a meeting now and then. Maybe go in the afternoons. Ask her to try an evening meeting. Then they could spend the morning chilling. She liked the people in the morning meetings though, said they weren't as intense as the evening ones. She didn't go out much. This was her only Paulie-time.

Paulie came back with the laundry, sat on the couch, and started folding.

Tom laughed, carrying Mel to the stroller. "We won't die if Mel's undershirts are wrinkled."

"I dunno," Paulie said.

"Let's just go. Okay?"

The day was already a scorcher. Paulie's hair was sleek and dripping down her back. Mel, skin shiny with sunscreen, clung to the snack tray, refusing to sit back. When she was hard to get down, they'd walk her to sleep in the stroller. She knew their tricks.

"Easy on the O.J.," Paulie said. "She's got a red bum."

"Gotcha," Tom said.

They kissed. Mel made smacking sounds and Paulie grinned. "See you later, girl. Mwah! Oh, you're tasty."

"Hee," Mel said, hunching her shoulders in pleasure.

Tom was going to miss these kinds of mornings when and if they ever moved. Paulie had ambitions to get them a house in a "nice" neighbourhood, but Tom loved East Vancouver. He'd grown up here, and yeah, it was a little rough around the edges, but they weren't exactly pruning roses and taking high tea. East Van's heart was Commercial Drive, a.k.a. The Drive, a coffee freak's paradise. He didn't care for the artsy stores popping up, but he rotated through a wide range of coffee houses that served everything from traditional joe to organic free-trade, shade-grown, bird-friendly beans.

Tom stopped in Turks for his morning Americano. Tom liked laid-back Turks because it was directly across from Grandview Park. Paulie preferred Joe's, because it had an attached pool hall, where she could rack up a few games with Jazz to unwind after her NA meetings. Tom thought Joe's had really good coffee, but he didn't want to crowd Paulie. She needed some space and, if he was forced to admit it, he needed not to be teased to death by her raunchy sobriety buddies.

"Morning, Tom-tom. Usual?" Kate said. Today she was wearing an orange bikini top and a sarong skirt, showing lots of latte-creamy skin. Kate studied ethnobotany at UBC. She shared a nearby house with six other students. On slow mornings when Mel was asleep, Kate gave him free refills and talked his ear off.

"Morning, Kate," Tom said. "Yup. Same as always."

Mel hid her face against the stroller, then peeked out at two girls sitting near the counter.

"Hel-lo, sweetie pie, hello," the brunette with facial tattoos said. "Peek-a-boo, I see you."

Mel squealed.

"I'm going to bite her," the bald girl said. "What's her name?"

"Melody." Tom rolled the stroller closer.

"Hi there, Melody. Hi there."

"Mwah!" Melody said.

31

"Hey, that's a first," Tom said.

"Is it?" The bald girl seemed tickled by this.

"Americano's up, Tom-tom."

"Thanks, Kate. Wave bye-bye, Mel. Bye-bye."

"Mwah! Mwah! Mwah!"

Mel blew kisses at the pedestrians and cars. When people ignored her, she stopped, sitting back. She braced her feet against the snack tray, wiggling her toes in her sandals. They rolled across the street. Grandview Park was on the side of a gently sloping hill, and from the top had a postcard view of downtown and Grouse Mountain. Houses crept up the distant blue of the mountains on the North Shore. Unlike Toronto, which could sprawl in all directions on the relative flatness of Southern Ontario, Vancouver was hemmed in by the mountains and the ocean. With space so squashed, downtown Vancouver glittered with skyscrapers and mushroom-like clusters of condos. Grandview Park had a playground shaded by tall trees, a wide stretch of grass near the local high school that was currently occupied by some junior gangbangers smoking up.

Bongo Man was going at it under a tree near the corner, grooving to his own rhythm despite the obvious irritation of nearby backpackers. They were stretched out on their sleeping bags on the other side of the tree, giving Bongo Man nasty sideways glances, muttering among themselves. Bongo Man had waist-long blond dreads dyed an uneven shade of purple. His eyes were half-closed, and an unlit joint spit-stuck to the side of his mouth. Mel was not interested in Bongo Man. He was old news. The water park held her full attention, causing her to sit up and bounce in her stroller.

Tom parked the stroller near an empty bench. On another bench nearby, a pale girl with kohl-rimmed eyes and flat-black spiky hair nodded at him as she breast-fed her baby girl. He nodded back. She was in his parenting group, but he could never remember her name, just her kids, Seraph and Truman. She shared the bench with an obese blond woman in black stirrup pants and a blue T-shirt, and a man in tight acid-wash jeans and a wife-beater who was sucking on his cigarette like he needed it to breathe.

"Brendan, that's enough. That's enough. Let your brother have a turn. I mean it," said Shirl, a petite woman in a tie-dyed sundress, a matching handkerchief holding her hair back. Paulie had met Shirl in a rehab years ago, and when they bumped into each other at a drop-in centre, they'd bonded over bad birthing stories. Shirl saw Tom and waved, walking toward the bench.

"Hi, Shirl." Tom swung Melody up.

"Mwah!" Mel said, bouncing.

"Oh, come here, kissy face," Shirl said.

"Where's Jim?" Tom said.

"Dental appointment." She squinted. "Brendan, get off the swing! Brendan Nathanial Dodson, you get your ass off that swing right now!"

"But Mo-om."

"Don't make me come over there!" She took a deep breath. "I'm going to kill them if they don't kill each other first."

"Gotcha covered."

Shirl stuck her nose in Mel's hair. "I get an estrogen rush just holding her. Want to trade?"

"Come by at three in the morning and we'll talk."

Shirl laughed, moved Mel to her hip. Tom sat on the bench and sipped his Americano as he watched them walk toward the water park. Eric pumped his legs. Brendan swatted his brother when he swung near.

"Higher!" Eric demanded.

33

A group of singing Hare Krishnas danced up the sidewalk, giving Bongo Man a run for his money. A couple of women spread blankets near the sidewalk and put out books and clothes for sale.

Because of its slightly seedy reputation, East Van was one of the last affordable places to live in Vancouver, so it attracted a mix of anarchists and activists, blue-collar families and immigrants. The hippies who couldn't afford Kitsilano had also migrated east, bringing organic co-ops and hemp shops into the mix. There were mom-and-pop restaurants everywhere and you could find a Jamaican jerk shack beside an Ethiopian vegetarian café beside a hydroponics bong palace.

Gentrification creep had started with a few condos, some spas and upscale junk stores, and a Starbucks, which had been bitterly petitioned against by the coffee shops on the same block. You could always tell the new condo owners, like the couple walking up the path – the slim woman wearing a chino pencil skirt and paisley blouse, the big guy wearing a chino suit and navy dress shirt. They stuck out like narcs at a boozecan.

"Hey!" Tom said. "Stop punching Brendan! Eric! Did you hear me? I'm going to call your mom."

The twins stuck their tongues out at him and ran to the slides.

Tom downed the rest of his Americano and walked over to the trash can.

"Look who escaped from Fraggle Rock," Chino Guy said.

Tom ignored him and walked back to the playground but Chino Guy blocked his way, grinning down at him. Something about him – the reddish brown hair, the freckles, the pointy chin – rang a bell, but Tom couldn't place him.

"Do I know you?" Tom said doubtfully. He didn't know that many human tanks.

34

"I hear it's good luck to spot one," Chino Guy said.

"Mike," Chino Girl said.

"McConnell?" Tom said. "Holy fuck."

"How the hell are you, Bauer?"

"What the hell have you been eating, man?"

"You haven't changed at all, shrimpola. You should start working out."

"I think the steroids have given you brain damage."

Mike laughed, his ratcheting hee-haw bringing back memories of lunchtime in high school, when they used to hang out in the hallways or cut class together.

"Just a sec," Tom said. "Eric! What did I just tell you?"

"He started it!"

"Liar!"

"You're begging for a time out, guys."

The twins waggled their bums in his direction.

"Yours?" Mike said.

"Thank Christ, no. They're my friend Shirl's. She's over there with my daughter."

Chino Girl cleared her throat. "I'm Greer, Mike's partner." She had a frank stare, unsettlingly light grey eyes, and a sculpted bob. She held out her hand, gave a firm, dry shake. "Pleased to meet you."

"You must be a very patient woman, Greer."

"Oh, yeah," Mike said, "you're still a riot, Bauer."

"Ah, shit. Just a sec. Put the rock down! Eric, you put that down," Tom said.

"So how have my monsters been?" Shirl said. Shirl and Mel were soaked. Mel reached for him.

"Pretty quiet." Tom lifted Mel. She yanked excitedly at his hair.

"Their colds are slowing them down," Shirl said.

"Hey, Shirl, this is Mike and his girlfriend, Greer. Mike, Greer, this is Shirl, and this is my girl, Melody."

"Hi. Er-RIC! Put the rock down!" Shirl shouted. "See you tomorrow, Tom. Now, Eric. I mean it!"

"Bye, Shirl."

Mike and Greer stood staring at him and Mel.

"Are you hungry?" Tom said as Mel chewed on his sleeve. He reached in the stroller for a Ziploc bag full of Cheerios. They sat on the bench. Mel stuck her hands in the bag and grabbed fistfuls and threw them on the ground. Tom pulled the stroller closer and rummaged around for a bottle. Mel leaned against him while she drank.

"She's adorable," Greer said, sitting beside him.

"Takes after her mother."

"Is she around?" Greer said.

"No, she's at a meeting."

"Where do you guys live?" Mike asked.

"We've got an apartment a few blocks from here. What are you guys doing in this neck of the woods?"

"One of Greer's friends has a show at Havana."

Ah, Tom thought. Havana was a popular Cuban-themed hipster restaurant. It had a small gallery exhibiting paintings and photographs of up-and-comers.

"It's Serena's first exhibit," Greer said. "She took Mike's picture –"

"All you can see are my knees."

"She's working with some haunting juxtapositions, the perfect and the disfigured –"

"She's into scars."

Greer checked her watch. "Compelling, very moving. We should get going, hon."

"Are you in the book?" Mike said.

"Yeah."

"I'll catch up with you later."

"Pleasure meeting you, Tom," Greer said.

"Likewise. Say bye-bye, Mel."

Mel popped the bottle out of her mouth. "Mwah!"

"Well, that was a blast from the past," Tom said, watching them leave.

Mel tugged on her ear, yawning. Tom changed her diaper, put her in fresh clothes, and brought her over to the swings. They swayed back and forth as the kids screamed through the park.

Paulie had wanted Mel to listen to Mozart, but Mel wasn't interested in the classics. She didn't pay attention to the children's tapes either, not a Barney fan, no Elmo. Paulie had played the radio one day around bedtime and discovered that Mel relaxed best to The Tragically Hip, Radiohead, and R.E.M.

Mel and her moody boys, she had said.

Tom sang a Hip song, low and slow, altering the lyrics to make them Mel-friendly. She knew the swing trick too and squirmed.

"Melo-dy-ee! Honey, are you mad at your dad?"

She found a comfortable spot, heaving a great put-upon sigh. Her eyes drooped.

"Honey, are you mad at your dad?"

An early afternoon breeze sent the leaves into a tizzy. Mel shut her eyes as the light on her face flashed gold and green, gold and green.

"Either your feet are freakishly small," Paulie said, lifting his left foot and pressing the sole of hers against it. "Or mine are freakishly big. Look, they're the same size."

"I love your elephant feet," Tom said.

Paulie kicked his foot and he laughed. She reached for her shirt, but found his instead and pulled it on.

"We should do something," Paulie said.

"Now?" Tom said.

"Get up."

"You go," Tom said.

Paulie bounced on the mattress. "Come on. Up. Up." She punched his leg.

"Ow."

"Come on."

Tom pushed himself up onto his elbows. "Paulie, you're killing the relaxing part."

"We're wasting the day," Paulie said.

38

"Paulie," Tom groaned. "I can't stay awake. You go. Bring Mel in here. We'll nap together."

She pulled on her jeans, leaning back to do the zipper up. She sat cross-legged beside him. His eyes slid shut.

He heard a high whine, felt the bed shake. Paulie ran the vacuum cleaner by his head. He turned over and put a pillow over his ears. Eventually, he heard the vacuum cleaner move down the hallway.

"I'm doing the sheets," she said, giving his ass a sharp slap. "Get up for a minute."

Tom stumbled to his feet and waited until she stripped the mattress before lying back down.

Mel woke him by sitting on his chest, reaching forward and lifting his eyelids.

"Daddy's awake," Tom said. "You can let go now."

"Hah," Mel said.

<hr>

The tattoo artist's bare chest and back were covered in tsunami waves, blue and green with white foam. The waves undulated when he moved, a human ocean. His earlobes were stretched to his shoulders, loops of pink flesh. The tattoo artist shaved the downy hair from a spot on Paulie's right forearm, halfway between her wrist and her elbow. He wiped the skin with an alcohol towelette and pressed the transfer paper against her skin. When he lifted the paper, a blue template of the tattoo she wanted was in place. The tattoo artist revved the tattoo gun, pumping the ink into the needle. "Last chance to back out."

Paulie flexed her hand, squeezed it tight, and then relaxed it, staring at the template for the tattoo, "1 July 1995" written in cursive script, bordered with a black ribbon banner. Paulie reached out to Tom with her free hand and he pulled his stool closer. She smiled at him. Her hand was clammy. He smiled back.

"I don't have another day one in me," she said. "I'm tired of going back to day one."

The tattoo artist nodded. "Strength, sister."

"I'm good to go," Paulie said.

He moved his reading lamp and spotlighted the tattoo. The needle drew tiny beads of blood that the artist dabbed away with a paper towel.

Paulie grimaced. "No more day ones."

▌▍▌

A squat, orange moon hung low, rippling as it hit the mountains. Downtown lights jittered in the heat. People sat on their porches and balconies, doors and windows open hopefully, ready for an evening breeze. A pack of kids ran around a front yard, screaming through the sprinkler. Traffic slowed on The Drive, cars crawling along to avoid the jaywalking pedestrians.

Tom and Paulie shared an iced coffee, hung out on a sidewalk patio to escape the oven they called their apartment. Paulie nodded off in her chair, a quick nap. Mel had long since passed out in her stroller. Tom waited as long as he could and then gently shook Paulie awake.

"Sorry," Tom said. "Duty calls."

The first fireworks thumped in the distance. Paulie frowned, turned her head to the TV inside. The waitress had switched channels to show the Canada Day festivities.

"You're really late," Paulie said. "Why didn't you wake me?"

"Lucky Lou's won't fall apart without me," Tom said.

40

Tom walked them home and, despite Paulie's protests, right up to their apartment.

"Don't forget milk," she said, before she closed the door behind him.

◫

Tom listlessly flipped through an old *Enquirer*. A woman in Kentucky, he read, had hired a priest to perform an exorcism on her toaster, because it left the mark of Satan in every slice. Apparently, the Prince of Darkness had his slow shifts, too.

Even though the coveted daytime shifts paid less and had a steady, irate flow of harried commuters, graveyard was the least-loved shift at Lucky Lou's. At night, after the neighbouring stores and coffee shops closed, Lou's glass wall overlooked a deserted, unlit parking lot on one side, and Commercial Drive on the other. Tom always felt like he was in a glowing fish tank and, given that Lou's had been robbed four times in the last two years, he doubted that the excellent lighting was a deterrent.

None of the women would work overnight. First, there was the safety issue, and second, there was Stan, the owner's tattooed and pierced nephew with a penchant for battle fatigues and semi-automatics. He'd originally run Lou's, but had been demoted until he was in charge of the graveyard. Stan tended to take hour-long breaks with damp and wrinkled mags like *Shaved Slaves* or *Commando Gang Bang*, which he left around the bathroom when he finished.

Not many of the guys liked working with Stan either. Tom hadn't been given an option for shifts since he had the least seniority. As fellow insomniacs went, even though Stan didn't pull his weight, even though he spent most of the time in the back on the coin-operated Internet computers playing games or visiting porn sites, at least he didn't give a shit what you did either.

Tom noticed a black van in the parking lot. He wasn't sure why he noticed it or why it gave him the creeps. It was a black van like any other black van, parked and dark, the driver hidden behind tinted windows.

"Knock, knock!" Mike's voice boomed.

They'd left the door open to air the place out between coats. Mike walked in, carrying a large fruit basket with a teddy bear on top. Tom stopped washing his brush and stood.

"Hey," he said, surprised. He'd thought the catch-up-with-you-later thing was a politeness. He hadn't expected Mike to call and certainly not to show up.

"Bad time?" Mike said, looking around at the tarp-covered furniture and the freshly painted walls.

"No, no. We're finishing up. Paulie! Company!"

"What?" Paulie shouted back.

"We have a visitor."

Paulie wandered into the living room, her baseball cap askew, her face smudged with Lemon Zing and smeared eyeliner. She stopped when she saw Mike.

"Paulina Mazenkowski?" Mike said.

"Yeah, that's me."

"Mike McConnell. We went to high school together."

She stared at him, frowning. "Sorry. Don't remember you. Mommy brain, I guess."

"This is from my partner, Greer," Mike said. "She insisted. I was all for beer and pizza."

Paulina stared at the basket. "Hey. Thanks. This is nice. Do you want something to drink? We've got Pepsi, apple juice, or milk."

"I'm fine, thanks. Where do you want this?"

"The kitchen would be great. Thanks."

"How you holding up?" Tom said.

She groaned. "Stick a fork in me, I'm done. I'm going to go crash with Mel."

"Got your keys?" Tom said.

She jangled them, walking away without looking back.

Mike returned, shaking his head. "How the hell did you hook up with Mazenkowski?"

"Dumb luck."

"Huh. Never saw her as the, uh, settled-down type."

Tom shrugged. "People change."

Mike looked around. "Where're you guys sleeping tonight?"

"The couple down the hall's letting us crash in their living room. Back in a sec. I need to scrub off a few layers of smell."

Tom took a bird bath in the bathroom sink. He towelled off and threw his shirt in the garbage. There was no saving it after the marathon weekend of priming and painting in the summer heat. He grabbed a relatively clean T-shirt from the bedroom, and a Pepsi from the kitchen, where Mike was sitting at the table.

"So," Mike said. "You're a dad now."

"Yup."

"How's that?"

"Not bad."

"What else are you up to these days?"

Tom popped the Pepsi. "Paulie's got the reno bug."

"I can see that."

Tom sat across from Mike, who pushed the fruit basket to the side.

"Where'd you go? You dropped off the map after Grade Ten."

"We moved around. How about you?"

"Bummed around Europe after high school. Bartended down under."

"Nice," Tom said.

"Yeah. Starting second-year psych."

"Bull fucking shit," Tom said. "You're going to be a shrink?"

"I'm thinking I'd make a pretty good shrink."

"Seriously?" Tom said. He waited for Mike to break out in his hee-haw laugh. "You're yanking my chain. Right?"

"You got a problem with that?"

"What happened to Rage Against the Machine, the suits are killing us, the –"

"All right, all right. I was a kid. I was mouthing off."

"What does your aunt say?"

Mike grinned. "Lots. She's trying to steer me into law. Civil. Corporate. Anything with a high snore factor."

"Good God."

"Yeah."

"Well," Tom said. "You could article with Evan's firm."

"They got divorced."

"Yeah?"

"Yeah, they waited until my grad year to have their big blow out. Fun times."

"What happened?"

"The usual. Hey, how's your mom doing?"

"No clue. We haven't talked for a while."

"Oh."

"You're too young to have kids . . . you're ruining your lives . . . blah, blah, blah."

"Oh."

"Are you sure you don't want a drink?"

"Any beer?"

"You're shit out of luck, bud. We're a dry household. Paulie's on the program and booze fucks up my meds. You can grab some beers though. There's a liquor store –"

"Pepsi's fine, Tom."

Tom got Mike a Pepsi from the fridge and tossed it to him. He stood in front of the fridge, wishing he could climb in and sit there.

"Are you going to school?" Mike said.

"Got a job at Lucky Lou's."

"Christ, Bauer. Why are you wasting your time in a corner store?"

"The shifts are flexible, and the store's right up the street. What are you up to these days?"

"Security guard at UBC."

Tom started laughing.

"What's so funny?" Mike said.

"After all the shit you pulled on the mall cops, don't you think it's ironic?"

"Shut up."

"You shut up."

A rumbling roll started downstairs, sounding like a bowling ball going down its alley over and over.

"Oh, boy," Tom said.

"What the hell is that?"

"The apartment below us has some skater kids. They were reasonable until one of them pulled up the carpets. They've turned it into a skate park."

"Have you complained?"

"Everyone's complained." He walked to the living room, taking the tarp off the CD player. He turned the speakers so they were facing the floor. "As long as the kids pay their rent, the owners aren't doing anything. The police already visited them a million times. The kids laugh it off."

"I'll go down and talk to them."

"No, no, Mike. Relax. We've got it covered." The phone rang. "Yellow."

"I have Albert on my cellular phone. He says he's ready," Mrs. Tsing said in her stately, carefully enunciated speech. "My stereo is cued as well."

"Just a minute. I can't find the CD. Up, here it is. Putting it in the drive, aaaaand I'm good to go."

"Shall I count down?" she said.

"Be my guest," Tom said.

"Three, two, one, and play."

After a second of silence, Celine Dion began crooning "The Power of Love." Loud boos from the apartment below, followed by banging and shouts of, "You losers! You suck!"

"Heh, heh, heh," Tom said. "Any of the divas are skater-repellents, but no one can touch Celine. Come on. Let's watch the rats desert the sinking ship."

They walked to the front window. Celine began to build. The skaters pumped their own music, but Celine rose above it, furiously passionate, slightly out of sync on three different stereo systems.

Tom leaned out the window, talking louder over the crescendo-ing offensive: "Paulie was in favour of an old-fashioned smackdown, but this way is surprisingly effective. There they go."

"You fucking losers!" The tallest of the boys shouted up at them from the lawn. "I'm going to kick you in your hairy cunts!"

"Come here and we'll see who kicks who, punk!" Mike yelled.

"Suck me off, motherfucker!" He grabbed his crotch.

"I'll kick your ass into tomorrow, you little punk!" Mike said, his face going heart-attack red.

"Fuck you!" Skater Boy said.

"Weird, huh?" Tom said, suddenly feeling nostalgic. "Five years ago, everyone was calling us the punks. Now we're the grown-ups."

"That was never me," Mike said, scowling.

Tom grinned.

"Hey, dickless wonder," Skater Boy said, "yeah, I'm talking to you, Bauer! You gonna sic your psycho bitch on me?"

"What?" Tom shouted, cupping his ear. "Did you say you're a Celine fan, too?"

Skater Boy pointed at him. "You're dead, motherfucker! Do you hear me? You're dead!"

"She's on TV tonight!" Tom said. "I'll tape it for you!"

"Faggot!"

"What? You want to hear this song again?"

"Go to hell."

"One more time for the Celine fan on the lawn!" Tom said.

The skater boy's friends nudged each other, having a chuckle among themselves.

Skater Boy went rigid with rage, his voice lifting an octave. "You goof! You fucking goof!"

"That's the spirit! Sing along with Dion!"

"Tad likes Di-on, Tad likes Di-on," his friends teased.

Tad chased his friends, who took off, howling.

"Tad's going to stomp you," Mike said. "You know that, don't you?"

"He's okay. He has no taste in music, but he's okay."

IIII

They pushed the furniture from the centre of the room back into its usual position. Mike did most of the heavy lifting while Tom acted as guide. Finally, they pushed the couch in front of the TV and flopped down. Tom studied the walls. Lemon Zing had a Day-Glo-green undertone that hadn't been noticeable in the swatches. Tom hoped the Zing mellowed when it cured. If it didn't, they'd have to put up lots of pictures to tone it down, because he wasn't painting again for a long, long time.

Mike checked his watch. "I should head'er."

"Drop by for dinner one night," Tom said. "We're not fancy cooks, but the food's hot and there's lots of it."

"We'll take you up on that. Greer hasn't mastered anything beyond the stir-fry," Mike said. "And I'm still working on KD."

Tom laughed.

"But seriously," Mike said. "If you need help with people bothering you, just call and –"

"They're good kids," Tom said. "They're just acting out."

Mike nodded, his eyes shifting around the room. "I hear your cousin's getting day parole next week."

Tom stopped smiling. "How'd you hear about that?"

Mike sighed. "I ran into your mom. She's worried."

"Forget it, man. You know her deal better than anyone. She wants attention, that's all."

"I remember Jeremy was a number-one freak show."

"You met him once," Tom said.

"After he moved in with you guys, you started showing up to school with bruises and burns."

"It was a bad year. Jer was the least of my problems."

"Bad in what way? Illegal bad or personal bad?" Mike said.

"Jer was an asshole," Tom said. "But he was there for us when no one else could be bothered. I owe him a lot. He and Mom are feuding. I don't want to play ref."

After a minute, Mike said, "Fair enough."

Paulie took the teddy bear off the fruit basket. "What was his name again?"

"Mike McConnell."

"Old boyfriend?"

"Just a friend."

"Are you sure?" She held the bear up. "I think he's sweet on you."

"Sorry to disappoint you, hon, but Mike is so straight he squeaks."

"And here I was all ready to be jealous."

Paulie handed the bear to Mel, who was sitting on the floor. She chewed its ear for a minute then tossed it aside and scooted for the tarps they'd piled by the door. Paulie followed her, lifting the tarps out of reach. Mel motored around the furniture, interested in the new arrangement.

"Well? What did Squeaky want?"

"He wanted to catch up."

"I don't remember him."

"He was my height back then. Scrawny. Enough attitude to lift-off the space shuttle."

"Nope. Nothing. *Mel.* No, baby. Tom, can you get her?"

Tom scooped Mel up before she tipped the garbage over.

"Maybe I'm getting Alzheimer's," she said.

"Me and Mike were under the radar in high school. I was anyways until . . . well, you know."

"Yeah," Paulina said. "I know."

|||||

Tom checked the clock above the front doors. Two more hours until the morning shift showed. The security buzzer bleated as a young guy in a baseball cap walked in. Behind the man, Tom noticed the black van cruising into the empty parking lot. The distance from the shop blurred the Crime Stoppers–worthy details like the licence plates, model, and make, but he was sure it was the same van that had been through the lot twice before.

Tom ignored the urge to lock the front doors. There were loads of non-robbing reasons people would wait in a deserted parking lot with their van's headlights off and the engine running. Maybe this was a lost tourist who kept stopping to check his map. Maybe this was some horndog picking up women. Maybe this was just some dealer waiting for a drop. The van turned out of the lot and disappeared down the deserted street. Tom massaged his temples. Or maybe sleep deprivation was making him bug-eyed.

Tom absently tracked the customer on the security cameras. He was a little taller than Tom, body-builder buff, black muscle shirt and sweats. When he turned his back, he had a thin brown ponytail tied at the nape of his neck. The guy lingered over the adult magazines, snatched a *Hustler*, and brought it to the counter.

"A 6/49 Quick Pick," the guy said. "How much is your Internet time?"

"A dollar for twenty minutes."

"Huh," the guy said. "Pretty quiet tonight. Is anyone on the computer or are you alone?"

Tom studied him. Overly tanned with wide-set brown eyes in a narrow face. No scars or tattoos.

"We've got two computers. Someone's using one, but the other one is free."

Stan suddenly said, "Eat that! Yeah!"

Through the security camera at the back, Tom could see Stan leaning forward as he exploded, burned, and decapitated mutant enemies galloping across his computer screen in *Alien Apocalypse IV*.

A young black man wearing shiny blue shorts banged on the window. "We won!" he screamed. "4-2 on the penalties! We won!"

"That's great!" Tom said.

The man banged the window a few more times then skipped away. The guy in the muscle shirt paid with a twenty and left. Must be a full moon tonight, Tom thought.

The same black van rolled into the parking lot. It parked near the street.

"That van's back," Tom said.

"Yeah?" Stan said, distractedly, still focused on his game.

"What if they're casing the store?"

"Fuck, don't be paranoid." Stan craned his head around a pile of canned pop and stared out at the van. "If it turns into a robbery, give them whatever's in the register. Insurance'll cover it."

"Glad we have a plan."

"Don't worry," Stan hunched down, grunting and swaying as he got back into his game. "You'll get used to it."

The van waited.

Stan emerged from the back as a parade of cars honked past. The passengers hung out the windows, wahooing, alternately in shadow or brightly lit as they passed under the streetlights. When Tom glanced back at the parking lot, the van was gone. On the hood of the last car in the parade sat a well-endowed topless woman with two strategically placed soccer-ball pasties, her upraised arms flying a large, flapping Brazilian flag. She sang along to Queen's "We Are the Champions" as it thundered out of the car's stereo system.

"Wow," Tom said. "You gotta love The Drive."

Stan said, munching Cap'n Crunch cereal from the box, "Brazil must have beat Holland in the semi-finals."

"Beat them at what?"

"The World Cup."

Tom must have still looked puzzled, because Stan said in exasperation, "We talked about this last week. When Beckham got red-carded. England in flames. Footballers rioting."

"Oh, yeah," Tom said. Afterward, Tom had deliberately kept asking which Spice Girl Beckham was dating because it bugged Stan. Which would be more entertaining if he wasn't so easily bugged. Still, anything to make the hours pass. "I thought you said it was soccer."

Stan glared at him.

"Weird time for a game anyways," Tom said, turning back to his *Enquirer*.

"It's in France," Stan said slowly. "It's a half a day ahead of us."

"Ah," Tom said. "Some guy said it was 4-2 on the penalties."

"Do you even know what that means?" Stan said.

"Nope. Not a clue."

"It means we missed a fucking great game because we're stuck in a shitty little hole in the wall, that's what it means."

<hr>

"It's not like I'm asking for the moon, am I?" Cindy said, tapping her high-heeled foot. "He's got a fucking forty-thou-a-year job. Bobby's clarinet lessons aren't going to break him, right? But, no-oo. Clarinet is a fucking girl's instrument. Bobby has to play sax. Well, I'll tell you what. Bobby hates sax."

A customer came up to the counter, and Cindy gave him a wide, insincere smile. "Twelve-fifty. Thanks, have a nice day." She turned back to Tom, chewing her gum furiously. "So that asshole won't pay unless Bobby changes instruments."

"What does Bobby say?" Tom said.

Cindy sighed. "I haven't told him. How do I tell him his dad thinks he's a weenie?"

"What does your mom say?"

"Please. What she always says. You made your bed, missy, you go ahead and sleep in it." She pulled a compact out of her purse and examined her eyes. "God, I'm so puffy." She clicked the compact shut. "Destiny's molars are coming in, and she's a basket case, an absolute basket case."

"I should get going," Tom said. "Paulie's waiting."

"How's she holding up?"

"She's wrecked."

"Oh, the poor hon. Did you guys try the clove oil?"

"Yeah. But Mel's got four teeth coming in and she's not sleeping –"

"Bauer," Stan said as he put on his jacket on the way out. "You're such a girl."

55

Cindy popped her gum. "Spoken like a man who hasn't been laid in years."

"Shut your pie-hole," Stan said.

"Stick it in your ass and rotate, perv."

"You're begging for it. You're just begging for it."

Cindy snorted. "When I want a pencil dick, yeah, I'll come begging for you, perv."

"Are you going to let her do your talking, Bauer?"

"You betcha," Tom said.

"You're both fired."

"What-EV-er, perv," Cindy said as Stan stomped out the door. "I don't know how you can stand working with him. He's such a creep."

"He's okay."

"If you think perverts are okay, yeah, I guess he is."

"See you Saturday," Tom said.

"Kiss your honeys for me," Cindy said.

As he walked, Tom swung the plastic grocery bag filled with milk, digestive cookies, and caramels. He wondered if he should get his Americano early or save it. The chill damp in the morning air was already giving way to a humid, glass-shimmering, smog-inducing heat. They'd have to hang out somewhere with air conditioning today, maybe splurge on a movie. Or take a ride to the beach. Sit in the sand and eat ice cream and screw everything else. He had three days off before he had to go back to work.

He yawned, his eyes watering as he fiddled with his apartment keys. Mel had a nasty habit of rising with the sun no matter how late she'd been up. He always hoped to find them both asleep when he got home, but Mel was usually playing on the living-room floor while Paulie sat blankly in front of the TV, waiting for him to come home so she could catch a few zees before taking a shower and heading off to her meeting.

The TV wasn't on, but he heard a telltale crash. The coats were scattered down the hallway and the coat rack was on the floor. Tom straightened it.

"Mel," he said. "What are you up to, my little monkey?"

She usually giggled when she heard him come in. He frowned. The coffee table was tipped over. The books were tumbled over the living-room rug. The recently reupholstered couch was slashed open and leaking stuffing. "Mel –"

A man popped up from behind the overturned armchair. It was the man wearing a muscle shirt he'd seen earlier in Lou's. Another man stepped out from the kitchen, grabbed Tom by the throat, and shoved him against the wall. He touched the barrel of a Glock, cool and hard, to the underside of Tom's chin. Glock Man wore a blue T-shirt pitted with sweat, his boxer's nose close to Tom's, half an eyebrow on his left side, greying brown hair, and brown eyes.

The grocery bag fell with a splat as Tom grabbed the burglar's hands.

"Relax, Tom," Glock Man said.

"Mel!" Tom shouted. "Paulie! Mel!"

"Shh," Glock Man said, pressing the gun into his flesh.

JAG

June 4, 1998

Dear Detective Pritchard,

Thank you for lunch yesterday. I hope you can help us. The three videotapes I found in Jeremy Rieger's apartment are lost and all I have are these transcripts. George seemed like such a nice private investigator, and he had such lovely offices. Honestly, he charged so much money to keep the tapes in his safe, I never thought he'd go out of business!

I am terrified of what will happen when Jeremy gets out of prison and no one seems to care! I am including the statement my son sent me in 1994, although I don't know why you want to see it. I told you it's all lies. Jeremy has my Tommy so terrified, he refuses to help me and he won't talk to anyone.

I pray that you find a way to keep my nephew in prison,

Christa Bauer

I, Thomas Eugene Bauer, reside at 943 Victoria Drive, Vancouver, British Columbia. My date of birth is April 3, 1977. My social insurance number is ■ ■ ■. I am making the following voluntary statement:

Jeremy Rieger is my first cousin on my mother's side. He lived with me and my mother, Christa Bauer, in apartment 304 of The Woodcourt Apartments at 1334 Woodcourt Street from the beginning of March 1993 to mid-April 1993. He had a cot in my bedroom. He was not home much. He used our apartment as a crash pad.

I was not aware that he had recently been paroled. He did not discuss his personal life with me. We argued about what to watch on TV and whose turn it was to do the dishes. Two days before he moved out, Jeremy bought a large-screen TV for my mother and paid off some bills we had outstanding. We were surprised and asked him where he got his money. Jeremy told us he had received an inheritance from his grandfather. I did not witness Jeremy Rieger selling illegal drugs to get his money. Jeremy had a pack-a-day Player's Light habit, and he argued with my mother about not being allowed to smoke inside. After he moved out, he would visit every two weeks or so.

We lost all our possessions when The Woodcourt Apartments burned down on May 26, 1993. My recollection of those events is hampered by a head injury I sustained when I fell off the drain-pipe I was climbing down to get out of my apartment. I became extremely paranoid and spent five weeks hiding in the Downtown East Side of Vancouver. I have epilepsy, absence and sensory seizures followed by convulsions, and require medication to be seizure-free. As the weeks progressed and the medications left my system, the frequency and duration of the seizures increased. A friend from high school who lived in the area found me and brought me to Emergency at Saint Paul's Hospital.

After this time, Jeremy offered to let us stay at his condominium, Suite 2702 of The Pacifica at 410 West Georgia Street, until we were back on our feet. Jeremy told us he was a stockbroker and he sold stocks, bonds, currencies, etc. He said you had to be a complete idiot not to make money in the stock market and rec-ommended we save our money and invest. After almost a year, we still did not have our own place. The relationship between Jeremy and my mother soured.

The thirty-seven-thousand dollars Jeremy Rieger spent for my mother to attend the Twelve Oaks Rehabilitation Centre was offered as a Christmas gift, not a loan. When she is not receiving social assistance, my mother makes minimum wage. She would never accept a loan of that magnitude. I have the Christmas card and the envelope that Jeremy Rieger gave her when he presented her with the chance to stay at Twelve Oaks. The handwriting is Jeremy Rieger's, and he dated the top-left corner of the inside of the card. I have placed the card and enve-lope in the custody of Julia Howlett-Danson, who is a volunteer from the Law Students Legal Advice Program at the University of British Columbia.

I will not press charges against Jeremy Rieger for an assault committed by Richard Patolmic. The bruises on my neck and arms in the pictures my mother showed the police were not caused by Jeremy. A day or two after my sixteenth birthday, I had been assaulted by Richard Patolmic, a man my mother had recently dumped. I did not press charges against Mr. Patolmic then, nor do I wish to press them now even if he comes back. His actions were not within the normal range of his character. Being dumped is hard.

Although my mother is currently a member in good standing of Alcoholics Anonymous, at the time she had difficulty admitting she had a problem and was frequently absent from our day-to-day life. I ran small errands such as picking up the dry cleaning and washing Jeremy's cars. I attended accelerated classes to complete high school early. At no time did I witness assault, sexual assault, "pump and dump" scams, money laundering, extortion, threats, unlawful confinement, kidnapping, or homicide while I was living in Jeremy Rieger's condominium. I believe my mother believes what other people have told her, but I'm not willing to say I saw things I didn't see.

I am sending notarized copies of this letter to the legal representation of Jeremy Rieger and Christa Bauer. I do not wish to participate in either of their cases. I think these problems would be better solved through family counselling.

I swear that the above statement consisting of this and two additional pages is true to the best of my recollection.

Thomas Eugene Bauer

August 18, 1994

VHS 1

Title: FRESH START IN *VANSTERDAM!!!*

Date: 02-03-1993

Duration: 00:59:18

[00:00:00]

Light levels in the van are low. Two unidentified Caucasian males
in their late teens sit in the front bucket seats. The first male
holds a black semi-automatic paintball gun across his lap. He sits
in the passenger's seat. He wears a dark windbreaker and has a
baseball cap over closely cropped blond or light brown hair. The
second male, the driver, wears a light short-sleeved shirt and
jeans. He has dark hair in a ponytail at the nape of his neck.

Jeremy Rieger is visible in the rear-view mirror reflection as he
pans his camcorder back to the 1st Male. Mr. Rieger is in his early
twenties with dark hair and wears a black T-shirt.

JEREMY RIEGER *[off-camera]*:   Her! Her!

A blond female in her late teens waits at a bus stop. The 1st Male fires at her with the paintball gun. The female stumbles backward. Green paint appears on her left breast.

J. RIEGER: Bull's eye!

[Laughter]

The van speeds off. The camera stays on the female until they turn a corner.

1st MALE: That rocked!

2nd MALE: Fucking watch where you point that thing!

[Laughter]

[00:02:12]

A tall, bald, heavy-set Caucasian male jogs along the road. He wears sweatpants and a white hockey jersey with a Vancouver Canucks logo. The 2nd Male is now in the passenger's seat. He sights the back of the jogger's head with the paintball gun. The jogger stumbles forward.

2nd MALE: Canucks suck, you loser!

The jogger gives chase to the van.

[Laughter]

1st MALE: Give me the gun.

2nd MALE: You couldn't shoot shit in a toilet bowl.

1st MALE: Jer, I want my turn.

2nd MALE: You fucking baby. I want my turn, I want my turn.

J. RIEGER: We'll all get a turn. Let him have his fun and then you'll have yours.

The engine starts. The 2nd Male is driving. Mr. Rieger is now in the front passenger seat. He holds the paint gun.

J. RIEGER: . . . anyone take him serious? What kind of pussy name is *Firebug*?

1st Male hoots. His laughter is distorted because he is close to the camera as he films.

2nd MALE: Never say that in front of him. He's real proud of that nickname.

1st MALE: Firebug fragged this shitbag –

2nd MALE: Use your fucking head. What if Rieger's a cop?

1st MALE: Or full of it.

J. RIEGER: I'm not a fucking cop and I'm not knocking over gas stations. Any halfwit can do that. I want serious action.

2nd MALE: You got to claw your way up the food chain like the rest of us.

J. RIEGER: I've paid my dues.

2nd MALE: Look, there's a drive-through Starbucks.

1st MALE: I want doughnuts.

J. RIEGER: Okay, Homer.

2nd MALE: D'oh! D'oh!

[Laughter]

1st MALE: Fuck you!

J. RIEGER: Get close to that cyclist.

2nd MALE: You have to watch the trigger.

J. RIEGER: Closer.

2nd MALE: It sticks on the –

The squeal of the door opening is followed by a loud thump.

1st MALE: Holy fuck! Holy fuck, holy fuck, holy fuck!

2nd MALE: What the fuck did you do that for!

J. RIEGER: Keep driving.

1st MALE: Man, oh, man, oh, man, oh, man –

2nd MALE: Shut the fuck up! I can't think with your shit!

1st MALE: We're screwed, man! We're so screwed!

J. RIEGER: I've had enough of amateur night. I want to see Firebug. Now, people.

00:00:32 elapses without conversation.

2nd MALE: Is there blood on the door?

1st MALE: Let's ditch the van.

2nd MALE: Maybe it's just dented.

1st MALE: Pull over, man.

The interior car light flares, and the open door chime goes off. 00:02:05 of shuffling and doors opening and closing.

J. RIEGER: Did you get that? Did you see her face?

[00:05:59]

The Woodcourt Apartments at 1334 Woodcourt Street have three floors. The apartment building is dark brown with white trim. A Skytrain is audible in the background, but not visible.

J. RIEGER: What a dump. *[pause]* Hi, Mom! Made it in one piece. There's Aunt Chrissy in the corner apartment, waving. I'm ready to start a new life in Vancouver! *[pause]* So stop phoning my fucking parole officer and get your own goddamn life.

A short, thin, brunette Caucasian female in her mid-thirties fries hamburgers in the kitchen. She wears a white apron over a knee-length, short-sleeved yellow dress.

J. RIEGER: Hi, Aunt Chrissy!

CHRISTA BAUER: You silly goose! Put that away!

J. RIEGER: I'm making a video for Mom. Say hi!

C. BAUER: Hi, Sis! Hope your new meds are working out! *[pause]* Um. Can you start over? I don't think I should mention her meds.

J. RIEGER: I'll just edit that out. Hey, where's Tom?

C. BAUER: He's not here?

J. RIEGER: He's been AWOL all weekend.

C. BAUER: Check the fridge. He usually leaves a note if he's staying at Mike's.

A tall, heavy-set Caucasian male with brown hair enters the kitchen and kisses Ms. Bauer.

RICHARD PATOLMIC: Hey, good-looking.

C. BAUER: Richard, have you seen Tommy?

R. PATOLMIC: Have you checked the jails?

C. BAUER: That's not funny.

R. PATOLMIC: What? It's the truth. He's a pothead with authority issues. You don't have –

C. BAUER: He was teasing you, Richard.

R. PATOLMIC: He's a mouthy kid.

C. BAUER: He's fifteen.

R. PATOLMIC: Stop coddling him, Chrissy. Set rules. Enforce them.

C. BAUER: Don't tell me how to raise my son.

00:00:14 silence.

R. PATOLMIC: My shift starts in an hour.

C. BAUER: Here. Take a burger.

[00:08:39]

The camera focuses on a wristwatch. The time is 3:42 a.m.

J. RIEGER: Tommy locked himself in the bathroom an hour ago. Let's see what kind of porn Tommy whacks off to, shall we?

Mr. Rieger picks the lock. He slowly opens the door. Tom Bauer – a mid-teens Caucasian male with blue, shoulder-length hair – reads on a bathroom floor. He bobs his head to music on his Walkman.

J. RIEGER: Not exactly Mr. High Alert, is he? *[kicks Mr. Bauer]* What 'cha doing?

TOM BAUER: You fucking freak! When the bathroom door is closed and locked –

J. RIEGER: Let's see what turns your crank.

T. BAUER: Give that back!

J. RIEGER: *Mechanisms of Drug Resistance in Temporal Lobe Dysfunctions: Lessons from Oncology.* Wow. You are one sick puppy.

T. BAUER: Mom!

J. RIEGER: She's not home. It's just you and me.

[00:12:22]

Tom Bauer sits cross-legged on the couch in the living room. He cuts marijuana leaves onto a dinner plate.

J. RIEGER: I would tape *Billy the Kid vs. Dracula* but somebody hocked the VCR.

Mr. Bauer makes an obscene gesture with his middle finger.

J. RIEGER: I'm assuming that's how you bought your pot.

T. BAUER: This? This is just some crappy shake we found in a dumpster, man.

J. RIEGER: We?

T. BAUER: The royal we. As in, "We are of the opinion that this movie is crap."

J. RIEGER: I happen to think this movie puts some much-needed edge in John Carradine's oeuvre.

T. BAUER: His oeuvre, huh?

J. RIEGER: I can explain it in small words.

T. BAUER: Man, his oeuvre needed to pay rent real bad.

J. RIEGER: Don't use words unless you know what they mean. It gives away your ignorance.

T. BAUER: Blow it out your oeuvre.

J. RIEGER: Why were you reading a medical textbook in the bathroom with the door locked?

T. BAUER: I said let it go.

J. RIEGER: Why would you want to hide that?

T. BAUER: Man, you're a bug.

[00:13:59]

Tom Bauer carefully soaps a silver 1992 Jaguar XJS coupe.

J. RIEGER: You shouldn't let Richard push you around.

T. BAUER: For a couch surfer, you got one fancy car.

J. RIEGER: You have to stand up to him.

T. BAUER: If I was you, I'd sell this car and get my own apartment.

J. RIEGER: Are you listening to me?

T. BAUER: Richard's a fling. She's already avoiding his phone calls. She'll –

J. RIEGER: Whoa, whoa, whoa. What are you doing?

T. BAUER: I'm rinsing off the soap.

J. RIEGER: How many times do I have to tell you? Rinse with the tepid water from the buckets.

T. BAUER: This is so not worth what you're paying me.

J. RIEGER: What did I just say? No cold water!

Mr. Rieger is hit with a spray of water. He tips backward and sits on the ground, shielding his face. Mr. Bauer laughs. Mr. Rieger stands and charges. Mr. Bauer drops the hose. Mr. Rieger chases Mr. Bauer around the Jaguar four times.

The camera tumbles and comes to rest, focused on a brick wall. Mr. Rieger and Mr. Bauer can be heard struggling nearby.

J. RIEGER: You're going to clean my car exactly the way I tell you to, when I tell you.

T. BAUER: Go fuck yourself.

J. RIEGER: You will do it.

T. BAUER: Or what?

J. RIEGER: I'll go to your school, find Paulina Mazenkowski, and tell her everything you told me. *[pause]* And a few things you didn't.

Mr. Rieger laughs. Footsteps approach the camera.

T. BAUER: You're such an asshole.

J. RIEGER: Paulina! I wooove you! I can't wiiive without you! When you put your big, pouty lips on your flute and blow, I –

T. BAUER: Shut up! Shut –

[00:16:17]

Two unidentified early-twenties females pose nude on a bed. The first female, a Caucasian with a small build and blond hair, is prone with two pillows under her hips. Her wrists are handcuffed behind her back. The second female, a slim Hispanic brunette, wears a brown strap-on. They both stare into the camera and wait.

J. RIEGER: Tell her what you're going to do.

2nd FEMALE: I'm going to fuck you raw, slut.

J. RIEGER: Hit her.

The 2nd Female repeatedly slaps the 1st Female's buttocks. They engage in intercourse.

[00:22:03]

Both women are unconscious. The 1st Female is handcuffed to the headboard. The 2nd Female lies beside her. Mr. Rieger adjusts the 2nd Female's left hand so it is on the 1st Female's genitals. He returns to the camera, and the picture focuses on the 1st Female's torso.

Mr. Rieger returns to the 1st Female and picks up a serrated buck knife which he traces between her breasts down to her belly button. From the camera angle, it appears as if he suddenly and repeatedly stabs her, but he stabs beside her. Mr. Rieger makes sound effects for the knife entering her stomach and for agonized screaming.

[00:29:41]

A Denny's logo is visible on the dessert menu, which is suddenly lowered. Guy Francis [a.k.a. Firebug], a tall Caucasian male with

73

closely cropped blond hair, has a slight muscle-bound hunch and wears a navy jacket.

GUY FRANCIS: Craig's solid. I've known him since high school.

J. RIEGER: I don't work for free.

G. FRANCIS: We're playing for shape. A good word from Craig will open all kinds of doors.

J. RIEGER: So we bag Rusty.

G. FRANCIS: No. Listen. We catch Rusty with his hand in the cookie jar. Craig brings a legit complaint to Daddy Jack. Daddy Jack – and only Daddy Jack – solves the Rusty problem.

J. RIEGER: So I sit around and wait for Rusty to rip me off so Uncle Craig can rat him out. *[pause]* I hate shit detail. The next job better be one for the resume.

G. FRANCIS: Ah, to be gung-ho again.

J. RIEGER: Don't patronize me.

G. FRANCIS: Pay up and let's –

[00:33:12]

A large, black suitcase is removed from under a rollaway cot in the second bedroom of apartment 304. A hand unzips the suitcase and opens it, revealing a black garbage bag that hides six packages of white powder wrapped in clear plastic.

J. RIEGER: Ta-da! The bait. One key of crappy coke and the rest is baby powder. In this stunningly original plan, I play the retard hiding his stash under his bed. *[pause]* Rusty must be one dumb motherfucker if you think this is going to work.

Mr. Rieger turns to show Mr. Francis, who is installing a surveillance camera behind a heating vent on the wall.

G. FRANCIS: Shut that off.

J. RIEGER: Speaking of dumb motherfuckers, this is the delusional geezer who thinks he's the boss of me.

Mr. Francis lunges at the camera. It comes to rest on the floor, showing Mr. Francis and Mr. Rieger as they fight, rolling around the floor and then over the camera.

[00:34:49]

Mr. Bauer carries his ten-speed bike out of the storage closet in apartment 304. He wears orange pants with brown piping. Mr. Rieger laughs off-camera.

J. RIEGER: The Great Pumpkin wants his pants back, Charlie Brown!

Mr. Bauer puts down the bike and makes obscene gestures with both his middle fingers and then exits the apartment.

[00:35:27]

Looking down at Woodcourt Street from apartment 304. A grey sedan idles across the street.

J. RIEGER: Here, mousey. Come get the nice coke.

The sedan drives off.

J. RIEGER: Rusty, you motherfucking lazy piece of shit. Fuck. Fuck, fuck, fuck –

[00:36:18]

Mr. Bauer mops the floor at Chuck Wagon Burgers. He wears a cardboard cowboy hat and an orange uniform with brown piping.

J. RIEGER: You know something has gone seriously wrong in your life when you spend your Friday night staking out a Chuckie Burgers.

G. FRANCIS: Rusty's following him. That means something.

J. RIEGER: Rusty wouldn't spit on Tom if he was on fire.

G. FRANCIS: Tom's a sneaky little shit. I've seen hundreds of little shits just like him. He'll rob you blind as soon as he finds out you've got money. You watch him.

[00:37:11]

Mr. Bauer dismounts his bike in front of The Woodcourt Apartments. A car honks. Richard Patolmic exits a green Pontiac Grand Am.

R. PATOLMIC: I'm talking to you!

T. BAUER: She's at work!

Mr. Patolmic approaches Mr. Bauer.

R. PATOLMIC: Are you giving her my messages? 'Cause if I find out you're not –

T. BAUER: Give her your own messages, dipshit!

Bauer enters the building. Patolmic pounds on the entrance door. He presses the buzzer for apartment 304 for 00:01:47. When there is no response, he stands under apartment 304.

R. PATOLMIC: Chrissy! I just want to talk! Chrissy! I just want to talk!

An unidentified middle-aged Asian male on the second floor leans out his window.

ASIAN MALE: Hey, shit-for-brains! Some of us have to fucking work tomorrow!

R. PATOLMIC: Chrissy! Chrissy! Chrissy!

ASIAN MALE: Read the clues, moron!

R. PATOLMIC: Chrissy, I love you!

ASIAN MALE: You see this? I'm phoning the cops!

R. PATOLMIC: I love you!

[00:39:27]

Christa Bauer lights the candles on a train-shaped birthday cake, which reads, "Happy Sweet Sixteen, Tommy!" Mr. Rieger laughs off-camera.

C. BAUER: Shh. You'll ruin the surprise. *[pause]* Tommy! Shake a leg! Your breakfast's getting cold!

00:00:21 elapses before Mr. Bauer appears in his boxers and a T-shirt. Ms. Bauer and Mr. Rieger sing "Happy Birthday." Ms. Bauer leads Mr. Bauer to the kitchen table and sits him in front of the cake.

C. BAUER: Make a wish!

T. BAUER: Stop taping this. Mom. Make him stop.

C. BAUER: Oh, don't be a grumpy bunny. Hurry, I have to leave for work soon.

Mr. Bauer blows out the candles. Ms. Bauer hugs him and kisses his cheeks. Mr. Rieger starts to laugh again.

Mr. Rieger has set up the camera on the kitchen table. He chuckles as he examines various bills and places them back in a shoebox. Mr. Bauer enters the kitchen of apartment 304.

T. BAUER: What are you doing? Those are private!

J. RIEGER: How much are you guys in the hole?

T. BAUER: None of your goddamn business!

J. RIEGER: They're cutting off your power in three days. What are you going to do?

T. BAUER: I can't believe you went through my things.

Mr. Bauer attempts to wrest the bill box from Mr. Rieger, who pulls it back. Mr. Rieger holds up a bill and then throws it on the table. He removes his wallet from his back pocket and covers the bill in fifties. He repeats this with four other bills. Mr. Bauer touches the money on the table.

J. RIEGER: I'll help with rent and food and bills and all you have to do is one itty-bitty thing.

T. BAUER: What?

J. RIEGER: I want you to be good.

T. BAUER: Define "good."

J. RIEGER: You listen to me when I tell you what to do. No arguing. No debates. No whining.

[00:42:10]

Mr. Bauer gawks at the drugs in the suitcase under the rollaway cot.

J. RIEGER: Impressive, huh? Am I hearing apologies?

T. BAUER: Jer. Jesus.

J. RIEGER: Your bills aren't going to break my bank, so if you're smart, you're going to follow my rules.

T. BAUER: You're out of your mind. You can't keep that here. What if –

J. RIEGER: Are you being good? Meep. Uh, no. Now I'm going to introduce you to Mr. Consequences.

[00:42:47]

Mr. Rieger does an inspection of apartment 304. Mr. Bauer polishes a shoe at the kitchen table. Mr. Bauer has had his hair cut very short. He looks up when Mr. Rieger approaches.

J. RIEGER: I'd make you do everything again, but, hey, it's your birthday.

[00:46:33]

Mr. Rieger knocks on a door.

J. RIEGER: Tommy. Oh, Tommy.

Mr. Bauer is not in the bedroom. Mr. Rieger enters the living room. Mr. Bauer has fallen asleep on the couch. Mr. Rieger reaches out and shakes Mr. Bauer's shoulder.

J. RIEGER: Hey. Wake up.

Mr. Bauer is not responsive. The camera focuses on the coffee table where three and a half lines of powdered cocaine, a credit card, and a rolled bill are visible.

J. RIEGER: Some people can't handle their mickies.

Mr. Bauer lies unconscious on top of the coffee table. His jacket and shirt have been removed. Mr. Rieger places Mr. Bauer's hands over his head. Mr. Rieger sits on the couch and picks up a serrated buck knife. He speaks quietly, and is inaudible to the camera's microphone. 00:07:10 elapses. Mr. Rieger makes no move to use the knife. The lock for the front door snaps open and voices can be heard.

C. BAUER: Hel-lo! I'm home!

Mr. Rieger leaps over the coffee table and pushes it against the couch. He rolls Mr. Bauer onto the couch and throws a blanket over him. He pushes the coffee table back into position, turns the TV on with the remote, and sits in the recliner beside the couch, tucking the buck knife into one of the recliner's side pockets.

J. RIEGER: Hey, Aunt Chrissy.

C. BAUER: Jer-e-my! *[pause]* Ah! Look at Tommy! How did you get him to cut his hair! Ah! I love it!

A dark-haired man of average height and weight follows Ms. Bauer into the living room. They are obviously intoxicated.

J. RIEGER: Who's this?

C. BAUER: Say howdy, Pete.

PETE: Howdy, Pete.

Ms. Bauer and Pete laugh. Mr. Rieger shuts off the TV. Ms. Bauer struggles to lift Mr. Bauer's head onto her lap as she sits down.

PETE: I thought we were going to party, Chris.

C. BAUER: Look at my baby. Isn't he handsome? Oh, he's such a sweet boy.

PETE: Come on, Chris.

C. BAUER: Just sixteen years ago, he was sliding into the world –

VHS 2
Title: SHE'S A LADY
Date: 04-04-1993
Duration: 00:58:10

[00:00:00]

Paulina Mazenkowski, a late-teens Caucasian female with long blond hair, poses with her arms raised in front of her parents' two-storey home at 1492 Empress Drive.

PAULINA MAZENKOWSKI: Welcome to the freak show.

Ms. Mazenkowski opens the front door. The camera follows her, panning the living room. Screaming can be heard. The camera points down at the floral area rug. Something shatters and heavy thuds can be heard.

J. RIEGER: Someone's being killed in your basement.

P. MAZENKOWSKI: Relax. That's just Mom and Dad.

J. RIEGER: They're fighting?

P. MAZENKOWSKI: Ignore them.

J. RIEGER: Should we hide the knives and guns?

[00:01:14]

Ms. Mazenkowski sits at her vanity table applying her makeup. The camera focuses on the bed's white wooden canopy covered with gauzy curtains, plastic butterflies, and roses.

J. RIEGER: Wow.

P. MAZENKOWSKI: I know. Mom was supposed to give birth to a doll and got me instead.

Someone pounds on the door. Ms. Mazenkowski continues applying her mascara.

P. MAZENKOWSKI: I'm busy, Daddy. Go away.

MR. MAZENKOWSKI: Who's in there with you?

P. MAZENKOWSKI: No one.

MR. MAZENKOWSKI: Then whose car is in our driveway? Don't lie to me! What are you doing?

P. MAZENKOWSKI: I'm fucking the football team, Daddy.

MR. MAZENKOWSKI: You fucking slut! Whoring around like –

J. RIEGER: Do you want me to take care of him?

P. MAZENKOWSKI: Don't bother. He'll pass out in a few minutes.

[00:02:29]

Ms. Mazenkowski sits nude on a chair at a desk in a hotel room. She practises scales on her flute.

J. RIEGER: I'm dating a band geek.

P. MAZENKOWSKI: Don't knock it. My parole officer eats this shit up.

J. RIEGER: Is that all he eats?

P. MAZENKOWSKI: Turn that fucking thing off.

[00:03:19]

Ms. Mazenkowski stands naked with her hands on her hips.

P. MAZENKOWSKI: Did you turn the camera on?

J. RIEGER: Relax, babe, I grabbed a condom.

P. MAZENKOWSKI: Jeremy. *[pause]* You know what? Never mind. I'm outta here.

Ms. Mazenkowski begins to dress.

J. RIEGER: Come on, Paulina –

P. MAZENKOWSKI: I said I'd leave if you turned the camera on and what do you do? You fucking turn it on.

J. RIEGER: I'd really like you to stay.

Mr. Rieger moves toward Ms. Mazenkowski who kicks Mr. Rieger in the shins.

J. RIEGER: Paulie! Come on!

P. MAZENKOWSKI: Bye, Jer.

[00:04:02]

Mr. Rieger is outside, crouching down behind a tree. He holds a semi-automatic paintball gun and wears a protective mask. He lifts his finger.

J. RIEGER: Be vewy quiet. We're hunting wabbit.

[00:04:14]

A blurry figure is visible through dense brush.
   UNIDENTIFIED MALE: Guys! *[pause]* Not funny, guys! Jer?
Snickering and laughing can be heard.

[00:04:34]

Rusty Letourneau, a Caucasian male in his late teens/early twenties with a heavy build and shoulder-length dark hair, holds the leashes of two large, barking German shepherds. He holds a piece of paint-stained clothing in front of their noses and then releases them. He laughs as they disappear into the bushes.

[00:04:48]

The remaining 00:00:03 of a previously recorded scene that has been taped over. Although the camera is moving fast and the images are blurred, screaming can be heard, and the sound of dogs growling and clothes ripping. This is followed by 00:05:29 of static.

[00:10:20]

A male of average height and weight struggles as two men in black balaclavas and clothes hold his arms, which are cuffed in front of him. The victim is of undetermined race as he is splattered in green paint. The men drag him along a trail.

UNIDENTIFIED MALE: Did you think that was funny? Fucking laugh it up now, you useless cunts. You better –

They reach a coffin with silver handles beside a grave-sized hole. The unidentified victim begins to scream.

[00:11:22]

The victim struggles to exit the coffin. He is held in place by Mr. Rieger, who has removed his mask.

J. RIEGER: Any last words, rat?

UNIDENTIFIED MALE: I didn't say anything! I will never say anything –

J. RIEGER: No, you won't. Close it up.

The victim screams as the coffin lid is shut and locked. Mr. Rieger shushes the other people who have begun to laugh.

The men lift the coffin up, shake it, and drop it beside the hole. They shovel dirt over the coffin. The victim screams louder and pounds the coffin lid. The males struggle not to laugh out loud, covering their mouths and moving away from the coffin. One of the men ties a thick white rope to the handles.

[00:13:38]

Rusty Letourneau rides like a surfer on top of the coffin, which is attached to a pickup truck. They drive down a gravel logging road.

J. RIEGER: Go, Rusty, go!

People laugh near the camera when Mr. Letourneau falls off the coffin and lands in the ditch.

Mr. Rieger is in a clearing. Five men wearing black balaclavas have formed a circle with the sixth man holding the camera. Mr. Rieger steps into the centre of the circle. He removes his pants. The other men begin to hoot. Rusty Letourneau steps forward and removes his balaclava. He smiles at the camera and aims his air rifle at Mr. Rieger.

J. RIEGER: Lower.

R. LETOURNEAU: Take it like a man, Rieger.

J. RIEGER: Maybe you like it in the ass, but –

Mr. Letourneau shoots Mr. Rieger in the lower legs. Mr. Rieger drops to the ground and screams.

J. RIEGER: Jesus fucking Christ! *[screams]* Fuck! Fuck that hurts!

The other men laugh. One by one they step into the centre of the circle and Mr. Letourneau shoots them and then, after initial screaming and swearing, they move back to their places. Mr. Rieger stands at the end of the sequence and shoots Mr. Letourneau in the lower legs. Mr. Letourneau hops on one foot, then the other, but doesn't scream or swear.

R. LETOURNEAU: That's how it's done.

J. RIEGER: Okay, John Wayne, you –

[00:31:49]

Paulina Mazenkowski screams. She jumps up and down and claps her hands. She poses on the hood of the Jaguar.

P. MAZENKOWSKI: What kind of engine does she have, Jer?

J. RIEGER: The manual's in the glove compartment.

P. MAZENKOWSKI: Manual? Let me peek under the hood. I'm a hands-on kind of girl.

J. RIEGER: Baby, anything you want.

P. MAZENKOWSKI: I want to drive this hot bitch.

J. RIEGER: Anything but that.

P. MAZENKOWSKI: Come on, Jer. Let me show you what I can do.

[00:33:53]

The camera is waist-high, pointed up. Paulina Mazenkowski leans over and stares into the camera.

P. MAZENKOWSKI: Are you sure it's working?

J. RIEGER: It's working. The hole is on this side of the duffle. Point and shoot.

Ms. Mazenkowski crosses the street and enters Chuck Wagon Burgers. Tom Bauer stands at one of the four tills. He wears an orange uniform with brown piping.

T. BAUER: Welcome to Chuckie Burgers. Can I –

P. MAZENKOWSKI: Hi, Tom.

T. BAUER: Oh. Hi, uh. Paulina.

P. MAZENKOWSKI: Missed you at practice this morning.

T. BAUER: You did? Hey. Um. A bunch of us thought. Um. You should have got the solo.

P. MAZENKOWSKI: Thanks.

T. BAUER: I mean it. I'm not just saying that cause you're, uh, you know, but you nail the runs. And Eileen fudges them. If she didn't suck like a Hoover, you'd have it.

P. MAZENKOWSKI: God, I know. "You're fifty-two? Really? I didn't think you were a day over thirty!"

Mr. Bauer laughs.

UNIDENTIFIED FEMALE: Can I get some service around here?

Mr. Bauer sighs.

P. MAZENKOWSKI: A small Diet Coke, Tom.

Mr. Bauer pours Ms. Mazenkowski's drink.

T. BAUER: I got it.

P. MAZENKOWSKI: Thanks. See you tomorrow, Tom.

T. BAUER: Later. *[pause]* Welcome to Chuckie Burgers.

Ms. Mazenkowski exits Chuck Wagon Burgers and returns to Mr. Rieger, who is waiting in a blue Ford pickup truck.

J. RIEGER: And?

P. MAZENKOWSKI: I dunno, Jer. This is creepy. Why –

[00:41:08]

Tom Bauer dismounts his black and yellow ten-speed at 2177 Granville Street, a salmon-coloured, two-storey stucco house with terra cotta roof tiles. He sneaks around the side of the house. He knocks on a basement window. The light in the basement goes on. Mr. Bauer proceeds to the back of the house.

[00:42:03]

2177 Granville Street viewed from the alley. Mr. Bauer exits the detached garage with Mike McConnell, a mid-teens, Caucasian male with a small build, and shoulder-length red hair. They shush each other, staggering to the basement.

[00:45:25]

Patricia McConnell wears a navy sheath dress. She looks behind her toward the open back door.

PATRICIA MCCONNELL: Anytime this century, Michael!

MIKE MCCONNELL: Don't get your thong in a knot, Patricia!

P. MCCONNELL: You will not use that tone with me, Michael!

M. MCCONNELL: Stop fucking yelling at me!

P. MCCONNELL: Get in the Jeep. Now.

M. MCCONNELL: I'll take the bus.

P. MCCONNELL: If you skip classes again, you are grounded! Do you hear me?

M. MCCONNELL: Fucking deaf people in Tokyo can hear you!

Ms. McConnell enters the garage. A green Jeep exits at a high speed. Mr. McConnell waits and then opens the back door. He punches in the security code. Mr. Bauer appears. They go to the garage and exit on their bikes.

[00:46:19]

Looking down at the Food Court in the atrium in the Granville Mall: Mr. Bauer, in a blue baseball cap, pushes through the lunchtime crowd. He bumps into a tall man who wears jeans and a Blue Jays jacket. They speak. Bauer continues to walk and, within a few feet, hands off a tan wallet to Mr. McConnell, who walks in the opposite direction.

J. RIEGER: Score one for the geezer.

[00:47:36]

Tom Bauer stares at the floor in front of the bathroom mirror.

J. RIEGER: See how the cut of the jacket gives you the illusion of shoulders?

Mr. Bauer sighs. He glances at his reflection in the mirror and then back at the floor.

T. BAUER: You put food in the fridge and you paid the bills. You've done enough, Jer. I can't accept these clothes. It's too much.

J. RIEGER: Nice try.

T. BAUER: Give my clothes back, you jerk! I paid good money for those clothes!

Mr. Rieger laughs.

T. BAUER: Jer, I'm not you. If I wear this crap to school, I'm going to get a shit-kicking.

J. RIEGER: You look great.

T. BAUER: Can I please, please, please have my real clothes back? Please. Please, Jer.

J. RIEGER: Dumpster divers have more sartorial sophistication than you. It's embarrassing.

T. BAUER: So? Why do you care? Why can't –

J. RIEGER: This discussion is over.

[00:48:57]

Mr. Rieger crushes four white tablets and sprinkles them into a can of Pepsi. The television plays music videos loudly in the background. Richard Patolmic is briefly visible as he strides past the kitchen. Mr. Rieger pauses and turns his head.

J. RIEGER: Tom?

Mr. Rieger gives the can of Pepsi a shake. A loud thump can be heard coming from another room, quickly followed by the sound of Richard Patolmic's raised voice. Mr. Rieger runs into the hallway.

T. BAUER: I don't know!

R. PATOLMIC: You're lying! Where is she!

Mr. Bauer shouts. Continuous thumps and shouts.

R. PATOLMIC: You smug, smart-mouthed little puke! You don't want to piss me off!

Mr. Rieger runs back into the kitchen. He carries a baseball bat. He pauses to shut off the camera.

[00:56:08]

Richard Patolmic lies on the floor of the storage room in apartment 304 of The Woodcourt Apartments. Mr. Patolmic is unconscious and has extensive bruising to his face and his leg rests at an angle that suggests it has been broken.

The camera swings quickly to show the hallway. Tom Bauer's face is slack. His mouth and nose are bleeding. His neck shows extensive bruising. He walks aimlessly through apartment 304. He appears to be sleepwalking. Loud knocking can be heard.

J. RIEGER: Door's open!

Mr. Bauer continues to move through the living room. Guy Francis enters the room and studies Mr. Bauer.

J. RIEGER: Spooky, huh? He used to do this when we were kids.

G. FRANCIS: What the hell's wrong with him?

J. RIEGER: Some kind of seizure. *[pause]* I've got a surprise in the storage closet.

G. FRANCIS: Are you fucking out of your mind?

VHS 3
Title: RABBIT SEASON
Date: 15-04-1993
Duration: 01:56:19

[oo:oo:oo]

Mr. Rieger pins Mr. Bauer to the floor in the living room of apartment 304. Mr. Bauer struggles, but Mr. Rieger is kneeling on his arms and straddles him. Fading bruises are visible around neck and lower lip.

J. RIEGER: Someone is still mad about Paulina.

Mr. Bauer turns his face from the camera.

J. RIEGER: Poor Tom. All rejected.

T. BAUER: Get off me!

J. RIEGER: You can't see it now, but I did you a favour. She is one wild –

Mr. Bauer frees an arm and the recording stops.

Mr. Bauer stands with his hands on his knees. He appears out of breath.

J. RIEGER: Let's make this interesting. If you can make it past me to the lobby, I will forgive all your debts.

Mr. Bauer stands straight and presses his hands into his left side. Mr. Rieger makes drum-roll sounds.

J. RIEGER: On your mark! Get set! Go!

Mr. Bauer does not move. He glares at the camera.

J. RIEGER: I said go.

Mr. Bauer attempts to sit on the couch.

J. RIEGER: Meep! Come on, Tommy. Let's see some go-get'um attitude!

Mr. Bauer turns his face from the camera.

J. RIEGER: Give up? Smart boy. You wouldn't even make it to the –

Mr. Bauer suddenly runs toward the hallway, but does not head toward the front door.

J. RIEGER: You moron! The other way! *[laughs]* He makes it too easy. Tick-tock, time's up!

Mr. Rieger follows Mr. Bauer into the bedroom, where the window is open. Mr. Rieger leans out the window. Mr. Bauer shimmies down the drainpipe. As he reaches the ground, he makes an obscene gesture before sprinting to the side of the building and disappearing from view.

J. RIEGER: Firebug, I owe you an apology. What a sneaky little shit.

[00:06:27]

Christa Bauer cries on the couch in the living room of apartment 304.

    J. RIEGER: Of course you can accept it. It's a gift.

The camera focuses on a large-screen TV and an entertainment centre.

    C. BAUER: You bought this with blood money!

    J. RIEGER: Blood money? What are you talking about?

    C. BAUER: I'm sorry, honey, but you have to leave. I can't have drugs in my house. How –

[00:07:05]

Guy Francis is in the driver's seat. The camera flashes by him as it follows Mr. Bauer, who is on his black and yellow ten-speed bike. Mr. Bauer appears unaware that he is being followed as he weaves through downtown traffic.

[00:10:57]

Mr. Bauer rides on Low Level Road beside the railway tracks in North Vancouver. There are no houses along this stretch of road. Bauer rides east toward the Ironworker's Memorial *[Second Narrows]* Bridge. Traffic is light. The reflective lights on Mr. Bauer's pedals circle as they are spotlighted by the vehicle following him.

    J. RIEGER: Get closer.

    G. FRANCIS: He'll make us.

J. RIEGER: Bring me right beside him.

The vehicle pulls over to the side of the road.

J. RIEGER: You're losing him!

Mr. Bauer's reflector lights disappear from view.

G. FRANCIS: Don't you think your aunt is going to go, "Hmm.
I kicked Jer out yesterday and today Tom's been squashed by a car."

Mr. Rieger turns the camera on Mr. Francis.

G. FRANCIS: Kick the shit out of him later. We need to move.
Now. Before this gets any more fucked up than it is.

J. RIEGER: Prioritize.

G. FRANCIS: Prioritize.

J. RIEGER: I don't know why he makes me nuts.

G. FRANCIS: Family does it to you every time.

[00:12:43]

Christa Bauer chews her nails. She realizes she's being recorded
and removes her fingers from her mouth. They are standing at
the arrivals lounge of the Vancouver Airport.

J. RIEGER: Relax. She's checking up on me, not you. I'm the
one with naughty friends.

C. BAUER: Then why does she want to stay with me? Why
doesn't she stay with you in the hotel? She thinks this is my fault.
Anything goes wrong and they all say, "Oh, that Chrissy."

J. RIEGER: You can't let her ride you.

C. BAUER: I hate to say this about my own flesh and blood, but
sometimes I wish she'd – oh! Look! Faith! Yoo-hoo! Over here!
Oh, my!

An attendant pushes Faith Rieger in a wheelchair up to Mr.
Rieger and Ms. Bauer. Mrs. Rieger rises out of the wheelchair

slowly. Her tremors are more noticeable. She embraces Ms. Bauer, who cries. She then embraces her son.

FAITH RIEGER: I'm so glad you're both sober.

J. RIEGER: Hello, Mother.

[00:13:39]

Ms. Bauer opens the oven door in the kitchen of apartment 304. She checks her roast.

C. BAUER: Go knock on the bathroom door and tell Tommy to hurry.

J. RIEGER: Will do.

Mr. Rieger passes the hallway and pokes the camera in the living room. Mrs. Rieger is watching television.

J. RIEGER: How're we holding up?

F. RIEGER: Are you sure you don't need any help?

J. RIEGER: We've got it covered. Sit, sit.

A hand knocks on the bathroom door. The sound of the shower can be heard.

J. RIEGER: Rear in gear, buddy. Chow time!

C. BAUER: The corn, Jeremy! Not the creamed stuff!

J. RIEGER: Got it, Aunt Chrissy!

[00:14:52]

Two patrol officers stand in the hallway of apartment 304. VPD constables Daniel Hanson and Edward Roglaski are recorded together and then individually.

J. RIEGER: I'm recording this now!

96

F. RIEGER: Jeremy, calm down.

J. RIEGER: I can't believe you're just standing there when someone stole my Jaguar!

DANIEL HANSON: Mr. Rieger, we've done everything we can do right now. We have –

J. RIEGER: No! Dust for prints! Canvass the neighbourhood! Do something!

D. HANSON: Mr. Rieger –

J. RIEGER: Could you be more useless? Could you try and be more useless?

Mrs. Rieger appears in front of the camera. She brings her hand up to cover the lens.

F. RIEGER: That's enough, Jeremy.

[00:15:56]

The camera is at waist-level and approaches a Caucasian male, late-twenties with long brown hair who wears a black leather vest over a black T-shirt with a toxic symbol in neon green on the front. He sits at a table in a bar. A hand reaches out and puts a pitcher of beer on the table.

UNIDENTIFIED MALE: Hey, thanks.

J. RIEGER [off-camera]: No problem. What was his name again?

UNIDENTIFIED MALE: He was pretty drunk. Wilber or Willy or something. He's got a twin, though, who's got the same tattoo, right here [points to his neck].

J. RIEGER: What else did he say?

UNIDENTIFIED MALE: Bunch of horseshit. Your boy's having a fine old time. Buying drinks for the ladies, cabbing it everywhere.

J. RIEGER: So you're sure about this address?

UNIDENTIFIED MALE: Your car is gone, man. Take the insurance and ride, baby, cause that Jag is toast.

[00:17:19]

The 1992 silver Jaguar XJS has been gutted. It sits in what appears to be a chop shop. To the left is a partially dismantled red Lamborghini. The camera examines the remains of the Jaguar.

[00:20:41]

The roof of a corrugated aluminum-sided industrial building burns against the night sky. The sound of footsteps on gravel grows louder and then stops.

G. FRANCIS: Our thief's name is Willy Baker.

J. RIEGER: Address?

G. FRANCIS: 1334 Woodcourt Street, apartment 206. Coincidence?

Emergency vehicles can be heard approaching.

J. RIEGER: Shall we be neighbourly?

[00:21:49]

Paulina Mazenkowski waves the camera away as she laughs. Guy Francis shakes his head and laughs. They are in an unfinished basement.

J. RIEGER: It's not funny. This isn't funny, guys.

P. MAZENKOWSKI: Not to you.

G. FRANCIS: I warned you, Jer. I hate to say I told you so, but sometimes you just have to. I told you so.

J. RIEGER: I don't understand how he could do that.

P. MAZENKOWSKI: Yeah, who knew he had balls.

G. FRANCIS: Tom's a gutless wonder. He got this piece of shit to do his dirty work.

The camera swings over to a Caucasian male, late teens/early twenties, shaved head, and a large, red dragon tattoo on the right side of his neck. He is tied to a weight-lifting chair with white rope. His shirt has been removed. He is bleeding at the nose, mouth, and ears.

P. MAZENKOWSKI: Not so tough now, are you, Willy?

She strikes him on the side of the head.

J. RIEGER: Pace yourself.

Ms. Mazenkowski blows a kiss at the camera.

[00:27:39]

Tom Bauer sits on the stone steps of an unidentified building. The camera views him from below. He is smoking a marijuana cigarette.

P. MAZENKOWSKI: Have you seen Jeremy lately?

T. BAUER: Nope. *[pause]* You can do better, way better.

P. MAZENKOWSKI: I can, huh?

T. BAUER: Shit, yeah. Even Shane was better than Jeremy, man.

P. MAZENKOWSKI: Shane was an asshole.

T. BAUER: I'll take asshole over homicidal any day.

P. MAZENKOWSKI: What'd he do?

T. BAUER: Man, let's get off Jeremy.

P. MAZENKOWSKI: Now you got me curious.

T. BAUER: You want another one?

P. MAZENKOWSKI: Sure.

Mr. Bauer lights up a marijuana cigarette and hands it to Ms. Mazenkowski. The streetlight flickers on above them.

P. MAZENKOWSKI: Do you need a ride anywhere?

T. BAUER: I've got my bike.

P. MAZENKOWSKI: We can put it in my trunk. *[pause]* Least I can do if I'm going to crash at your place.

They finish the marijuana cigarette. The camera faces forward, bouncing as they walk.

P. MAZENKOWSKI: Home, James?

T. BAUER: You don't have to. You really don't.

P. MAZENKOWSKI: There's my car.

They walk toward a dark brown 1970s model four-door Chevrolet Cavalier.

P. MAZENKOWSKI: Let me pop the trunk.

Mr. Bauer loads his bike into the trunk and shuts it. The camera points toward the dashboard. The sound of a door opening can be heard.

P. MAZENKOWSKI: Don't slam it too hard or it'll fall off.

The door squeals closed. Ms. Mazenkowski turns the radio on to a classic rock station.

P. MAZENKOWSKI: I need a Slushie. Do you mind?

T. BAUER: Nah.

The engine starts and then stalls.

P. MAZENKOWSKI: Fuck.

T. BAUER: I can double you.

Ms. Mazenkowski laughs again. The engine starts and then stalls two more times before it starts.

P. MAZENKOWSKI: If I can get my car started, you want to come to a party on Friday?

T. BAUER: Sure.

P. MAZENKOWSKI: Hey, Grandpa Sunday! *[honks]* Pick a lane!

UNIDENTIFIED MALE: Up yours!

P. MAZENKOWSKI: Fucking dink in his fucking lame-ass bug. *[honks]* Turn already! *[honks]*

UNIDENTIFIED MALE: Get bent!

P. MAZENKOWSKI: Jesus on a crapper.

T. BAUER: I don't think we should – holy fuck!

The tires squeal and other cars honk.

P. MAZENKOWSKI: That's better. *[The engine stops]* You coming in?

T. BAUER: Let me squish my guts back down my throat first.

Ms. Mazenkowski laughs. The camera is jostled and then the recording stops.

[00:37:20]

Jeremy Rieger removes Tom Bauer's jacket. Mr. Bauer struggles to get away. They appear to be in an attic with dark wood panelling. A bare bulb hangs from the middle of the ceiling. The only other furniture is a bed. Mr. Rieger then removes Mr. Bauer's shirt. The camera is bumped continually.

J. RIEGER: I think you'd better leave.

P. MAZENKOWSKI: I want my stuff.

Mr. Rieger releases Mr. Bauer, who staggers toward the door.

J. RIEGER: Christ. What's the matter with him?

P. MAZENKOWSKI: Gave him some stuff.

Mr. Rieger grabs Ms. Mazenkowski by the hair.

J. RIEGER: You stupid bitch. I wanted him sober.

The camera rocks as they struggle, bumping into the tripod. Ms. Mazenkowski also appears to be intoxicated. Mr. Rieger throws her to the floor and kicks her in the head three times. Mr. Bauer is struggling with the door, which appears to be locked. Ms. Mazenkowski remains curled on the floor.

Mr. Rieger reaches into a duffle bag and removes a pair of handcuffs. He pauses and looks at the camera. He reaches toward the camera and the recording stops.

[00:49:50]

00:50:11 has been erased and replaced with a partial recording of the movie *Scream, Blacula, Scream.*

[01:40:01]

Tom Bauer sits on the kitchen counter. He has small, round burns on each shoulder. His nose is bleeding, and he has a large bruise over his left eye. The camera zooms in on the burns. He raises his hands to cover his face. The cuffs of his shirt are stained reddish-brown. Mr. Rieger opens his wallet and hands some bills to Mr. Bauer.

J. RIEGER: Go get yourself some pot.

Mr. Bauer does not move to accept the money.

T. BAUER: Jer. *[pause]* I can't . . . I don't . . .

J. RIEGER: As far as I'm concerned, we're even-Steven.

Mr. Bauer does not respond.

J. RIEGER: I'm forgiving you, you dumbass.

T. BAUER: You're forgiving me.

J. RIEGER: You took it farther than most people would. I'm giving you credit for balls. So I'm letting you off the hook. For now. But you're going to be good, Tom. If you fuck up again, I won't be so forgiving.

[01:52:37]

The view is grainy from low light exposure. A fire alarm rings loudly in the background. Smoke limits the range of the camera to a few feet. The light from the camcorder suddenly illuminates a set of dark, wet footprints leading to the bedroom window. The camera follows the footprints backward, pausing at a clump of what appears to be hair at the bathroom door. Near the clump is a broken toilet-tank lid stained dark red.

The bathroom floor has a large, red puddle near the wall, which has multiple arches of what appear to be blood splatter. The camera tilts up to examine the ceiling, which also has been sprayed.

J. RIEGER: You think you know someone. You live with them. You eat with them. You fight with them. And then they go and surprise you.

The camera pans the bathroom. The bathtub is filled and the shower curtain has been ripped off. The camera pans the walls.

J. RIEGER: Look at what he can do.

G. FRANCIS: Fire trucks!

J. RIEGER: Look at the rage. Written all over the walls. Like a haiku.

G. FRANCIS: Move your fucking ass, Rieger! I'm not carrying these damn –

2nd BLOOD

The sun hit their apartment every day at three. By this time, Mel needed two bottles, two snacks, breakfast and lunch. Hearty eater, Mel. They were weaning her, so only two short boob-sessions. If it was hot, she needed less. Maybe two bottles. A juice. A Popsicle. But she definitely needed a big breakfast. Always woke with an appetite.

Tom could hear them ripping things, breaking things, the tinkle of things coming apart. The burglars hadn't demanded valuables but they hadn't asked any questions either. They'd said shut up, sit down, stay still.

In the evenings, Mel needed a small dinner: a piece of chicken, some rice, maybe a little broccoli or peas if they bribed her. She liked dessert, understood the words *cake, cookie, candy, grapes, strawberries*. Like her daddy, a sweet tooth. Paulie was greasy-salty oriented – chips, grilled cheese sandwiches with bacon, hamburgers – except for caramels. Paulie had a weakness for caramels.

Through the pillowcase over his head, Tom had a gauzy view of the living room and a blurry view of the kitchen. The shaft of sunlight (finger of God, finger of God) appearing through the gap in the curtains highlighted the landscape of overturned, dismantled furniture. The burglars had taken apart the living room, moved into the kitchen, and were now in the bedrooms.

The duct tape had no give. His forearms and chest and legs were taped to an armchair he and Paulie had found during an ambitious dumpster dive. It smelled of old sweat, the avocado-green upholstery grey with the grime of many owners, the seat pale from the pressure of many bums. Heavy armchair. Tom had dragged it six blocks, Paulie laughing as he flopped down on the sidewalk, flailing, "I can't give you any more power, Captain! The ship's breaking up, she's breaking up!"

Paulie had held her hand to the small of her back, her belly jutting out. "Suck it up, buttercup. Two more blocks."

He was willing to give them the money hidden in The Regina if that was what they were looking for. More than willing. He would deal with Jeremy when Jeremy got out, when Jeremy was released (dancing to the jailhouse rock) and free to come and kick his butt. But Glock Man had taped his mouth shut. The slime of sweat oozing down his face did not loosen the layers of tape as he'd hoped it would. Sweat making his pants stiff, making his shirt clammy, the sting of sweat dripping in his eyes, blurring his vision. They had not opened the windows. The men did not seem inclined to turn on the old-fashioned fans that he and Paulie had nervously bought from second-hand stores, worried about the fan blades and Mel's chubby fingers interacting. The men did not seem to mind being slow-cooked as they burgled.

Maybe Mel and Paulie hadn't been home when the burglars came. The apartment was hot. Maybe Mel had heat stroke and

Paulie had taken her to Emergency. Maybe Mel had been hard to get down last night and Paulie had taken her for a long stroller ride. Maybe they were in the park, right now, waiting for him.

Paulie in a fury was not quiet. Even if they'd gagged her, Tom would have heard something. Duct tape was no match for Paulie. Mel. Mel. Mel would not be this quiet this long. Mel would not be still. Mel wasn't quiet even when she slept.

(Blubbering does not help us, does it?)

Maybe Paulie had needed to go to a meeting. She would bring Mel to a meeting. Maybe they were at a friend's place. Maybe they were safe with some friend that Paulie had not introduced Tom to, that she had never mentioned before. Maybe she'd gone in search of air conditioning. Maybe she was visiting her parents. (Paulie shot, in the bedroom, Mel beside her. Paulie unconscious, Mel tied up and dying of dehydration.)

"Shut up," Muscle Shirt said, coming over to hit him on top of the head. "Do you hear me, snitch? Shut up."

(Blubbering does not make us look tough, Jeremy used to say. God, Tom, no one likes a crybaby.)

"Leave him alone," Glock Man said. "For the love of – fucking go do the bathroom."

He tugged the pillowcase off Tom's head. Tom flinched.

"Are you thirsty?" Glock Man said.

Glock Man crossed the room, opened the duffle bag on the table, and brought out a sports bottle. He popped off the lid, stuck a bendy straw in the orange Gatorade. Then he put the bottle down and unsheathed a Bowie knife. With the bottle in one hand and the knife in the other, he walked over to the chair. He put down the Gatorade. Glock Man lifted the knife and brought it slowly to Tom's face. Tom pulled back, yanking against the duct tape. Glock Man carefully poked a hole in the duct tape between

Tom's lips. He wiggled the knife tip to widen the opening. He pulled the knife back and stuck the straw in the hole.

Tom drank the lukewarm Gatorade, uncertain about where to look, glancing at the overturned and dismantled furniture, glancing at the closed curtains, finally focussing on Glock Man's forehead. He stared steadily at Tom, concern or curiosity, Tom wasn't sure.

"Settle down, Tom," Glock Man pulled the straw out of Tom's mouth. "Let's give you something to take the edge off."

Tom shook his head.

"Don't worry," Glock Man said. He took a Visine bottle out of his pants pocket and squeezed the contents into the Gatorade bottle. "It's not Visine."

Tom yanked harder against the tape. Glock Man clamped a hand on Tom's forehead. He shoved the Gatorade bottle against Tom's mouth, tilting it up, trying to pour it into Tom's mouth. Tom twisted, but Glock Man caught a handful of hair and yanked his head back. Tom pressed his tongue against the hole. Glock Man shifted, tucking Tom's head under his arm to free up that hand so he could plug Tom's nose until he gasped, sucking back too much Gatorade, choking and straining for breath.

"Good boy, Tom. Good boy."

▥

He'd brought home a box of Freezies last week. Tom thought of them as the slanting, early evening light hit his knee. He dozed, startled awake by the sound of cordless drills or heavy thuds. Things you take for granted: getting up and walking over to the fridge and getting a Freezie.

They reminded him of Sno Cones, migraine-inducing cold and kid-friendly sweet, favourite flavour, Rocket Raspberry.

Walking through the Pacific National Exhibition with Paulie, Mel strapped to his chest, only a few weeks old, Labour Day weekend. The crush of kids, of couples and seniors buying lottery tickets for the Dream Home on display. They'd toured it, tried to imagine owning a house with four bedrooms. They couldn't afford the tickets, though. They'd spent seven-fifty each getting in. Paulie determined to get out and do something, sick of staring at the walls. Blew the rest of their budget on food: Paulie had a bag of mini-doughnuts and Tom had a Sno Cone. They wandered through the Marketplace, window shopping, snacking on samples, watching the salesmen and women hustling their buns. Paulie would lean over and slip him tongue, moving the raspberry-flavoured ice back and forth between them, their mouths numb and stained Kool-Aid red.

▐▌

They were on the bus in search of snow. The bus packed with kids with snowboards and skis, with sightseers like themselves. As Mel clutched Paulie in the front seats, Tom stood over them so the skis and snowboards wouldn't fall and hit them. The bus driver wore a Santa hat, wished everyone a ho-ho-ho Mer-ry Christmas as the passengers trooped on, paid their fare, and crammed into the aisles. Tom refused to move, even though he got dirty looks.

They wound through North Vancouver, past the Capilano Suspension Bridge, another site on Paulie's Mel-must-see list. But not until she was older. Not until she could walk by herself. They'd watched the coverage of the woman who'd accidentally dumped her Down's syndrome kid over the side. (The woman's flat reaction when she was told the kid had survived.) Paulie wasn't taking any chances. No kid falling from her arms, plunging hundreds of feet to the ground.

III

"End of the line, Grouse Mountain," the bus driver yelled out. They waited for the crush to pass them, and then followed the crowd up the hill to the Skyride ticket counter. The line snaked down the sidewalk.

"I'll wait," Tom said. "Go sit down."

The tram was packed. Paulie elbowed her way up to a window. Tom stayed in the centre, queasy as the swaying tram (Italy: low-flying plane snaps the tram wires and everyone dies. French Alps: old wire breaks and everyone plunges to their deaths) chugged up and up. Mel squealed and hit the window. Paulie's girl, no fear of heights. Tom was perfectly content to not have a view.

The sun disappeared behind a rolling bank of grey cloud. The first snowflakes, fat and wet, stuck to the north side of the tram as it shuddered and came to a stop.

Mel squinted at the sky as they stepped off, shaking in surprise when a snowflake touched her cheek. Mel looked puzzled and serious as they walked through the snow, the skiers tromping all around them, booted footsteps as heavy as astronauts'.

A shadow blocked the light from the window. Tom raised his head.

Glock Man changed drill bits on the cordless screwdriver and put the TV back together. Muscle Shirt righted the coffee table. He threw a blanket over the couch. They sat, arguing over what to watch, *Wheel of Fortune* or *Wild Weather Week* on the Discovery Channel. Glock Man won by slapping Muscle Shirt upside the head.

"As the tropical storm unleashes torrents of rain, the weakening dam bursts," the deep-voiced host said, thumping danger music accompanying the scene of a family eating supper in their dining room. "The villagers are unaware of the wall of water rushing through the deforested hills above them."

"Do you want to order a pizza?" Muscle Shirt said.

"Don't be any dumber than you have to be," Glock Man said.

"Phone him then. There's nothing here. I'm not fucking spending the night in this heat trap for nothing. I need air conditioning."

"Go fucking stick your useless head in the crapper. That'll cool you down."

"At least open a window. One window."

"I'm not warning you again, idiot."

"Maria Santos is trapped on the highest branch, her frantic family unable to reach her as the water rises."

"I'm taking a shower," Muscle Shirt said.

"Good. Go do that."

Glock Man put his feet up on the coffee table as Muscle Shirt disappeared down the hallway. He turned the TV's volume up.

Tom's tongue felt too big for his mouth, felt dry and strange like a piece of rubber. He didn't feel hot any more. Cold thoughts had worked. Mind over matter. Mel is okay. Mel is fine. Mel is somewhere else.

He remembered a news story where a woman with five children left her baby in the car seat. She thought the babysitter had taken her baby girl out with the other kids. The baby girl was asleep. The mother was tired and late for work. The mother came back six hours later. In the Arizona sun, with the family van's windows closed –

Think cold. Think Arctic. Polar bears. Midnight sun. A documentary he'd seen with Paulie: two scientists studying polar bears had lived in Churchill, a town directly in the path of migrating bears.

The first scientist grew a patch of sunflowers indoors. Sun-flowers turn their heads to follow the sun, and he was wondering what would happen if the sun never set. As the midnight sun began, he planted the flowers outside, and they followed it around and around, followed it until they twisted their own stalks so tight they strangled themselves and died.

▌▌▌▌

"At the top of the hour," the news anchor said, "Good news about the softwood lumber dispute."

Bedtime for Mel: bath, brush teeth, change into a nightshirt, change into fresh diaper, read two books, and kiss good night. One stopperful of Tempra if she was teething.

The phone rang. Glock Man and Muscle Shirt exchanged glances. They let the answering machine pick up, Paulie's voice saying, "We're busy. Leave short messages, people."

"Pau-lina," Jazz sang out. "Where are you? Missed you this morning. I'll bring the book tomorrow. Again. Phone me back or I'll kick your butt. Buh-bye."

Tom's neck had a crick from the angle he'd been sleeping. His hands and feet and ass felt numb. He kept drifting, jerking awake when the commercials came on. Muscle Shirt sipped a Pepsi – the snap of the tab, the sigh of pressure being released, cold pop can in a hand, throat-aching Pepsi going down. Glock Man leaned forward to watch a tornado smash through a military base.

"Sarge?" a guy's tentative voice, off-camera. "Maybe we should go down to the basement now?"

"In a minute, in a minute. Whoa! Do you see the power of that thing?"

▌▌▌▌

A baby's shriek woke him. Then he heard tiny, quick footsteps. Under the doorway, fast-moving shadows dimmed the light coming from the hallway and then passed. He knew he was back in the old apartment he'd shared with his mother, the old Woodcourt Apartments.

"Hello?" Tom said. "Is anyone there?"

The footsteps stopped. He heard a high giggle, like a naughty little kid chuckling over something. Another giggle joined it, and another. The baby cried.

He sat up, disoriented. Across from him was the cot where Jeremy had slept those first few months he'd lived with them when he moved to Vancouver. Tom pushed aside the blankets and swung his legs over the bed. The linoleum was chilly against his bare feet.

"Hello?" Tom said.

He couldn't tell which room the baby was in. He started looking in his mother's room. It was overturned, as if she'd been hunting frantically for something, probably clothes or keys, before she left. He heard the shower running, so checked the bathroom. When he slid the shower curtain aside, the tub was filled. Something crashed, and the footsteps ran.

"Damn it," Tom said.

He poked his head out of the door, saw nothing. The baby's squall became staccato as it started hyperventilating.

In the kitchen, he opened all the cupboards but there were only sluggishly moving cockroaches inside. The fridge was empty. The oven held a shrivelled piece of burnt meat that had white things growing on it. A man was passed out under the table, but it wasn't anyone he recognized. He knew he was going to have to wake him up and kick him out, but he wanted to find the kids first before they wrecked anything else or hurt the baby.

The phone rang. As he walked down the hallway, the phone kept ringing and the answering machine didn't pick up. He ignored it. The storage room had a sliding door. When he pushed it open, cold air ran out. A tiny man, barely coming up to his knees, skittered past him.

Paulina shakily reached out and grabbed his forearm. She was wearing the skin-tight jeans and the white leather jacket with fringe she used to wear in high school. Her hair was strawberry blond again, the way he used to love it, fluffed high in sharp crimps, except for a fist-sized spot above her right ear where it was matted with blood. She pulled him in the storage room and slid the door shut behind them. Her mascara was clumped under her eyes and tracked along her nose as if she'd been crying. She put her index finger to her cotton-candy pink lips and said, "Shh."

As suddenly as the baby had started screaming, it stopped. The footsteps made their way down the hall to the storage room. The door rattled. Paulina let go of him so that she could hold it shut.

"Shh," she said.

"Okay, listen up, kiddies. Once upon a time, this cunt had a magic goose that shit golden eggs. She was rich and happy until her daddy ripped the bird a new ass to see if he could get all the gold. Goose died, gold died, cunt and daddy died poor in the fucking gutter. Got it?"

"Yeah, yeah," Muscle Shirt said.

"Loud and clear," Glock Man said.

A hand grabbed Tom's chin, turned his head. He blinked slowly, trying to focus. Blurry man in front of him, buzz cut, khaki shirt, large, square face. The man was someone he knew.

He had a name that slipped and slithered around his brain as Tom struggled to keep his head up.

"Anything?"

"Nada," Muscle Shirt said.

"Clean as a whistle," Glock Man said.

"Tom." Someone slapped his face. "Did you give him anything?"

"Firebug, man, relax," Muscle Shirt said. "We wouldn't start the party without you."

"Fuck," Firebug said. A slap, nothing hard. "Tommy-boy. Wakey, wakey. You morons. Get me some water. Now, kiddies, before our goose bites it."

Firebug's arm held him up, helping him through the parking lot to the Ramada Inn near the highway.

"I don't think Mel has enough diapers," Tom told the clerk. "She's eating lots and she needs lots of diapers. And wipes. Does she have any snacks? Did you pack her any snacks?"

"My friend's had a bit too much," Firebug said.

The clerk handed back Firebug's credit card, not amused. "Enjoy your stay."

"Thanks."

The elevator was mirrored, and Tom watched himself sway. He did look like he'd pulled an all-nighter, a real humdinger of a binge.

"Is Paulie here?" Tom said, starting to slide down. "Paulie? Paulie?"

Firebug hefted Tom up. "For fuck's sake, shut up."

Tom tried to stand by himself and fell into a mirror, the glass cool against his cheek. "Does Mel have enough diapers?"

"I'm giving you some slack now, Tom, because you're out of it. But I'm going to come down on you hard if you keep bugging me about Mel. Clear?"

"Mel's teething."

"Yeah? That's great. That's just fucking peachy."

<hr/>

"Hey, hey, hey," Firebug said, grabbing his arm. "I told you to stay in the room."

"Firebug?" Tom said. "What are you doing here?"

"I'm on a fucking convention. Come on."

Firebug took him by the elbow and led him back to the open door of the hotel room. Firebug sat him on the chair at the desk and opened a ginger ale. He put two white caplets in Tom's hand and the can of pop in the other.

Firebug leaned in close as if he saw something tiny on Tom's face and wanted to get a good look at it. "You are one sneaky little shit, Tom Bauer. Are you awake?"

"I think we left Mel in the car seat."

"Or are you faking it?"

"She's not here. I checked. We have to go get Mel."

Firebug gripped Tom's arms and gave him a shake. The ginger ale sloshed onto their pants. "Mel's not in the car seat. There is no car seat. Stop talking about the fucking car seat."

Tom cocked his head. "Can you hear her crying? I can hear her crying. Paulie must be asleep. We have to go back to the car. I think we left Mel in the car seat."

Firebug sucked in a deep breath. "Up. Get up."

Tom followed Firebug into the bathroom. He blanked for a moment, and when he came to, Firebug sat him on the toilet.

Tom stared at his clothes. Firebug folded them and put them in the trash can. Firebug left the bathroom and came back with a dry-cleaning bag and pair of clippers. He draped the white plastic bag around Tom shoulders.

"Hold this," Firebug said.

Tom held the bag in place as Firebug sheared his head. His hair fell in clumps, looking lank and greasy, coiled into half-moons on the bleached-white floor tiles. The buzz from the clippers rattled his skull.

"All pretty for your big scene tomorrow."

Firebug took the bag and put it in the trash. He used his hand to scoop the hair on the floor into piles and then he trashed that too.

"Something's wrong," Tom said.

"Get up," Firebug said. "Good Tom. Very good. In the shower."

In the mirror over the bathroom sink, he watched Firebug turning the shower on. The water that hit him was lukewarm. He tried to step away from it, but Firebug held his left wrist, took a white bar of soap and lifted Tom's arm. Firebug scrubbed one pit then the other.

"I know something's wrong."

"Figured that out all by yourself, did you?" Firebug soaped his chest and stomach. "Yeah, you're a regular Sherlock Holmes."

Daylight crowned the hills in the distance, but the vault of the sky was blue-black with a wispy ring of pearl-white light at its centre. In the false night of the total eclipse, the birds stopped singing, the bees stopped droning, and the cows in the field lined up and headed back to the barn. His cousins ran screaming through the front yard, bug-eyed with dark goggles as Uncle Lowell chased them. Aunt Faith and his mother stood on the porch, laughing. Tom put his hand in Jeremy's because Jeremy was smiling down at him. He felt safe.

|||

"The mood is set," Jeremy said. "Candles, soft music, a horny teenager, and his hot babe aaaaand action."

Tom sat on the grey suede sofa. Lilia sat beside him in a blue dress, the artfully tattered hem spread around her like ruffled tulip petals. Jeremy held up the camcorder and waved his hand. On the large-screen TV in front of the sofa, he could see duplicates of him and Lilia. Lilia's manicured hand touched his hair. She was not his type – too sharp, all cheekbones and collarbones, and long arms and legs, and bored, hooded green eyes. Her mass of blue-black waves (one peek-a-boo wave over her right eye) was too retro, too cool for school, and he felt uncomfortable touching her, like he was fondling a really expensive vase that he'd have to pay for if he broke.

"You're sitting beside a beautiful woman who's willing to pop your cherry," Jeremy said. "So you should probably look a tad bit excited instead of like you're swallowing a bug."

"I don't want to do this," Tom said. "I don't think we should do this."

"Lil, give the boy some encouragement."

"I think the star has nerves." Lilia sat back. "I'm feeling kind of antsy myself. Do you want to do some blow?"

"Go for it."

"I'm serious, Jer."

"Once the star's blown, you'll get your blow."

Lilia scratched her face. "Come on, Jer. The teamsters demand a refreshment break. At least give Tom a hoot."

"No hoot for the star. Come on, we're wasting precious time here."

"A couple of lines," Lilia said. "That's all. Come on, Jer. You want us to fly, don't you? You want to watch us fly?"

"Oh, all right. The director caves to the unreasonable demands of the union."

Lilia and Jeremy snorted lines off the glass coffee table. Jeremy reached over and wiped the fine white powder off Lilia's left nostril.

"How about Tommy-baby?" Lilia said, smiling wide. "Let's get Tommy-baby on board."

"Tommy-baby can't handle anything. You give him anything and he passes out."

"Do you want a hoot?" Lilia said to him.

"Yes."

"I don't have any pot," Jeremy said.

"I've got some in my purse. Right back, don't go anywhere." With a flirty toss of her hair, she strode out of the room.

"Jeremy," Tom said. "Could you not tape it at least?"

"You'll thank me later when you want to watch it."

"But I won't want to watch it. Jeremy. There're some things you don't record, you know?"

"Like what?"

"Like this! You don't videotape your . . . your . . . stuff. You don't see people going to funerals with camcorders and sticking them in the caskets, do you? You don't go around videotaping your dog taking a dump, do you? You don't go showing people your colonoscopy, do you?"

"Ugh. I think Lil's right. You need a couple of hoots."

"Here we are! A baggie full of sunshine!" Lilia said.

He smoked a joint while Lilia and Jeremy watched him. Jeremy went back to his director's chair, and Lilia put her hands on Tom's shoulders.

"Lie back," she said. "And think of England."

"You're ruining the mood, people," Jeremy yelled at them as they rolled around the sofa, laughing their asses off. "We had a mood going, and you're ruining it."

Tom's hands tingled. The pain dragged him out of sleep. He heard birds. Leaves shushed. He peeled his cheek off the plaid cover of the bench seat he was lying on. His handcuffs clanged against the exposed metal of the steering wheel as he sprang upright. He wasn't sure if it was early morning or twilight. He couldn't remember falling asleep or how he'd gotten into the truck.

"Paulie!" he shouted. "Mel! Paulie!"

The old Ford was parked on the shoulder of a narrow gravel road crowded with trees. The road wound up a hill and had a puffy line of browning grass marking the centre. Tom tugged at the cuffs that were threaded through the wheel. The cuffs were steel and double-hinged. The steering wheel's rubber cover was attached to the metal core with duct tape.

"Paulie! Mel! Paulie!"

If he wanted to, he could honk the horn. He could kick the parking brake off. He could open the door. He was reasonably sure he could yank the steering column off. Instead, he leaned forward and rested his head on the wheel as his chest tightened and his breath came in shallow gasps. He could get them killed if he did something stupid. He could get them killed if he did nothing. He could sit here and be good and hope for the best. They might not even be here. Or they might be twenty feet away.

The windows were open. Tom leaned out as a wave of nausea emptied his stomach down the side of the truck. Stringy bile sparkled against the dark blue rust-splotched paint. His head ached, a steady, heavy throb in his temples.

Paulie would do something. Paulie would not sit obediently like a dumb dog. Paulie would take the truck apart to stay in the game.

Tom pressed the horn but it didn't make a sound. He pressed both sides of the horn, and then slammed his hands against the wheel again and again in a fit. This isn't helpful, he told himself. Calm down.

Bracing his feet against the dashboard, he grabbed the steering wheel and tried to pry it off. He'd seen it done somewhere, a movie, something with Arnie or Sylvester or Jean-Claude. Nothing happened, except his wrist bones were scraped raw. He paused, trying not to hyperventilate.

He used his foot to pull off the parking brake. The truck didn't move. Tom slammed himself forward and then back, forward and back. The truck rolled slowly backward until it rested against a fat-trunked tree that showered brown needles in the cab.

A hiker could be nearby. Or a hunter. Tom opened his mouth, but couldn't bring himself to yell for help. He didn't know why it was embarrassing, even now when his life literally depended on it.

"Fire!" he shouted. "Fire!"

The truck smelled like old sweat, like a gym locker, funky like socks that could stand by themselves. The dashboard was faded where the sun hit and dark blue underneath. The floor was pebbled plastic, dusty blue with dirt and gravel. The bench seat was worn on the driver's side so Tom tilted toward the door. His wrists were shredded from his attempts to pull off the steering wheel. He had managed to crack the plastic on the left side. He let his head fall back. The sun had cleared the tops of the trees. Tom wondered what time that meant.

He'd left them at six. He'd checked in with Paulie during his coffee break at nine, and she'd sounded fine. Annoyed and tired, actually. Mel had been hard to put down. The TV had been loud in the background, Mary Hart's polished chirp accompanied by the *Entertainment Tonight* theme song. Paulie had mumbled responses and finally'd said she needed to get to the dishes but Tom knew she really wanted to veg and wasn't up to distracting him from work's soul-crushing monotony. A full day and night had passed since they'd been snatched.

He caught his reflection in the rear-view mirror, startled again by his baldness. He remembered a motel, or a hotel, a clerk. A potential witness. Firebug could hardly be planning to kill them if he was dragging Tom in front of potential witnesses. Firebug wasn't sloppy. Something, something, he couldn't understand why his thoughts were so scattered, why everything was jumbled and jerky.

Jazz would check in, would make sure that no backsliding was taking place on her watch. She had phoned, Tom remembered that. Jazz had left a message, something about a book. Shirl would miss them in the morning. She might not be alarmed enough to visit. Maybe after a few days, she'd wonder where they went, be annoyed that she had no recess from the twins. Stan would call tomorrow when he didn't show for work, but wouldn't be too concerned. People quit Lucky Lou's all the time without giving notice.

Paulie wouldn't go down without a slugfest. Maybe one of the neighbours had seen or heard something. Maybe they'd already called the police. Maybe someone had gone to their apartment and seen the mess and put two and two together and there was an all-points bulletin out for them.

But Paulie wouldn't do anything that would get Mel hurt. If they got Mel first, Paulie would bide her time. The neighbours might have heard the commotion but assumed he and Paulie were still renovating. They'd banged around like crazy these last few days.

It didn't make sense. Muscle Shirt had called him a snitch, but Tom had kept his mouth shut. Paulie'd never go running to the cops, not with her record. They were such small fry, it wasn't funny. It had to be a sick, stupid joke.

But Firebug lacked a sense of ha-ha. Personality type A-B, All Business. Everything in its place. Firebug's perfectly tidy writing, textbook cursive. A dot for every "i" and a cross for every "t." Firebug wasn't random. Doesn't make any sense, doesn't make any sense, doesn't. Sense.

He pounded on the steering wheel, willing it to break. He braced his feet again. He would run up the road to the top of the hill and see what he could see from there. He would circle the truck, expanding his search in widening circles in case Paulie and Mel were nearby. He would find them. They were alive. Firebug wasn't random.

Something popped. Tom scrambled for the door, kicking off his sneakers to fit his toes under the handle. The door swung

126

open with a loud creak. Tom slid outside, braced himself on the running boards, and, grabbing the wheel, used his weight and all his strength to pull. The steering wheel groaned, and then clicked, and he could feel a minute shift.

Then he heard heavy footsteps crunching on the gravel. Tom raised his head to look over the door. Firebug walked down the hill. He was wearing fatigues and black boots. His holstered gun bulged under his shirt. His sunglasses glinted as he turned his head, his attention caught by something in the woods. Tom yanked on the wheel, yanked and twisted and bounced, trying to make it break faster.

The footsteps stopped near him. Tom listened. He turned to find Firebug watching him. He stood, swallowing.

"Hey," Tom said. "Firebug, I –"

"You don't speak until you're spoken to," Firebug said.

Tom found himself babbling, unable to stop. "Please. Please, can I see them? Please, Firebug. Please, I –"

"Paulie's right there," Firebug said, making a small movement with his head.

The road was empty. Tom turned his head back in time to see Firebug's fist. Tom spun, still tethered to the steering wheel, falling back against the bench seat as he tasted old pennies, blood in his mouth from where he'd bit his tongue. It felt like his scalp was too tight, like he had a rat bite above his ear. Firebug shook out his hand, his solid silver ring washed with blood.

"I ask the questions," Firebug said.

The bile rose up so fast, even though Tom tried to avoid it, he ended up spraying Firebug across the chest. Tom coughed, shaking, his throat burning. Firebug lifted his shirt. He stared at the vomit and then at Tom.

"If you were anyone else," Firebug said, "I would have shot you long ago."

IIIII

"Stop here," Firebug said, poking Tom's ribs with the tip of his .45 Para-Ordnance pistol, Betty. ("The only woman who was ever faithful to me." Firebug in the maudlin stage of drunk, rubbing Betty along his cheek in a smoke-hazed kitchen. "Good, old Betty.")

The clearing was about a hundred feet from the truck. The trees surrounding the clearing were tall and had white, peeling bark. Tom didn't know what kind of trees they were. Their crowns were high overhead and their leaves flashed dark green and then light green, dark and light as a breeze blew through the canopy. The trunks were thin. Firebug unsnapped Tom's cuffs.

"Please remove your shirt," Firebug said. He held out a black garbage bag, keeping the pistol trained at the centre of Tom's guts. The handcuffs glittered and clinked at the bottom of the bag with his sneakers. Firebug had coils of thin, white rope thrown over his shoulder.

Tom struggled to make his fingers work. They were cold and Novocaine-numb. He was shaking. He pulled his T-shirt over his head and dropped it in the bag.

"Your pants, please," Firebug said.

He dropped his eyes. Just like a doctor's office, visit to the doctor, he told himself even as he felt heat creeping up his neck.

"Tom," Firebug said. "I don't want to repeat myself. Do you understand?"

Tom nodded. He undid his button and then his zipper and pushed his pants down his legs and stepped out of them. He bent over, picked them up, and dropped them in the garbage bag.

128

"Good," Firebug said. "Socks, please."

Tom lifted one foot and then the other.

"Underwear, please."

He didn't think about what he was doing. He kept his eyes on a spot past Firebug, and then on the truck. Firebug put the garbage bag down.

"Please back up," Firebug said.

Tom stepped back and then back again until he felt a tree trunk behind him. The trunk wasn't thick, but the tree was solid and didn't move when he leaned against it.

"Kneel," Firebug said.

The ground was dusty. Firebug pushed him into position, legs apart, back resting against the bark. Firebug folded Tom's forearms behind the trunk. His joints popped in protest, the muscles across his chest and down his arms twinged from the stress.

"I'm going to keep the pressure off your wrists," Firebug said. "Don't want to risk nerve damage, do we?"

Jaunty. Very jaunty. Things were going well in Firebug's world. Rope went around Tom's stomach, around his chest, and finally around his neck.

"Be quiet," Firebug said, patting Betty who was safely back in her rig. "Or I'll shoot your kneecaps."

Firebug picked up the garbage bag and slung it over his shoulder like a Santa sack. He strolled back to the truck as if he had all the time in the world. Tom could wiggle, could shift his legs, but if he moved too much, the rope tightened around his neck and he quickly stopped.

His heart, his heart, his chest hurt because his heart was vibrating like a rung bell. Trees and sunshine, leaves, fierce summer light, smooth dusty ground. Paulie and Mel, somewhere, alive, please, alive and unhurt. His breathing rapid and loud in the clearing. He wanted to memorize his location. Two kinds of trees. Deciduous. Leafy trees. Needles and leaves. The sad total of what he remembered from high-school biology.

He jerked at the whine of a small motor. Firebug leaned into his truck, hand vacuuming. Tom's guts iced, clenched. All the "i"s dotted, "t"s crossed. All evidence of his existence hoovered up and tossed into a plain black garbage bag.

▦

Firebug walked back and forth between the truck and Tom. First, he brought back a camcorder and a tripod. He adjusted the tripod so the camcorder was level with Tom's head. On the next trip, he brought back a green camp chair, which he set up in front of Tom. He placed a tackle box on one side of the chair and a navy blue duffle bag on the other. He snapped open the tackle box. The top layer was all lures and spoons. He lifted the fishing stuff off, and underneath were Firebug's real tools, neatly compartmentalized: a mini-torch, the kind that caramelized crème brûlée; a pair of red-handled needle-nose pliers; stainless steel surgical scalpels; thick needles, the kind that Paulie had used to sew canvas.

Firebug pulled a small bag of white powder out of his pants pocket. He opened the bag and then reached into the tackle box and picked up a tiny spoon that he used to scoop up the powder. Coke or crank – either way, it wasn't promising.

"Bump?" Firebug said, offering Tom the spoon.

Tom shook his head.

Firebug snorted the bump and sat back, tapping the spoon on the chair. He closed the bag and put it and the spoon in his pocket. He admired the clearing before he bent over and picked up one of the needles. He rolled it between his fingers. "I'm not a big believer in chainsaws. Jer . . . well, Jer's watched *Scarface* one too many times. I say once you hack off a limb, you've peaked."

"Anything you want," Tom said. "Anything."

Firebug stuck the needle in the back of his hand like it was a pin cushion. Firebug picked up the pliers and the mini blowtorch. He patted his pockets until he came up with a lighter. The blowtorch hissed and then whooshed to life as Firebug brought the lighter close to it.

If Tom was standing, he would have fallen. He felt boneless, his bones had dissolved. He sagged against the ropes, hoping he'd pass out.

"Anything," Tom said. "Anything, Firebug. Anything you want. I have money. Do you want money? I have seventy thousand dollars. I have three keys of coke. They're yours."

Firebug plucked the needle out of his hand with the pliers. He passed the blowtorch along the needle until it glowed orange. The air above the flame quivered.

"Did I do something?" Tom said. "I'm sorry. I don't know what I did. You have to tell me what I did. Please. Please, don't. Please, Firebug. Please."

Firebug shut off the torch and put it beside the chair. He reached over to the camcorder and turned it on. He stared into the camera. "Jer, old buddy, old pal. You have something that belongs to me. And now I have something that belongs to you. Look at the camera, Tom, and beg Jeremy for your life."

Tom launched himself up, trying to stand. He could kick then. The ropes creaked. He could hear himself grunting as he strained to make the ropes move.

Firebug's arm pulled back. Sunlight showed the thinning spots at his temples, shining with sweat. Lips pursed in concentration, eyes wide and fixed, Firebug jabbed.

For a moment, Tom thought he missed. But the needle hadn't connected yet. The skin of Tom's left nipple sizzled as the needle touched. He could hear it, the sound like a match being pinched out by wet fingers. His chest exploded. He convulsed. His back arched and his body went rigid as Firebug forced the needle in until it grated against bone.

Nothing existed. Nothing had ever existed but the pain. He squealed, he heard the sounds ripping through his throat, and he fought the ropes. He screamed and he screamed and he threw himself forward so the ropes would tighten and it would end.

ROLL

Roll the drunks passed out at your mother's party. Since they've trashed the apartment, they might as well help with rent. Never take all the money. The tricky part of rolling in your own home is facing a jonesing boozehound who's sure he's been ripped off. Take just enough to cause doubt: did I spend it or did I get rolled? Practise looking innocent in the mirror. If you can't manage innocent, settle for slack-jawed, drooling stupid. Blink slowly and nod a lot.

Roll your mother's boyfriend first. He's got a decoy wallet in his pants. The real wallet is tucked into a hole in the lining of his black leather vest. He's been claiming poverty, but he's sporting almost seven hundred dollars. He has an emergency twenty in his right shoe. You once found a tooth, a large metallic molar in a shoe. It left an angry red indentation in the man's heel. Another time, you found a faded black-and-white picture of a pretty, pigtailed girl holding a doll. Leave the boyfriend's twenty. You just wanted to look. You're always curious to see what people are afraid to lose.

2.

"Someone out there must be missing you by now, baby." The woman tilts her head, tries on a smile. She has a fine web of wrinkles around her eyes and two deep lines bracketing her mouth. "You got a name?"

"Yeah," you say.

"Yeah? Yeah what?"

Watch the tea kettle rattle on the hot plate. "I can't remember."

"Huh," she says, pulling her sleeve over her hand to pick up the kettle. She carefully pours two mugs. Her teaspoon ting-tings as she stirs. The hot chocolate has floating lumps of powder, circling. They burst open on your tongue, gritty and sweet.

A fat fly bounces off the window. A silver suncatcher spins, a winking happy face hanging on a white thread tacked to the window frame. Your nose drips again. Bright red drops splatter the rim of the mug. Black gunk under your fingernails. Dirt or old blood.

"You need fresh clothes. There's a T-shirt in the pile by the door." She's wearing a light blue sweatshirt with soft-focus kittens on the front. The kittens are rolling around in a basket, playing with a ball of pink yarn.

Even if you get stared at, at least the bloody shirt looks tough. "I'm good."

She sips her hot chocolate, staring. "At least wash up. You look like hell."

"I'm sorry," you say. "I forgot your name again."

"Lorraine."

"Thanks, Lorraine."

"Bathroom's down the hall. Towel and soap are in the hallway closet."

Lock the door and sit on the toilet. Take the raggedy pink towel hung over your arm and a small bar of cheap hotel soap and put them on the edge of the sink. Peel off your shirt to wash it. Pause to touch the footprint-shaped bruises around your ribs. This explains the stitch when you take a deep breath or try to lift your right arm. Two patches of gauze are taped to your shoulders. Lift an end to peek. It's been feeling like someone's got their fingernails and they're digging them in and wiggling them under the skin. Peel off both patches and scratch the scabs oozing sticky, clear fluid. The burns are small and round, cigarettes most likely. They'll leave raised scars. Your mother has one on the back of her hand. *Brand of a love gone bad.*

The bathroom is humid but you're cold. Stall over your mother's name. Cindy. Carol. Cathy. Memory skitters away.

Touch the side of your head. You have an egg. Look in the mirror above the sink. You have a Fu Manchu moustache in varying shades of dried and drying blood.

137

Scrub your face until the water runs clear. Take a shaky breath. Hold what you have and wait for the past to come crawling back from its bender. Your mother has terrible taste in men. Lorraine has terrible taste in clothes and you're drying yourself on her pink towel.

███

"You got a stash, baby. Let's see what you stashed." Lorraine reaches down through the hole under the armpit of the jacket you handed her. She pulls out a thin wallet.

"Let me see."

She's opened the wallet. Three crisp one-hundred-dollar bills are inside. Lorraine whistles. "Baby's flush."

Take the wallet and pull out the I.D. The student card has a picture of a sullen boy with lank, shoulder-length blue hair hiding his face. He's wearing a plaid shirt. Thomas Eugene Bauer is in Grade Ten and his bus pass is going to expire at the end of June.

"What month is it?" you ask Lorraine.

"Did you get clocked and good. It's June, honey." Lorraine says, continuing her search of the jacket lining. She pulls out a little baggie. "Maybe you owe someone money."

"You think that's me?"

"That's you, baby."

"Maybe I jacked Thomas. Maybe Thomas kicked the crap out of me."

"Uh, yeah." She doesn't roll her eyes, but the sentiment is clear on her face and it irks. "Thomas or Tommy or Tom? What'd'ya think?"

"Tom."

"Hello, Tom. Pleasure to meet you."

"The pleasure's mine."

▓

"And this is Sheldon," Lorraine says.

Force your eyes open as the parade of school pictures continues. Sleep is heavy on your shoulders. You can barely remember your own name, and she is giving you the lowdown on her grandkids. She has this tentative smile that makes you fight sleep.

Taste something metal. The hot chocolate isn't sitting too well. The room goes tilt-a-whirl. Lorraine stops talking and watches you. She does not appear surprised when you face plant the floor.

Realize Lorraine hasn't been telling you about her grandkids at all. She's been explaining that she is not all bad. She's going to roll you now, but she's got her reasons.

3.

The crash church lets you sleep it off. People leave, arrive, settle down, wake up, scrounge, and just plain chat, a background hum punctuated by belligerents. Take comfort from the noise. Grow uneasy during the lulls. The crash church has many exits, many rooms, and a maze of dark corridors with hidey holes, but most people crash in the pews. Hide in the middle of everybody. Cover your head with a sleeping bag even though the day is hot and the sleeping bag reeks.

"Rick?" a man says. He shakes shoulders, turns back blankets and sleeping bags to look at faces. "Rick?"

Examine the man. He's very clean, which makes you suspicious. He's wearing black jeans and a black windbreaker.

"Has anyone seen Rick?"

"Fuck off," someone grumbles.

They are coming for you. They are coming down the hallway. Sneak behind the pulpit and crawl into it. Listen to the man make his way through the pews calling out for Rick. Even after he leaves, do not move. You're spotted by a woman who is cutting through the pews to get to a corridor. Put your finger to your lips and soundlessly shush her. She speeds up to get away from you.

▒

"Get out, get out, get out," the woman says, shooing you out of the corner store. "Don't come in my store."

"Someone's following me," you say.

"Someone always following you. Scare away my customers. Get out, get out, get out. Go take a bath."

Just in case you weren't sure she meant it, she locks the door behind you and flips the sign from "OPEN" to "*Sorry*, We're Closed."

The grey car is gone. Make a run for cover. Ignore traffic, ignore cars honking, cross the street while the grey car is gone.

▒

Across the hall of the drop-in centre, the TV in the seniors' room blares the evening news. Tammy-Lynn is missing. She lived two blocks from her school and hasn't been seen since yesterday. Her parents weep on TV. Volunteers sweep the nearby woods, calling out her name. They comb the ground for clues. A police chief faces a media scrum stoically. A hotline has been set up, and a reward for information leading to her return. Tammy-Lynn is thirteen. Her school picture shows a buck-toothed girl with braces, crooked bangs, and large, green eyes.

Sip your coffee and turn your attention to the guys playing pool. Time is a slippery fish. But you're sure it's been a while since you were home. They aren't exactly breaking out the sniffer

141

dogs for you. No one holds your teddy bear on TV, sobbing for your safe return.

◫

"I gave you a sleeping bag last night," the guy says, peeved. He stands in the back of a black van with a big red cross on the side. He holds a green sleeping bag out of your reach. "What did you do with it?"

He doesn't look familiar at all. "Are you sure it was me?"

"Don't give me that," the guy says. His blue T-shirt sleeves are rolled up to his shoulders, his jeans are creased, and his brown hair is short. He has a bulgy red nose that you believe you would remember.

"Lorraine took everything," you say. "She even took my shoes."

"Bullshit. I saw you drop it. That's the third sleeping bag I gave you this week."

Frown. "Are you sure?"

"I have eyes. I'm not stupid. I'll give you a sleeping bag this time, but don't let me catch you lying again."

"I think Lorraine took it. She took everything."

"There wasn't any Lorraine. You dropped it, you bullshitter."

"Give him the fucking sleeping bag already," the driver says, crushing his smoke under his boot.

"But he keeps throwing them away."

The driver has one black eyebrow that lifts in the middle. "Look at him. He's a spaz. That's why he's out here."

"No more sleeping bags," the guy says, lowering his head to glower at you. "You hear? You're not the only person who needs them. I can't keep wasting them on you."

The driver rolls his eyes. "Yeah, you tell him."

Turn to walk away. The man behind you glares. He wears a black eye patch, like a pirate.

"There was a Lorraine," you insist.

His eye could burn holes. The man swallows hard, making the dragon tattoo on his neck ripple. He shifts on his aluminum crutches, moving closer to you. He has a snow-white cast on his right leg from his thigh to his foot.

"Hey," the guy in the van says to Eyepatch. "What can I do you for?"

Eyepatch swings his head and focuses his venom on the guy in the van. Eyepatch shuffles out of line and grabs your arm, holding it tight.

"You set me up," he says.

Eyepatch has a bruise gone green showing under the eye patch. He has a shaved head which shows other bruises going yellow and green. You're sure he has the wrong person. You'd remember the dragon tattoo. It's large, vermilion with yellow eyes. Shake your head. He watches you for a long time and then lets you go.

"Where's your sick fuck of a cousin?" he says.

A car honks. Duck.

"See! See, he dropped it again!" The guy in the van is ecstatic to have caught you in the act. "You bullshitter!"

Pick up the sleeping bag. Hold it tight. The floor of the crash church will be hard without it. "I'm sure there was a Lorraine." Think about it. "I'm almost sure there was a Lorraine. She was nice, but she took everything. I think she was real. She must have been real. I don't know why I'd make up a wo –" Realize you are babbling. Bite your lips shut.

Eyepatch stares at you and stares at you. You can't move when he's staring at you.

"Don't get hung up on what's real or not real," Eyepatch says. "That's just another straitjacket."

A man stops beside Eyepatch. They are the same height, the same weight, and have the same beer-coloured eyes in the same face. They are like before-and-after pictures: before the eye patch and after; before the leg cast and after. No-Eyepatch has the same tattoo, but on the other side of his neck.

"This him, Willy?" No-Eyepatch says.

Willy shakes his head.

No-Eyepatch says to you, "Do you know this kid named Tom? Tom Bauer?"

Wonder if they're real. Ask, "Are you real?" just in case you are standing on the sidewalk staring back at nothing.

"Are you a schitz?" No-Eyepatch says. He turns to Willy. "Do you know this guy?"

"I thought I was Tom," you say.

"You're not the Tom we're looking for," Willy says.

"If you were the other Tom, I'd kick your ass to Kingdom Come," No-Eyepatch says. "No one sets up my bro and gets away with it."

▐▐▌

Crawl back up the drainpipe. Move backward in the logic of dream time. Crawl back through the window. Look up then down the street as you back into your bedroom in your mother's apartment. Your hands draw blood from the curtains. Your feet pick up blood from the carpet as you creep through the hallway. The shadowy figure of a man in all black examines something through the front-door peephole while someone pounds on the other side of the door. Back into the bathroom where another man in a black ski mask lies on the floor, one arm stretched over his head, the

144

other over his chest. Your hands steady as you place them on his neck and find no pulse. His burly chest rises suddenly. His bright blue eyes flutter open. Blood runs off your feet. Blood streams back into his face, back into a hole where his brains show through.

The lid of the toilet tank flies from the floor into your hands. The centrifugal force of your fear spins you. The bits of hair and skull on the lid leap to the man in the black ski mask, who slides up the wall, his face snapping forward. Knight him again, closing the rip in the mask that will hide his brown hair. Each time the tank hits him, he stands straighter. He tucks his snub-nose six-shooter back in his waistband. Replace the tank lid slowly, sitting down. Water streams from the floor back to your hair, back up your nose, you suck it in in great gasps. The other masked man jogs back into the bathroom.

"I'll go check it out," he says. "Watch him, Rusty."

But he grips you, pressing a semi-automatic to your forehead, his attention caught by pounding on the front door.

"Bauer! Bauer, you motherfucking set me up!" Willy Baker screams from the hallway. "Bauer!"

They lift you off the toilet. Water streams back into the bathtub, off your shirt, off your face as they grip your arms and press you into the overflowing bathtub.

———

The pounding is distant and steady like a heartbeat. It kicks you out of sleep so you're sitting, shoving the blankets back.

Shout, "Mom! Mom, wake up! Mom!"

"Shut up, you fucking doorknob."

Mom is hard to wake. She might not hear them kicking in your front door. Go wake her up. Run around the apartment trying to find her.

Shake her hard. "Get up, get up. I hear something."

There's a man in your mother's bed. Sometimes they sleep over.

"Where's Mom?" you ask him.

"Get this freak off me!" the man says.

The room is full of beds. Men flinch from the lights as they go on.

"I'm going to have to ask you to calm down," a large man in blue overalls says. "You can't go around screaming –"

They're coming down the hallway. You hear them marching down the hallway. Run for the bedroom window and crawl out. Run. Run down the street and hide.

4.

Open one eye.

"Tom?" the voice says again.

The tree above you nods, agreeing with the breeze. The sky is army-blanket grey. The grass itches your cheek. The clouds have rolled in, and you are hearing voices.

A girl squats down beside you, her knees showing through her ripped jeans. She has long, reddish-blond hair falling around her shoulders in big curls. She takes off her sunglasses. Her eyes are dark blue.

If you're going to start seeing things, pretty girls are always a bonus, even if they look at you sourly.

"Do you remember me?" the girl says.

Shake your head.

"What do you remember?"

Men in black ski masks. Water running. Dreams. Streets. Nothing that makes sense. "Nothing."

▓

"This way," she says.

She makes move-along gestures like a traffic cop.

"A traffic cop, huh?" she says.

"Did I say that out loud?"

"No, I'm psychic," she says.

"Oh."

"What're you on?" she says. "Are you stoned?"

Stop. If you go up to Lorraine's room, she's going to roll you. When she found you lost on the street, she acted all friendly but she took everything, even your shoes.

"I'm Paulina," the girl says. "I don't know who this cunt Lorraine is. I'm bringing you to your apartment."

"I don't know," you say. They haven't exactly been combing the woods for you. Doubt they want you back.

"Big old mama's boy like you? Shit yeah, she wants you back."

▓

The girl leans against the driver's door, one hand on the steering wheel, the other supporting her head. She glances at you. The rain makes patterns on the windshield.

"This is your street. Anything look familiar?" she says.

Shake your head.

"Maybe something will come back when you get to your place," she says. She sits up, alert. The car has turned a corner, and there's an apartment building at the other end of the street. Half of it is still brown with white trim, although the black shadow of flames has been burned around the windows. The other half

148

rests at a lazy tilt, the walls burned down to struts and supports, a cobweb of black wood bending in on itself. She stops the car in front of the lobby doors, which have been boarded shut and criss-crossed with yellow tape that flaps in the wind.

"Crap," the girl says.

          |||||

The girl parks her car in front of the only house on a block filled with boxy warehouses. The downstairs windows are boarded up.

"This way," she says. She walks around the side of the house. Follow her up steep, creaking fire-escape stairs. The stairs shudder as you walk.

The room has a single bed on a rusty white frame. Beside the bed is the kitchen, a cocktail fridge, a sink, and a hot plate. The bathroom is separated by a shower curtain, and the counter is a dresser. The kitchen window has a view of an empty parking lot.

Repeat her name. She gets annoyed if you call her Lorraine. She is not Lorraine, although Lorraine seemed nice and offered you a towel just like the girl is doing right now. She pulls back the flowery shower curtain separating the bathroom from the living area. The shower is a grey stall with a blue shower curtain.

"Scrub everything," she says.

          |||||

The nurse at the Emergency admissions desk has a toy train on her desk. Stop staring. It's hard, because you remember some-thing: the blue train with the sunny face is Thomas the Tank Engine, and the fat conductor thinks Thomas is really useful. The nurse picks up the toy.

"I'm having a harder time letting go than my son is," the nurse says with a wry smile. "He's moved on to Power Rangers."

"Uh, yeah," the girl says after a long silence.

"Anyhoo," the nurse says. "Do you know what kind of drugs your friend gave you, Tom?"

The girl nudges you.

Say, "I don't know."

"I think it was mushrooms," the girl says. "It might have had a sprinkling of acid, too."

"Hmm," the nurse says.

"I'm remembering things better now," you say. "I don't think I need to do any tests."

"Better safe than sorry," the nurse says.

▌║

You can see only their eyes. They're wearing ski masks.

"Where's the coke?" one of the men says.

"I don't know," is not the answer they want.

Don't scream. They slug the side of your head when you scream. Mrs. Tupper must have heard you by now, must have heard something and will call the police. Your downstairs neighbour complains when you cough too loud. She has to have heard something before they made you stop screaming.

The man with the deep voice whips the shower curtain open. The bathtub is filling.

"I don't know. Jer took it. When he left. I don't know where it is." This is all you have to say. They aren't going to believe you yet.

"Tie his arms, Rusty," the guy to your left says as they bend you over the side of the tub. They press your face toward the water.

"You dumb fuck. You used my name," Rusty says. "Now we're going to have to kill him."

▌║

"Shh," the girl says. "Shh."

She lowers the railing of the bed, lifts the sheets, and crawls in beside you. Her arm is heavy on your side. The nurses whisper in the corridor. The man in the bed beside you groans.

"Shh. You're okay now." Her breath tickles your neck as she speaks.

Believe her. For the first time in your memory, let go and believe that someone is watching out for you.

"Shut up," she says.

5.

You are on the floor in the upstairs room of a rundown house. Handcuffs pin your wrists behind your back. Your fingers fall asleep under the combined weight of your body and Jeremy's as Jeremy straddles your waist. In your peripheral vision, underneath the bare bulb that hangs from a yellowed ceiling, Paulina crawls near the camera tripod, her dress transparent, wet from the rain, one side of her blond head matted with blood from Jeremy kicking her head and kicking her head and kicking her head. As Jeremy lights the first cigarette, you're flooded with disbelief so strong, feel sleepwalking calm. Jeremy tenses like a sprinter waiting for the gun, his hand pinching your neck as he holds you still.

"Did you think you could get away with it?" Jeremy says.

Remember the first time you felt this way. You were ten. On a small hill near your school, you hit a patch of black ice and the bicycle tires slipped sideways. You hurt your wrist trying to break your fall, but it didn't matter because a very large truck was behind you. The truck came to a stop on top of you, but it had monster wheels that lifted it high enough so nothing touched you. If you had moved, if the driver had tried to swerve, you would be under the wheels. Stare up at the undercarriage and – in the same calm – crawl out, dragging your bike behind you.

Move back an hour before you entered this room. Remember instead how Paulina's hand felt as she led you up the stairs, how you could make out the line of her thong, the dress cotton and light blue, mid-thigh. She wasn't wearing a bra and her nipples were hard, dark points. A bulge pressed against your jeans, sudden awareness of your own skin, anticipation made you light-headed.

Move ahead a few hours. Jeremy will press you to have pancakes as if that was going to make everything all right. Jeremy will take you home in a cab. He will chat and laugh like you went to a movie together, like you grabbed a bite to eat. The cab driver will not speak during the trip, nervously examining you both in his rear-view mirror. You will try not to bleed on his seat.

But the moment you start to believe that you could die is like a lighthouse. The searchlight circles back and back to that moment when Jeremy takes the first cigarette from his mouth. Jeremy's face shadowed by the light from the bulb, the tip of the cigarette a red dot in the dim room.

You hate getting your cavities filled, hate the moment when the chunks spattering your mouth are bits of your tooth, when the smell from the drill is you, burning. This thought does not go through your head while Jeremy lowers the cigarette tip. This thought comes later. Before the tip touches your skin, feel a pinpoint of warmth on your shoulder, sudden like sunlight through the clouds.

If you had a time machine, you would go back to the moment when you agreed to wash Jeremy's silver 1992 Jaguar XJS coupe for quick cash. You would not take any money from Jeremy. You would not tell Jer about Paulina, and Jer would not seek her out and you would never see them kissing in the Jag at school.

Better yet, you would not deke out on a family dinner to go downstairs with a set of spare car keys. You would not hand the keys to Willy. You would not tell Willy the security code to the car alarm and Willy would not say, grinning, "Your own cousin, hey? Fuck, you're cold, man."

SURRENDER

October 9, 1993

Paulina-baby,

I imagine you wrapped in a quilt. My granny and my aunties would make quilts and every time me and my sisters were scared or hurt they'd wrap us up tight and hug us and we'd be warm and safe.

I'm not your judge. You aren't sitting in my court, and I don't pass my punishments down to you. You did the best you could with what you had. The things that keep you confused and miserable you put into the hands of your Higher Power. Let go and let God.

Hugs and much respect,
Jazz

October 12, 1993

Dear Tom,

I can't stop thinking about you. Not in a sexy way. Not that you aren't. You're cute, but, you know, you're goofy. It's not a bad thing. But I don't find that sexy. I don't want anything from you. I'm not writing to

crap

Hey Jazz,

Thanks. I needed that. I wish you could come every day. I don't get anybody here. Or they don't get me. I don't know. I'm only here because my ex-friend from high school Carrie Fucking Lanstrum thought I was hot for her useless boyfriend. Her lame-ass Barbie gang in matching mini-Ts and belly-button rings tried to swarm me at the Broadway Sky Train station. Had to laugh, hahahaha, save me! I'm being threatened by stick figures.

We're going to teach you a lesson you are going to carry on your face forever, bitch. Carrie Fucking Lanstrum, spouting bad trash talk, flashed her dinky switchblade. Her anorexic Barbie gang moved in to grab me.

Hahahaha. God, it felt good to laugh. Everything felt good. Kind of buzzed. First hit after three sober days. Slummed it in a McDonald's toilet stall. Snorted off a steel Never Out toilet paper holder. Never Out. Never Out. Never Out. It meant something deep, and I was the only one who knew. Finally felt human after three days of trying to go straight. Late-night streets wet and black and shiny and dazzling. The escalator taking me up to a higher plane. Carrie Fucking Lanstrum, at the other end of the Sky Train platform, whispered to her friends. Last train for the night due in five minutes.

Missing my Chevy. What a piece of shit that thing was. Wasn't even worth the coke I got for it. Busted up and handed down through all the Mazenkowski boys until it got to me. You couldn't make that car cool to save your life. Jake's big loser flames on the hood – took three cans of spray paint to cover that mess. Matthew's big-boobed mud-flaps and playboy dice. Dan stuck a huge muffler on it, trying to make the engine sound mean.

Jake had two surviving eight-track tapes, *Dr. Hook* and *The Best of CCR*, and one or the other'd be playing as we tooled around the driveway. Jake's crabby-ass car-care lectures: Your oil's filthier than your mouth. When was the last time you fucking checked your fluids? Don't fucking laugh. This is serious. Your tires are flatter than Dad's ass. What's your pressure? Fucking get a gauge, you cheapskate. This is your fan belt. Faaaan. Belt.

I heard you blew Brandon for a dime bag, Carrie Fucking Lanstrum said. Is that true? Are you a whore?

I heard he fucks you up the ass because your cunt could swallow a bus, I said. Is that true? Are you a less-than virginal asshole?

They were all quiet. I think they were trying to menace me. I wanted to tell them they'd have to work a lot harder. I have been menaced by the best. I have been worked over and worked under and worked and nothing you can do can touch me.

But while my brain was putting together that speech, I bull-dozed Carrie Fucking Lanstrum. Tackled her like she was holding a football. She flew backward. We rolled off the platform as her Barbie gang leapt out of the way. We landed between the tracks. Her Barbie gang shrieked as the Sky Train headlights rounded the corner, bearing down. Carrie Fucking Lanstrum fought to get me off her.

Do you think it'll stop? I said.

Her Barbie gang all holding out their hands to her.

Carrie! Get off her, bitch! Get off her!

None of them are jumping down for you, I said.

Carrie Fucking Lanstrum was too busy crying to answer. Crying and screaming. She caught me with a sucker punch and I rolled off. But I grabbed her around the neck and held on as her friends dragged her back. One of them tried to kick me off, but the rest were too freaked to bother.

The second I was on my feet, I connected my fists with noses, eyes, guts. They would have kicked my ass in the end. Ten to one. But the train had pulled into the station by then. I could see the security guards jogging past the stray passengers who paused to watch the fun.

October 18, 1993

Dear Tom,

This is the hardest letter I've ever had to write. Except for the one I wrote Mom. And the one I wrote Dad. And my ex-friend Carrie. Okay. This is still a hard letter.

It kind of is the hardest letter because you already forgave me in the hospital and I lost respect for you. But everyone here says forgiving someone is actually a sign of strength and that weak people can't forgive anybody, especially themselves. But it felt codependent. You know? I know your mom's a big alkie so I think you're trained

crap

Hey Jazz,

Mom visited today. She's moving in with my good old brother Matthew and his dishrag wife. She's supposed to stay a couple of weeks. Wayne Baker paid Mom a visit a few days ago. He said he was looking for me, but she'd do in a pinch. A mere eight months after the fact, Wayne figured out where my parents live and then he punched in the front-door window in full view of the neighbours. I think that's what got Mom upset. Not the tooth for a tooth, leg for a leg bullshit. Mom wanted me to look her in the eye and tell her The Truth. Crying away for the guards. What happened to you?

Dad's all excited. He went out and bought a security system and a shotgun. He's been practising at the range. They want Mazenkowski blood! They'll have to pay for it!

Please. Willy stole a Jag from a certified psycho and then he *bragged* about it. He's lucky he's breathing instead of chopped up and dumped in garbage bags around the city. Wayne pulled a nickel in Haven because he forgot to gas up the getaway car. Yeah, we're being menaced by criminal geniuses here. I told Mom to phone Wayne's parole officer and report him. She stopped crying.

Look what you've done to us! Look! We're living in terror and you don't even care!

I'd lay odds on you, Mommy. Liquor you up and hide you in the basement with a kitchen knife. Wayne doesn't stand a chance.

She couldn't leave fast enough. She can dish it, but she can't take it.

Dear Tom,

It's late. I can't sleep. My roommate snores. I would wake her but she outweighs me. She threw her pit bull against a wall and broke its back. She cried about it in group today. Her turn to share and boy, oh, boy, did she share. Mandatory rehab broke her and she surrendered. Holy roller born again sober. Either that or she's working it to get visitation privileges with her boyfriend. We had a fake wake for Pepper the pit bull to help Roomie's grieving process. You were. Just. Play-ing. Pepper! Pepper! Roomie in full-throttle howl. The facilitator made us write down our reactions on lavender paper. R.I.P., you bitey fucker.

Hey Jazz,

I met Jer at a house party a friend was throwing. Jer stuck out. He was the only guy who showed up wearing a suit. Not a stuffy old business suit – a sleek black Armani suit, his shirt casually unbuttoned at the top. Light tan on his face except for a faint outline of sunglasses. His dark brown hair had that just-stepped-off-my-yacht, didn't spend a lot of time (yes, I did) on my hair look. He seemed familiar, and later, I'd remember his Jag driving around our school when he used to drop Tom off. Oh, those sweet lines. First Jag I ever drove.

We fucked in the bathroom against the wall because the floor was disgusting and the pedestal sink was too flimsy. My back was against the switch, and the light kept going on and off and we were too horned up to care. People pounded on the door.

He even looked good nose to nose. Some guys look fine until they're on top of you, and then you notice the big, clogged pores, the stray nose hairs, and the start of a jowl. Jer had beautiful skin, the kind you want to lick when it glistens. Ripped body, sinews moving as we moved. I couldn't stop touching him. Wrapped my legs around his waist and he didn't tell me to get down, you aren't a butterfly, honey. Didn't faze him. His hair, his muscles, his skin, the lights, the wet smack of the condom, the angry people yelling for us to get out of the bathroom – my reflection stared at us as Jer threw his head back, open-mouthed grunts.

Dinner with the folks. Jer brought a dozen roses each for me and for Mom. Cuban cigars for Dad. Everyone pretending they'd just met.

My parents loved him. I've never brought home anybody they loved. I think they loved the Jag. Mom apologized over and over for the dry roast and lumpy gravy.

Don't screw this up, Mom said, catching my arm before Jer brought me out to a "movie."

I'm sorry about that, Jer, I said as we left the house. Thanks for pretending you didn't, you know, see them in high gear before.

He put his hand on the side of my face. Leaned in for a kiss.

Let's shake it off, babe.

I got hooked on Dexies at fat camp, Jer said in the black-out curtain dark of a hotel room.

Fat camp? I leaned my head on one elbow, touching his hair with my other hand. Playing with it. He used something that smelled like smoky oranges.

I was a chunky monkey until fat camp. When I got home, Dad thought the Dexies were cheating, so he cut me off. Said drugs would ruin my character. But Mom would sneak them to me in my lunch. It worked. Dad got off my back about being a porker. Mom got off his back about being on my back. Everyone was happy. And then Dad caught us. Poof. Chunky-monkey redux.

I never believed in soulmates until I met Jer. Long nights fucking, coking, and sharing war stories.

Dad brought me to his gym. He'd play drill instructor and I'd play new recruit. He'd be screaming in my face and I'd be thinking, if I hit him hard enough, right there, I could say he had a heart attack and hit his head on the weights when he fell. But the next summer, all the fat-camp kids were snorting Ritalin. They taught me how to get a prescription, how to grind the pills in a pill crusher. I was golden again.

Aren't you proud of yourself, son? DI Dad said. I know I was hard on you, but wasn't it worth it?

We'd go out to a club or restaurant where you had to know which fork to use and Jer would use the right one and I'd think, Man, if Mom saw that, she would cream. We could be doing the dirtiest, filthiest things in private, and she wouldn't care. Jer knew how to act in public. He knew how to talk to waiters, how to pick a wine, and how to chat while we waited to get the Jag out of valet parking. We'd look deep into each other's eyes over appetizers and he'd give me an if-they-only-knew smile and I'd smile back and we shared secrets and I thought that was love.

Tom has a crush on you.

Who?

Tom. My brother goes to your school.

Your brother's in my school?

He sits right behind you in band. Small world, huh?

If I'd had my eyes open, I would have read the signs. But I'd found Prince Charming and a little thing like freaky-ass family dynamics wasn't going to get past my blinders.

Mom likes these historical romances where the heroines never realize how beautiful they are. Hahahaha. Bullshit. If there are Nobel Stupid Prizes, women who don't realize they are beautiful would win them. You have to be damned dense not to notice the little things like other people's eyes, glazed, wandering all over you when you're talking. You could be telling them the cure for cancer and it wouldn't matter. You are beautiful. Your job is done.

I turned around in band practice and there was Tom, blushing like crazy because I caught him mooning. His eyes snapped down to his music sheet. He was wearing a suit, something Jer would have picked out, but on Tom, it looked like he'd gotten dressed in a hurry to go to church. Except for the fat lip, swollen and bruised. And his turtleneck, out of place for a warm spring day and not quite covering the bruises at the top of his neck.

Caught up to Tom in the hallway.

Hi, Tom.

Very faint answer, Hey.

Tell your bro he'd better be on time tonight or I'll kill him.

Tom blinked very fast, frowning. My bro?

Jer. The brother who cares enough to check up on you.

He blinked faster. You're seeing Jer?

If he's lucky.

He's not my brother.

Don't be that way, Tom.

No, seriously. He's my cousin.

I think it's sweet, I said. You guys must be close if he's calling you his brother.

Be careful, Tom said. He's delusional. He –

Later, Tom! Thinking to myself poor, jealous Tom and his secret crush all envious of Jeremy! Strolled away carefree, la la la, as if the lies hadn't registered, as if they weren't important.

Hey, Jer?

Yeah, babe. Jer had his eyes on the road, one hand on the wheel, one hand holding a cigarette as we waited at a red light.

I saw Tom in band today. He said he's not your brother. He said you guys're cousins.

Huh.

Why would you say you were brothers?

We are. Actually, we're half-brothers. He's not Dad's kid. Dad took a long tour after I was born, and Mom got mad and fooled around with an army buddy of his. The family kept it hush-hush. Poor kid. Did he really tell you he's Chrissy's? Well, whatever keeps you sane.

December 5, 1993

Dear Tom,

I don't know where to send this letter. I don't know what good it'll do giving it to you. I don't know what to say to you.

I went back to the hospital the day after they kicked me out. Your bed was empty and no one knew where you'd gone. Or they weren't telling me. I sat in the TV room for a long time. And then I left.

Hey Jazz,

Mostly booze, until I found coke. Even then, I was pretty func-
tional until Jer. Mom and Dad got all the boys a new car when
they graduated. Nothing fancy. Toyota hatchbacks, Honda Civics.
My brothers were holy hell, and they all got cars and a party and
cake. The only thing keeping me in that house going to school like
a good little girl was the promise of a new car to take off in.
Instead, I got a purse and a set of granny underwear with the days
of the week embroidered on the front. The kind of undies my
grandmother sent my mother every year for Christmas.

Jer had coke everywhere. Never had to ask for it. Bowls and
bowls of stuff. Before Jer, I had a level I was comfortable at. A
weekend sniffer. I slipped past it faster than I thought I could.
Found myself tearing through my room in the middle of doing
homework. I had a little bit left somewhere. I knew I had something. A little something to clear my head.

Mom came in and asked what I was doing. I looked up and
realized I'd turned my room upside down.

Jer gave me a pair of earrings, I lied. I lost one side.

She tsk-tsked and left me alone.

I'm tweaking, I thought, going cold. I'm tweaking. I can't believe I'm tweaking.

I didn't stop. Completely convinced I had some magical stash somewhere. I'd missed it and all I had to do was keep looking and it would appear because I needed it.

The restaurant bathroom was all white, all enamel and tile, scented with a woodsy air-freshener, cedar and pine. One of his whores sat on the counter, her back reflected in the mirror, the drape of the scooped dress revealing the small of her back, the bones of her spine. Her expression reminded me of a cat, neutral and interested. Jeremy knelt over me, his cock dark pink and bobbing in the chilly bathroom air. One of the urinals flushed continuously.

When the night started, I had no idea this was in the plan and part of my brain was shocked, and focused on the tiles, the air-freshener. My fingers wanted to sink themselves into his eyes and had tightened into fists. Jeremy held my wrists near my face. He rubbed the head of his cock along my jaw, leaving a sticky trail of pre-cum. His hands tightened on my wrists as he brushed the tip on my lips. Jeremy's mouth opened jaw-cracking wide as if he was the one pinned to the floor.

After we kicked the crap out of Willy Baker, we left him at the side of a road and went for sushi. I fixed my makeup at the table, and Jer snapped my compact closed, saying that was crass.

Every punch, every hit, every spit I rained down on Willy was meant for my parents. I was worth a purse Mom probably got as a gift-with-purchase and re-gifted underwear.

I want you to get Tom to trust you, Jer said.

Why?

Payback's a bitch and you are her stand-in.

Jer cut off my supply saying I'd get more after. Lame-ass plan. I hated it. So easy to get in with Tom. Saw him in the hallway at school. Tom, you got any weed? Man, I'm hard up.

. Tom drove me around when I was sick and shaking. Always ten clicks under the speed limit. Seat belt, Paulie! Checked both ways two or three times before he turned. I had told him I felt better in my car, and he'd said, why don't we go for a spin? Aretha Franklin on the radio. Freeway of Love. Bopped his head as he drove. His voice all high and out of tune. Waving out the window, deliberately cheerful to the people who'd been stuck behind us as they honked by. Nice day, isn't it! Take care! Drive to stay alive! Na na na, freeee-way, na na –

You're going to get us shot, I said.

Freeee-way. Huh?

Why are you signalling?

Don't you want to watch the planes?

The exit's a mile away.

I like to give people lots of warning.

I spent a few nights at his apartment, but nothing much happened. When we first got in, he filled the tub, made a bubble bath for me. Nothing sexier than a junk-sick chick. Shaking so hard the bubbles wobbled. Miserable and tired and trying to be seductive. He came back with a mug of Ovaltine and a stack of magazines – *People*, *True Story*, *High Times*.

I thought I'd ask first because I didn't know if you wanted marshmallows or not, he said, handing me the mug.

Not, I said.

He sat on the toilet and held up the covers so I could see. What'd'ya think? Roseanne and Tom get hitched. Married to the Wrong Brother. Blueberry Bonanza Confiscated in B.C.

Why don't you climb in with me? Said as I played with the bubbles around my breasts.

Lengthy, awkward pause where he dropped his eyes to the floor. You don't have to do that, Paulie.

You fucking freak of nature, I said. I was trying to be nice.

I don't need a pity fuck.

Normally, we'd fuck and that would be that. Instead, I thought, I'm stuck trying to make nice with this prissy little mama's boy. If I wasn't on the clock, I'd punch him and take off. Trying to calm myself down. Trying to think sexy thoughts when all I wanted to do was die.

When me and Mom moved to Vancouver, we didn't know anybody, he said. We didn't have anything. She hooked up with any guy that would give us a roof and regular grub. The guys that would take us in were always these assholes who treated her like a blow-up doll. I hated them so much it felt like I was breathing hate, like it was running through my veins. You're hot, Paulie. You know you're hot. But . . . I dunno. If all you need is a crash pad and company, then stay.

His bedroom looked like no one lived in it. No posters, no pictures, no mess of clothes on the floor. Even his socks were in order, folded together and lined up in their drawer. Fuck that bugged me. That's what you do when you're always getting farmed out. You try to be invisible. You try not to cause any trouble or call attention to the fact that you exist. Because then you're an inconvenience. When you depend on strangers for food and a place to stay, the last thing you can afford to be is an inconvenience.

Jeremy's camera was near the ceiling in Tom's bedroom. I knew Jer was going to watch this in a few days. No way was I giving him more of a show than I had to. I lay down on the couch. Tom fell asleep in the recliner. Jer wanted updates, and I couldn't be bothered.

Early in the morning, I crawled into the recliner with him. He turned sideways to make room, facing me. Boner making him shy. He was about to get up when I reached over and pulled the elastic on his briefs and took a peek.

Hey! he said, slapping my hand away.

Just checking, I said.

His mom came home on the fourth morning I was there. She stood at the entrance of the living room, blinking like she didn't believe what she was seeing. She perfumed the room with stale cigarette smoke and sweet, skunky body odour but mostly eye-watering booze fumes.

Later, she took me aside when Tom was taking a shower.

Aren't you Jeremy's girlfriend?

We broke up.

Tommy doesn't have any money.

I wasn't awake yet, didn't catch the dig for a minute or two. Then I wanted to shove her head through the wall.

Yeah? I said. Did you drink it up?

She got this flat stare. You're selfish. You're lazy. And you think you can use Tommy to get Jeremy back.

Fucking relax. We're just friends.

Do your parents know where you spent the night?

You're one to talk.

Get out.

I'll go when I'm good and ready.

I said get out. Now. Before I call the cops.

Go right ahead.

She stalked me through their apartment as I picked up my things. Cunt, I thought. Thinks I'm not good enough for her freak show. She slammed the door behind me. Jazz, every doubt I'd been having vanished. I could have shot Tom right there just to spite her.

Tom tilted his head up to the sun as we sat on the hood of my crappy old Chevy parked on the shoulder of a road in Richmond near the airport, the silver bellies of planes passing over us.

I saw this movie once, he said. This boat capsizes and this guy hops on his wife's back because she's a better swimmer. He drowns her and then spends the rest of the movie whining about his pain. Tom looked at me. It may not feel like it right now, but you're better off without Jer.

December 14, 1993

Dear Tom,

I brought you to a boozecan in Surrey because Jer promised me a pound of cocaine for a pound of flesh. I knew what he was capable of. I helped him beat up Willy Baker a week after you guys stole the Jag. I knew you were in trouble, and I didn't warn you. No excuses. What I did was wrong and I'm sorry.

I saw you at school the next Tuesday, and you ignored me. I thought it was over. I didn't want anything to do with you or Jeremy, and it looked like you wanted nothing to do with me. I thought you got off easy. Two cigarette burns and a head punch? Jer was planning on taking you apart. I thought, Tom can take care of himself.

When you didn't make it in for the last week of school, I was relieved you weren't at band practice. I could feel you staring at the back of my head. I wanted to tell you it was your own fault for stealing Jer's Jag when you knew he was a freakazoid. Then it was June and finals started.

I graduated. I moved out. I paid for my place for six months with the money I made from selling part of my coke. I knew

Mom and Dad weren't going to give me anything but the boot. I was supposed to make enough money to pay for tuition and expenses for the first year of university, but I ended up spending most of the summer in my bachelor suite. Head right in the bag. My own best customer. Then it was all gone, and my nest egg was drying up, and I bought the cheapest shit you can imagine.

Dad used to drive me down the worst alleys in East Hastings to show me the junkie prostitutes and the people who feed off them. This is what sin gets you. All their fears poured in me and festering. You are going to end up on skid row if you fuck boys. Toughening myself up for what seemed like a sure future strolling the razor-wired industrial sections where the freaks chase down women no one's going to bother looking for.

I saw you in Pigeon Park. Didn't know it was you. I hate it when people leave junkies to die like stray dogs. Everyone walking past you like you weren't there. I thought you were someone OD'ing, last convulsions. And then I got close enough to make you out, and I left you there. I walked away. I made it three blocks practically running before I turned back. I helped put you there. I thought you were being sarcastic at first, and then I felt relief when you didn't remember anything.

I heard an old woman in your building burnt down the place, but it seems too tidy. I should have left you in Emergency. I didn't mean to blubber all over you in the hospital. You had enough problems without me dumping on you. But when you remembered what I did, you could have been an asshole.

No one's forgiven me for anything. You are the first. I didn't even ask you to. You just did. It should feel better than it does. I guess. You are supposed to feel good when someone forgives you. Right? Maybe it's the newness that's weirding me out. Is that a word? Newness?

Hey Jazz,

Thanks for the smokes. I throw them at my new roommate when I need space. God, she's clingy. Hi. Hi. I was named after my grandmother. Who were you named after? Where you going? Are you coming back soon? What're you doing? Can you help me with my hair? Are you awake? Is that how you fold your socks? I've never seen socks folded like that before. If she didn't run off to the smoking lounge every once in a while, I would rip off her arm and beat her to death with it. I'm supposed to find five qualities I like about her and focus on the positive. Group has been on my back about my attitude.

But she's getting on my nerves, I said.

The things you don't like about other people are the things you don't like about yourself, the anger management facilitator said. When you point your finger, four fingers are pointing back at you-ou!

She's so chirpy, she makes group feel like remedial cheerleading. Does that mean I secretly loathe myself for being chirpy? What a lame theory. I am not chirpy. Or *clingy*. I am angry, resentful, bitter, quick-tempered, grudge-bearing, unreasonable, but I am not clingy.

There was that one time with Tom, but that was the coke psychosis. Instead of seeing snakes, I clung. Curled up to him in his bed. Hung around the hospital and waited for him to get out of his tests. Put my head in his lap while we watched TV. And cried nonstop. Bawled like I'd shot Old Yeller and the gun was still warm. I'm so embarrassed. I don't ever want to see him again. God. It was the coke. It was the summer of coke. I've never done that with anyone. Never. Even Jer couldn't make me cry. And he tried really hard.

If his mom hadn't shown up three days later and had security boot me out, I think I'd still be bawling at Tom's feet. God. God. I want to scrub the memory from my brain. That's what scared me. That's what made me try to go cold turkey. His mother's expression, so disdainful. The nurses. Looking at me like I had no self-respect at all and I didn't. He barely had his brains in his skull and I was so needy.

I was shocked sober. Miserable. So sick. I finally gave in and sold my car and then Carrie Fucking Lanstrum and her Barbie gang tried to jump me. I got held for psych evaluation. And then plead guilty to minor possession and got sent here.

I can't face Tom. I can't. I can't even write his fucking amends letter. Mom's letter was easier to write. It wasn't what he said or the way he said it or the look in his eyes or him. It was the coke. I was in coke psychosis. It had to be the coke. Either that or buried deep, deep down, I am a squishy, weepy weakling and that is just not possible.

3rd BLOOD

"That should be enough for now," Firebug said, shutting off the camcorder.

Tom hung against the ropes, writhing slowly. With each breath, pain spiked his sides like stitches from a long run. Firebug had drilled five needles into the muscles between his ribs. Tom's thighs were freckled from shallow puncture marks where Firebug had poked him awake when he was on the verge of passing out.

Firebug cut a plastic, beige patch into quarters. He peeled one of the quarter patches and stuck it above Tom's belly button.

Tom waited, tensed. Firebug placed the three remaining quarters in a small plastic bag, which he tucked in his tackle box beside the blowtorch. The patch tingled. Tom thought it was a nicotine patch but then someone was pouring warm honey over his belly and his chest and down his arms and his legs. Air caressed his skin. He could still feel the needles and the burns and the punctures, but they became pleasant, interesting as the honey sank under his skin and through his muscles and bones right down to his marrow. He closed his eyes and took a slow, deep breath.

"Nothing beats opiates," Firebug said.

The crickets sang in the yellowed grass in the nearby meadow, and Tom was lost in the sound, nodding. The trees glowed, their white bark golden in the slanting late-afternoon sunlight. Mosquitoes brushed his skin, tiny sparks when they bit the soft flesh of his face and chest and thighs. Sensation stopped at his shoulder joints, which felt hot and sore. It was like he didn't have arms any more. He found that cool.

Firebug brought his pliers to the needle in Tom's nipple. Tom felt a tug, and then blood ran down his chest like tears, warm, warm and absorbing. Firebug studied the needle and the flesh baked on it. He picked the needle off the pliers and dropped it into a white, plastic kitchen bag crumpled and open beside them. A fat black fly with glossy wings landed on the needle. It was joined by another fly, and another, and they danced around each other as they swarmed and whined. Tom rocked as Firebug jerked the needles out one by one. A squirrel spiralled up the trunk of a tree. Tom's head fell back as he watched the squirrel disappear into the canopy. The sky he felt he could fall through, blue etched by the white wake of a jet.

He heard sizzling. Felt a wash of lukewarm water and lowered his head. Firebug poured hydrogen peroxide on the open wounds and they foamed, rabid.

Panic. He felt panic, but distantly, as if he were a supersonic jet leaving his boom a minute behind.

"Boom," Tom said. "Boom."

Firebug half-carried, half-dragged Tom to the truck and hauled the passenger door open. Waves of heat wafted out of the cab. Firebug waited a moment and then lifted Tom onto the seat and slammed the door shut. Firebug walked around the front and the driver's side squealed open. The truck started with a rumble. Dust rose behind them as they climbed the hill.

Tom fell against the door, his head lolling, drowsy. He wanted to see where they were, to try to fix a location, but there were only more trees and the road. They crested the hill and the logging road dipped.

His head snapped up as the truck jerked to a stop. He wasn't sure if it was a short trip or if he'd dozed or blanked out. They were parked on a gentle slope in front of a squat stone building with shuttered windows. Solar panels shone black on the roof. An ancient, rusty white satellite dish almost the size of the house dominated the yard. A hedge of cedar trees formed a high wall around the fence. They parked beside a black Land Rover. The engine rumbled into silence. One of the burglars from yesterday, the man in a black muscle shirt with a brown ponytail hanging down his neck opened the front door and walked up to the passenger's side. They stared at each other.

"What the hell have you been doing? You had him all fucking night," Muscle Shirt said, yanking the door open. "Stop pussy-footing around."

"Leo," Firebug said. "Back off and let me handle this."

"This is how you get Jer to pay us what he owes." Leo slugged Tom in the stomach.

"You fuck-wit, stop –"

"Get the camera!" Leo said. "Get the fucking camera!"

Tom covered his head as Leo dragged him from the truck and threw him to the gravel. Tom curled into himself as Leo kicked him, screaming for the camera.

▐▌▌

They lifted him onto the butcher's block in the middle of a kitchen straight from the seventies – avocado appliances, orange counters, and dark-stained cupboards. The curtains were drawn even though the outside shutters were closed. The only lighting came from a block of fluorescent lights humming above them.

Leo rested his hand on the revolver he had tucked in the waist-band of his pants. He moved close, trying to stare Tom down. Firebug rummaged through the cupboards and pulled down clear plastic tumblers. He put them on the counter and then took a Brita water filter from the fridge.

Tom looked down at himself and realized he was still naked. Pain crept back into his body, biting through his haze. Paulie and Mel had to be in the house, maybe in a backroom or the base-ment. Glock Man must be with them, he thought. He wondered how close they were and if they could hear him if he shouted for them. Adrenalin woke him the rest of the way up. The kitchen opened to the hallway and across from the hallway was the living room. He hadn't been paying attention enough to notice a stair-case or other rooms in the back. He could say he needed to use the can and check out the backrooms. Leo's revolver looked like it had come out of a cereal box. If they were alone, Tom would gouge Leo's eyes before he introduced the cast-iron frying pan on the stove to the bastard's skull.

Tom touched the patch above his belly button. He knew how much it was going to hurt when the drugs wore off. He wasn't interested in suffering, but he couldn't do anything if he couldn't think. If they had any hope of getting out of this, he had to have his brains back. Tom pretended to scratch, peeling off the patch and letting it drop to the floor.

"He took something off," Leo said, pulling his revolver out and aiming at Tom. "Look, he threw it on the floor."

Firebug sipped his water.

"Did you hear me?" Leo said. He half-turned to face Firebug.

Firebug placed the tumbler on the counter. He turned in a smear of motion, punching Leo so hard he folded as he flew back against the butcher's block and his revolver clattered to the hardwood floor. Leo gasped for air, staggering.

"You agreed to do what I say," Firebug said. "Do you want to quit the crew?"

Leo sullenly shook his head.

"Good," Firebug said.

Firebug picked up another tumbler and brought it to Tom. He held it up in offering and Tom took it. Water sloshed over his hands as he tried to bring the cup to his face and Firebug patiently steadied Tom and helped him drink. Leo hesitated before he tucked his revolver back in his pants.

"When you're tempted to shoot Tom," Firebug said. "Imagine yourself in a beachfront hotel in tropical Aruba as you and two nubile whores frolic in a bed full of money."

Leo's expression went slack, his mouth opening just slightly in wonderment as if an angel or a UFO had landed in front of him.

"Tom alive gets you to Aruba," Firebug said. "Tom dead means you keep knocking over snack shacks. We'll let Jer take care of him. Okay?"

"Okay."

"Get my tackle box out of the back of the truck."

"Sure," Leo said.

"I have money," Tom said. "I have seventy thousand dollars and three keys of coke. They're yours if –"

"How'd a grimy little shit like you get that kind of money?" Leo said.

"Leo," Firebug said. "Don't get distracted by the quarter on the sidewalk when you're holding up a bank."

"Money's money," Leo said. "How much is the coke stepped on?"

Firebug slapped Leo upside the head. "Get my tackle box out of the truck, fuck-wit. Now. Goddamn Jesus fucking Christ in a sidecar. You make gum look smart."

▐▌▐

Firebug stood in front of him, talking, but Tom found himself straining to catch Paulie and Mel noises. Then his legs cramped and there was a long, long time he thought he was going to throw up on Firebug again, but he came back to himself to find Firebug holding his arms so he didn't fall off the butcher's block. Leo did not seem to be in a rush to return with the tackle box, and Tom hoped he had fallen off the steps and broken both legs.

"Goddamn useless no-brain dickskinning fuck-up," Firebug said. "Christ. It'd be faster sending a monkey."

Tom could feel the promise of the needle punctures now, the twinges in his side, the pinch in his thighs, and the throb in his left nipple. He looked down. The nipple had stopped bleeding, and the blood had crusted on his chest. The burn looked wet and the hole gaped. The needle marks between his ribs were closed and puffy, sticky with a clear fluid like sap. The ache in the small of his back was new. Thankfully, Leo had been wearing socks or the shit-kicking would have been worse.

"I need to use the bathroom," Tom said.

Firebug slung one of Tom's arms over his shoulder and helped him off the block and across the kitchen into the hallway. No stairs going up to an attic or down to a basement. Two rooms in the back, one with the door open, the other closed.

"Did you have a good cry?" Firebug said, swinging Tom around to face Leo, who carried the tackle box and the reek of cigarette smoke. "Did you phone your mommy and say I was being mean?"

"Don't get your panties in a twist," Leo said.

"Should I make your part less complicated? Here. Take Tom to the bathroom."

"I didn't sign up to ass-wipe Gomer."

"Gomer beat a biker to death with a toilet-tank lid," Firebug said. "Which is less impressive than it sounds because he is a dumb fuck like you."

"Stop calling me stupid."

"Go to town on him, Tom," Firebug said, patting his shoulder as he handed him off to Leo.

It was tempting to reach over and pull the revolver's trigger. But Firebug's trash talk was just that, and it wouldn't get Tom closer to Paulie and Mel. Firebug in a mood was something to avoid.

Tom expected the open room to be a bathroom, but it was a master bedroom, wide and dark, lit by four TVs lined up on the dresser to the left. The camera to the far left showed the logging road behind the wall of cedars. The two middle cameras slowly surveyed the front and back yards. The camera to the far right stopped Tom cold.

Paulie was bent over, finger-walking Mel across a room with a mural of a grassy hillside filled with bunnies and puppies and rainbows. One wall of the room had been replaced by bars. Glock Man sat on a chair on the other side of the bars and read a book. Paulie wore a yellow summer dress with spaghetti straps and her mouth was moving, but there was no sound. Mel strained forward, trying to go faster.

"Paulie!" Tom shouted. "Paulie!"

Paulie didn't react.

"Move it," Leo said.

"Paulie!" Tom screamed.

"She can't hear you," Leo said. "It's soundproofed, dumb-ass."

"Paulie! Mel! Paulie! Paulie!"

Leo yanked him past the TVs and dragged him to a bathroom on the far side of the bedroom. He flipped the light on and tossed Tom in.

"Where's Paulie?" Tom said. "Where's –"

Leo pulled his revolver and aimed at Tom's groin. "Finish your business."

Tom sat on the toilet and Leo sat on the edge of the tub. Leo pressed the gun against one of the needle punctures on Tom's ribs.

"Where's your stash?" he whispered.

Tom could still see the TV screen from the open bathroom door. Paulie lifted Mel onto her hip and brought her over to the bed in the corner. Leo used the gun to turn Tom's face.

"Neil watches them in the day," Leo said. "And I watch them at night. Do you want me pissed off, Gomer? Where's your stash?"

"In The Regina," Tom said. "In the washroom on the third floor. Five feet above the bathtub. In the wall above the end of the tub away from – away from the faucets. In a stainless-steel brief-case hanging on a hook."

"Motherfucking son of a bitch," he said, shaking his head and chuckling. "Hiding coke in a crack palace." Leo stopped chuckling and forced the tip of the revolver into Tom's mouth. "If it's not there, I'm going to take it out on your bitch and your baby."

The sound of Tom urinating was loud in the bathroom.

"Our little secret," Leo said.

Tom sat on the wingback armchair. Firebug struggled to hook the VCR to the ancient TV. Leo was in the hallway. Tom could hear him pacing. The flowery polyester furniture was shrink-wrapped in heavy plastic that squeaked against Tom's bare skin whenever he moved. The grandfather clock ticked in the corner. The room was air-conditioned cold but Tom was sweating.

Paulie and Mel were in a large room. Tom couldn't be sure, but it looked too large to be the room at the end of the hall. The basement then. He'd have to find the staircase. Maybe it was in the closed room. Maybe it was outside.

"Got it," Firebug said. He went and sat kitty-corner to Tom on the couch.

Tom recognized Grandview Park, himself and Mel sitting on a bench with Mike and his girlfriend nearby. They were all smiling.

"Spot the cop," Firebug said.

"Mike's not a cop," Tom said. "He's a friend from high school. We just bumped into each other."

"Constable Greer Johnson," Firebug said. "I hear grumblings she's on the promotional fast track. Daddy's an old street cop calling in favours from every rookie he's trained in the last twenty years."

"I don't even know Greer," Tom said.

The video jumped to Tom and Mike framed by the living-room window. Celine Dion belted out "The Power of Love" as they laughed and talked.

"Loose lips sink ships," Firebug said.

Tom rubbed his arms, wishing he had a blanket or some clothes. "I haven't said anything."

"Why isn't Rieger all over you? If you know where the bodies are, why doesn't he just whack you? What have you got on him?"

"Nothing. We're family, that's all."

"Rieger owes me a lot of money," Firebug said.

"I've got money," Tom said. "You can have it."

Firebug tapped his knee. "Do you think I'm a pooch?"

"No, no, man," Tom said.

"We're talking hundreds of thousands of dollars, Tom. Rieger thinks I'm a pooch."

"He doesn't. I don't. No one does."

"You've got people hunting through your garbage, people asking for wiretaps. Ambitious young things trying to be your friend. You could make a deal for Rusty. Self-defence. What would you be able to give them if Jer comes after Paulie and Mel?"

Tom closed his eyes. He wanted to lie down. He couldn't sit any way that gave him relief. He heard the snap of locks and opened his eyes in time to see Firebug pulling a patch out of the small plastic bag.

"I'm okay," Tom said. "I don't want –"

"Leave this one on," Firebug said. "Or we go back to the needles."

▌█▌

The back of the house had a greying, mouldy deck. Leo grumbled while he dragged chairs out from the kitchen. Firebug lit a citronella candle in a galvanized pail. Leo disappeared inside and came back with three sweating bottles of Kokanee.

"You don't get to party," Firebug said. "I don't want you drunk on the job. Take your shift."

Leo spat before he gave Firebug the beers. Firebug put them down. He picked Tom off the deck and sat him in a chair. He put a beer in Tom's hand. They stared at the setting sun like they were old friends catching up.

Tom couldn't remember which way the sun set. Japan was the land of the rising sun. And that was in the east. Time zones went east to west. So they were looking west. Front of the house was east.

Which told him nothing. He still had no idea where they were. Tall trees and the logging road. Where did they log? He had been outside Vancouver once or twice since he'd moved here as a kid. Put him anywhere in Vancouver and he could tell you where they were.

"Hey, boss," Glock Man said, knocking on the door frame. "Need anything?"

"We're good," Firebug said. "Get some shut-eye, Neil."

"Night."

"Night."

The sun flared behind the trees. The sky faded milky blue. Tom dropped his beer as the drug hit. Heard the bottle roll across the deck. Heard the fizz of the beer. Firebug didn't seem upset. Tom swallowed hard. He had to . . . he was supposed to . . . get Paulie and Mel. Go home.

Firebug sipped his beer. Tom watched the citronella candle burn. The cold left him; the shakes and the sweats left him. The sky was Creamsicle orange, electric and sweet. A jagged black line of trees circled them like a fort.

"I helped a friend build this place," Firebug said. "He believed in the End of Days. But his wife got sick of milking cows and plucking chickens while they waited for the Apocalypse, so she took his three kids and moved back to Surrey. My friend turned the basement into his own little prison. Snatched his kids first. Caught his wife in the parking lot when she came to pick up the kids. Not one person noticed they were gone.

"Then one day he went out to get some firewood just over there beside the stream. Tree fell on him. He died. By the time I dropped in to ask him a favour, his wife and the three kids were puddles of fat and piles of bone. Took forever to get the stink out." Firebug turned his head to watch Tom. "Rieger's going to take care of you, Tom. You're never leaving the basement, so to speak."

The orange faded into pink, and the pink faded into dusty white and then grey and it seemed to take a second but it must have been longer. He had put his fear down and forgotten where he'd put it.

"What would you give me to let Paulie and Mel go?"

"You wouldn't let them go," Tom said.

"Paulie's a good woman. I was sorry to see her mixed up with a slacker like you. Rieger's going to give me a lot of money for you. But if you have anything on Rieger, I'll drop Mel and Paulie in the Metrotown parking lot. Paulie's ex-con sobriety buddies'll make Jer a priority. You'll keep them occupied while I make a run for it."

It sounded good. But all the cold, thinking parts of his brain were occupied by the colour of the sky and the way the shadows fell and the memory looped in his head of Paulie in the yellow sundress and Mel's frustrated expression as she tried to run and couldn't.

IIII

They ended up in the kitchen. Firebug killed his bottle of beer, laying it on the butcher's block and rolling it under his palm like he was making a pie crust. Tom pretended to sip his, hefting the weight of the bottle in his hands. It wouldn't do much damage. But it might make a temporary distraction. They swayed in sync on their stools like drunks at closing time. Tom leaned his elbows on the butcher's block and rested his head in his hands.

"Why are you protecting him?" Firebug said. "Tom? Why do you care what happens to the shitbag?"

Tom raised his head and stared at Firebug. He was holding them hostage, but Tom doubted Jer would give Firebug the spare change in his pocket in exchange for them. Firebug wanted the goods on Jer. The second Tom gave him what he wanted, Tom didn't see why Firebug would want them around. And once Jer knew for sure they had his videotapes, what would he do? Would he believe they hadn't watched them, hadn't told anyone about them?

"He's a cheating, lying, homicidal son of a bitch who wouldn't let go of his toothbrush if his life depended on it. You have something. Or you know something. The cops think so. Rieger thinks so."

"I don't know anything and I don't have anything."

Firebug sighed. "Do you want to take a break? Get some shut-eye?"

Tom studied him, waiting for the punchline. "Sure."

"I didn't want to do this," Firebug said, "but you aren't leaving me with much choice. We're going to take this to Paulie."

197

Tom covered his face with his hands, pretending to cry to buy time. Firebug kept talking while Tom judged the distance to the stove. Four feet behind him. Take Firebug out. Get Betty. Take Leo out. Deal with Neil. One of those things that looked good on paper. Doing it was something else. But the thought of Firebug going at Paulie made him cold.

Tom threw his beer in Firebug's face. He pushed himself off the butcher's block with both hands, tipping the stool over to give Firebug an obstacle. He spun as his foot hit the floor so he faced the stove. He spotted the cast-iron frying pan turned over on the back burner. He lunged for it, brushing the handle of the pan with his fingertips a moment before Firebug punched him on the side of the head and sent him sprawling across the kitchen floor.

Firebug dragged him back to the living room, where he rummaged through the tackle box until he came up with a pair of handcuffs still in their plastic bag. He stepped on Tom's neck to hold him still. He ripped the plastic open and caught the keys as they fell out of the bag. He struggled to open the cuffs as Tom grabbed a leg of the coffee table and yanked it close.

"Fuck," Firebug said as the coffee table hit his shin. He took his foot off and Tom rolled over and scrambled for the hallway. Firebug caught him by the arm, snapped a cuff on one wrist. Tom kicked and punched and twisted. Firebug sat on him, grabbed his arm and pulled it down, tightening the cuffs until Tom's hands tingled. Firebug caught his breath, and then stood and hauled Tom up by his arm. He turned Tom around, bringing his face so close he went cross-eyed.

"Not funny," Firebug said.

Firebug pushed him into the couch. He took a wad of rags and shoved them in Tom's mouth and then wound a roll of duct tape around and around Tom's head. He put the duct tape down and picked up the lighter. He sat beside Tom, a friendly arm over his shoulders. Firebug flicked the lighter open and closed, open and closed, watching Tom. He brought the lighter to Tom's left nipple and flicked the lighter open. He held Tom still while he burned the skin around his bleeding nipple until the flesh was blackened and bubbling.

Tom's head bounced against Firebug's back as he tried to hold himself up, tried not to let his seared skin touch Firebug's shirt. Firebug carried him over his shoulder. They went down the hallway and into the master bedroom. Firebug pushed the bed aside. Beneath it was a trap door. The unpainted wooden stairs creaked as Firebug brought him down.

Bars to the right, lit by a night light. Paulie and Mel curled together on the bed. Paulie lifted her head. Leo lay on the floor, tapping his fingers on his stomach as he listened to a Walkman.

"Finally," Leo said.

Firebug dropped Tom. He turned him by the shoulder and then unsnapped one cuff. He shoved Tom face first into the bars and pressed on his shoulders until he knelt. Paulie sat up, pushing her hair out of her face.

"Tom?"

Firebug forced Tom's hands through the bars, hooking the right one on top of a vertical bar and the left one below so Tom couldn't stand. Firebug snapped the cuffs closed on the other side of the bars.

"Paulina," Firebug said. "Could you come to the bars, please?"

Paulie checked Mel before she reached for a bathrobe over a chair and put it on as she walked toward them.

"Tom?"

He shook his head, trying to speak through the duct tape, trying to warn her away from Firebug, but she came, frowning, tightening her bathrobe belt.

"God, look at you," she said, touching his face and kneeling in front of him.

Her eyes were puffy and bloodshot, but he couldn't see any bruises. She held his hands and kissed them. She was still whole and he'd fucked that up. He'd fucked up. She was in trouble and she didn't know it and he couldn't tell her.

"Go get my gear and my rig," Firebug said.

Leo sighed heavily before he trudged up the stairs and out of sight.

"How did a cokehead like you end up with a pothead like him?" Firebug said. "That has always mystified me, Paulina."

"Firebug, please," Paulie said.

"Tom is currently enjoying a pain patch they give end-stage cancer patients. A quarter patch to be exact. One tiny quarter patch and he's flying. I bet it wouldn't even tickle you, would it?"

Paulie touched Tom's face, testing the duct tape.

"Leave it," Firebug said.

She glanced at Firebug before she touched Tom's cheek.

"You clawed your way back," he said. Firebug kicked Tom's foot. "Cupcake here, he's a different story. I don't know if he'll come back. We'll start him off on a quarter gram of smack and work our way up."

"You're going to kill him," Paulie said.

"I know about Rusty," Firebug said. "Rieger collects his debts. He would make you pay. You and Tom know something or you have something and I'd like you to share."

Paulie's hands tightened on his as Leo came tromping down the steps. Leo handed Firebug a rolled towel. Firebug pulled a chair to the left of Tom. He carefully unwrapped the contents, some needles still in their original packaging, carefully folded paper packages, rubber tubing, a spoon.

"Hold him," Firebug said.

Leo wrapped his arm around Tom's neck and pulled him back until the cuffs clanged against the bar. Paulie covered his arms with her own. Firebug flicked the side of Tom's neck, tapping like a carpenter searching for studs in the wall.

"You chased the dragon," he said. "But you never injected. Why is that, Paulie?"

"Guy, let's talk about this," Paulie said. "Let's stop for a minute. And talk about this."

"Did you have rules? No continuous use. No injecting. Only on weekends. Just a nice, lovely come-down from coke. Like a beer after a long, hard day."

Tom heard the click of the lighter and swivelled his head around, alarmed. Firebug held the lighter under a spoon, moving it back and forth until the liquid turned golden like caramel.

"He can't take that much," Paulie said. "Guy. Listen to me. You can't give him that much. You'll put him in a coma."

"Talk to me, Paulina," Firebug said. "Tell me a story."

PENANCE

1. Do ye indeed speak righteousness, O congregation? Do ye judge uprightly, O ye sons of men?

At the granite footsteps of the Carnegie Centre, a crowd of rough-looking dealers usually milled around, offering drugs to passersby. Today the dealers and sex-trade workers were scattered west along Hastings, sheltering under the awnings of convenience stores and pizza shacks. Tom walked past a police car parked on the wide side-walk on the north side of the Carnegie. The two officers in the car watched the hammering rain as morosely as anyone else.

Inside, the Carnegie was warm and damp, had a tired smell, old sweat and pee. To the right of the entrance was a spiralling marble staircase, a reminder of better days when the Carnegie had been a posh library. To the left, the lobby's tables were filled with people playing checkers or chess, reading or just staring out the window waiting for the rain to stop. Straight ahead was the information desk where Paulina stood, dressed in a loose black sweater and black jeans, speaking to a guy with a garbage-bag rain jacket. She leaned against the counter, pointed to a piece of paper that they both studied.

Tom stepped into the alcove and pretended to be in line for the pay phone under the stairs. The last time he'd seen Paulina was almost a year ago, moments before she was dragged off the Neurology ward by security guards at Saint Paul's. The new Paulina was pale and primly free of makeup, her hair in a severe bun like a cartoon librarian. Tom had changed, too. But not in ways he wanted to share with the new Paulina.

"I don't understand you," was his mother's new mantra, repeated as she avoided his eyes. "I don't know who you are."

||||||

Paulie spun herself tightly into the starchy hospital blanket and then fought her way free, shivering, cramming her hands under Tom's back. She flailed, collapsing face first in the mattress, one arm over his waist. She was light and bony, cold and sticky; her breath was worried, quick; she smelled funky, low-tide beach-y. He'd given her his Valium so she could sleep. The nurse who gave him his pills watched him closely, and he knew she suspected but was too tired to call them on it.

Early, in the dull grey light, Paulie went still. She woke suddenly. She pushed herself up onto her elbows, watching him watch her. She looked down at herself. She tasted her mouth, smacking. "What time is it?"

"No clue," he said.

She pulled a blanket over her shoulders as she settled facing him, her breath warm on his face. "This is weird."

"What?"

"Me being here. Don't you think it's weird?"

"My weird-o-meter is broken," Tom said. "I can't tell what's weird and what's not weird any more. I am weirdlexic."

Paulie frowned. "Why do you do that?"

"Do what?"

"Make everything into a joke."

Tom laughed.

She punched his arm. "I'm serious."

"Ow." Obviously, Paulie was not a morning person.

"I should leave. The nurses are giving me looks."

"I'm sick of pills."

"I think they know," Paulie said.

She raked her hair back, pulled the black elastic off her wrist, and put her hair back in a low ponytail. Paulie shrugged the blanket off her shoulder and spread it over him. She laced her fingers behind her neck. She stared at the ceiling, her eyes moving back and forth as if she were watching a movie only she could see.

Tom shared a four-bed hospital room and a toilet with three other patients. The wing shared a shower and bath at the end of the hall. The tub had a thick ring of greenish-beige scum. Tom opted for a shower. He had a hard time taking the hospital gown off. He'd ended up sleeping in an awkward position, and his left shoulder didn't want to move.

He scrubbed himself down with the anti-bacterial soap from the sink. He didn't have a towel, didn't know where the towels were, and couldn't be bothered to ask. He used paper towels, dabbing the yellowing shoe-shaped bruises on his torso. The egg on the left side of his head was quiet now unless Tom touched it. The round scabs on his shoulders were starting to peel away.

One month and a bit. Zip. Gone. As if aliens had abducted him and he was missing time. What he did remember he didn't trust because it felt unreal, like a TV show he'd watched while he was stoned, losing chunks of the plot to snack runs during the commercial breaks.

Tom jumped as someone knocked on the washroom door.

"You still alive in there?" Paulie said.

"Yeah," Tom said, wondering how long he'd been washing up. It didn't feel like that long, but he couldn't be sure.

Doctors and nurses came and went; specialists and technicians popped in and out; patients left and were replaced. Everyone spun in a blur of coming and going except Paulie, who was never more than five feet from him. Not counting the bathroom trips when she'd return wired and bright-eyed, Paulie was always within earshot and if he wasn't sure he was tracking what someone was telling him, he'd call for her and she'd straighten things out.

They waited in the hospital room for a nurse to wheel in another round of blood tests. Paulie sat in the visitor's chair she'd dragged in from the hallway. It did feel weird having Paulie around. But he was afraid if he admitted it, she would leave. She hunched into herself, wrapped her arms tight, and hugged herself. It wouldn't take much to make her leave. He should. If she could give him up once, she could do it again. Judging from the shakes and cutback on trips to the bathroom, she was probably running low. It looked like she was hurting, a lot, and she was still here. She was going to be disappointed if she was expecting another reward from Jer. If Willy could hunt him down, Jer would have had no problem finding Tom if he'd wanted to. But all that was over. She had to know that. She wasn't an idiot.

So here they were and, for whatever her reasons, Paulie had bothered to drag him to the hospital and had stuck around while he got his shit together. Paulie didn't like fuss and he appreciated that. He wanted to know his mom was safe, was being taken care of, but the only people he could call to find out where his mother was were the people he didn't want to go into detail with: Jeremy's mother, Faith. Aunt Rhoda. Uncle Jeremiah.

When life gets you down for the count, it's not a sin to rest for a while, his mom always said when he was sick and restless. As long you pick yourself up before the ref calls the match, you'll be okay.

Paulie rolled the table tray over and sat on the side of the bed. She lifted the plastic cover, and they surveyed the selection. Lunch was beef broth and saltine crackers, mashed potatoes with a pat of butter, some kind of brown meat and green beans. Dessert was Jell-O, red today. Paulie claimed the tea first, drinking half before she handed it back. He sugared it up and she made a face.

"You're ruining good tea," she said.

"You want the broth?" Tom said.

"Sure."

He ate the potatoes. The menu said the meat was Salisbury steak, but it looked like meatloaf. He pushed it to Paulie's side of the tray, and she split it and pushed half back. He cut it into chunks to make eyes and a nose in the gravy, adding a set of green-bean lips. Paulie scowled, resolutely chomping on a piece.

"I'm mel-ting," Tom said, moving the lips. "What a world! What a world."

"Why don't you hate me?" Paulie said.

"What?" he said.

"Open your eyes, Tom," she said. "People keep looking at me. They're scared. They're disgusted. They can't get away fast enough."

He looked up and caught two nurses in the hallway watching them. "So?"

She sighed. "Tom . . ."

"If you're the scariest person they've seen," Tom said, "they must live in Care Bear land, man."

The nurses pretended to be examining a chart, but kept looking up from behind their station. Paulie inspected her fingernails, her expression carefully composed. "I did some horrible things. To you. I . . . I wish sorry was good enough . . ."

"It's history," Tom said. "I'm sorry you got dragged in, but I'm not sorry you're here."

The sides of her lips pulled down further and further until she turned her head toward the window, gulping. He pushed the tray out of the way and pulled her in for a hug. He expected her to slug his shoulder but she slumped back against him, turned her head into the crook of his neck, and pulled her lips back over tightly clenched teeth, her body heaving like she was throwing up.

█▏▐

"Maybe it's just my pits," Paulie said, pushing herself up and wiping her nose on the back of her hand. "I should hit the showers."

"Want to borrow a shirt?" Tom said. He had a selection of T-shirts from lost and found.

She shook her head.

"I'm going to watch some boob tube," Tom said.

"Meet you there," Paulie said.

Tom settled into the TV room. A puffy-faced woman with a big white bandage around her head and over one ear was watching

Oprah. He didn't care. He needed background noise to shut his brain up.

A tall, brown-haired orderly with a beer gut wandered in and sat in the chair beside Tom's even though there were lots of chairs empty. Tom considered moving, but the orderly didn't look like he wanted to chat.

"Get your damn hands off me!" Paulie shouted.

The orderly lunged to grab Tom's forearms and held him to the chair.

"Tom! Tom!" Paulie shouted. "Get off! Now! I mean it! You cunt! You dirty, lousy cunt! You get –"

"Could you turn the TV up?" the orderly said.

The puffy-faced woman shot a worried glance at them both, and then turned the TV up before going to stand in the doorway. The TV's speakers distorted as the audience clapped its approval. Paulie's voice grew fainter and farther away and then stopped.

"It's okay, Tom," the orderly kept saying. "Everything's okay."

▐▌▌

The private room seemed small and closed off. He'd gotten used to hearing the other patients, their monitoring machines, their visitors. The tranks made his head wobble. His mother pulled her chair close to the bed and held his hand as if he was dying and she was comforting him.

". . . silly, old Mrs. Tupper left her frying pan on," his mother said, indignant. "She denies it, of course, but the firefighters knew. Well. Our place went next –"

"Did anyone die?" Tom said. "Did they find a body?"

"A body?" his mom said. "No, sweetie, no one died. Just me! Oh, I thought you were burned to death! I couldn't find you anywhere! I went to Mike's! I phoned the police!"

He did imagine it then. The attempted robbery and bashing the guy's head in were part of a hallucination. Unless the guy's partner had dragged out the body. But you'd think someone would have noticed that. Especially if the building was on fire. Maybe they hadn't happened on the same day. "When did our building burn down? What day?"

"When? Oh! I tried to get BCTV to do a story on you! And *The Province*! I called every day." She lifted her purse onto her lap and pulled out a crumpled piece of paper. "Look. I put up posters everywhere. I went to your school. They let me make a speech in front of all your friends at assembly! Oh, I couldn't stop crying! And they were all so kind. But nobody knew where you were, honey bunny. You just disappeared after the fire –"

His mother talked and talked, and he waited for her to pause so he could break in, but she didn't.

"Where's Paulie?" he finally said.

"She went home," she said. "I told you that already, honey bunny. Remember?"

"Does she know I changed rooms?"

"I'll leave a note with the nursing staff," she said. "Paulina will know where to go."

"I want to sit in the hall. She might come back."

"Gosh, here I am yakking your ear off when you should be sleeping."

She kissed his hand, leaned her cheek against it, and sighed. Tom struggled to keep his eyes open.

"Did you see her leave? Did she say anything?"

"Were you with that Mazenkowski girl the whole time, Tommy?"

Tom pulled his hand away from her. "She found me, Mom.

She brought me here. You shouldn't have done that. She was trying to help."

Her lips thinned and she sat up, ramrod straight. "Herself. She was trying to help herself, Tommy."

He pretended to sleep until his mother left, and then he sat in the hallway and pretended to read an *Enquirer*. He stared at the pictures, nodded off, and then snapped awake. After a long doze, he found himself in bed, tucked under the sheets.

He noticed he wasn't alone, caught a small movement from the corner of his eye. A guy in his early twenties wearing a black suit with a brown shirt unbuttoned at the top sat in the visitor's chair, watching him the same way you'd watch an interesting zoo animal.

"Jer-e-my," Jeremy said slowly and loudly. "I am your cousin. Cousin Jer-e-my."

"Where's Paulie," Tom said. "Where'd Paulie go?"

Jeremy sighed. "I thought you were faking it for the jury. Now I know you're nuts."

▌▌

They drove against the Sunday-night traffic. Cars and SUVs and tour buses headed back to Vancouver formed a conga line of headlights. Everybody returning to their normal lives. The Sea to Sky Highway took a serious climb. The air conditioner in their truck didn't seem to be working. Jeremy kept his window open so he could flick his cigarette ashes out. He wore cammies and a khaki fishing hat, with "Don't touch my fly" embroidered in blue thread. Tom wore a baseball cap and a vest with a hundred puffy pockets over his hospital lost and found T-shirt.

Earlier that day, they'd loaded the back of the truck with two large, metal coolers and assorted fishing and camping gear.

When the truck came to a sudden stop, the bones in the coolers rattled like stones tumbling in the surf. The truck smelled like it had been washed down with the contents of a septic tank. Tom had retched as he'd helped Jeremy drag the coolers up a thick plank and push them into position by the cab.

"We're going to get caught," Tom had said.

"People are dumber than a sack of hammers," Jeremy had said. "They believe what they see. As far as anyone knows or cares, we're going fishing."

They stopped in Squamish at a roadside greasy spoon. Tourists in athletic gear of various styles ranging from Hollywood starlet tight and pink to skateboarder loose and grimy lounged with their après tour beers.

"This is obstruction of justice," Jeremy said as the waitress walked away with their order. "Eighteen months. Maybe less. Depends on how hard you cry and how many grannies you get on your jury. Grannies cream over your kind of face."

Tom glanced at the nearby tables, nervous. Jeremy whacked a packet of sugar against the back of his hand before he opened it and poured it in his coffee.

"No one's listening," Jeremy said. "And no one cares. You could stand up right now and confess and it wouldn't matter. Rusty Letourneau was scum. You're scum. What scum do in the pond stays in the pond."

Jer was suddenly propping him up by the shoulders, and Tom didn't remember seeing Jeremy move. Jer shoved him back against his chair.

"Tom, he was skimming off his uncle. And flaunting it. That put him past his best-before date, not you."

"Who's in the other cooler?" Tom said.

Jeremy considered him for so long Tom wondered if he'd said it out loud or if it had stayed in his head.

"His partner," Jer said. "Forget him. His daddy's a janitor at Wal-Mart. No one's going to put a biker hit on us for killing him."

The logging road narrowed until it was two tire tracks in the gravel. Morose brown-needled trees leaned over the road, drooping in the heat. The headlights arbitrarily spotlighted tree trunks, yellowed brush, and the occasional set of red eyes.

Tom took streetlights for granted. Their absence made him uneasy. The dashboard lights made Tom's reflection glow green against the flat black surrounding them. The darkness behind them was tempered with a faint halo of light from Whistler.

The truck rumbled down the road, finally slowing. At the end of the tracks, a shack with a green roof stood in a clearing, the windows sparking as the headlights passed over them. Jeremy cut the engine. He reached under the seat and brought up a flashlight. He opened the door and stepped outside, sucking in a deep breath. Tom hunched into himself.

"Grab the gear," he said.

Tom turned to stare at the shack. The lopsided porch gave the shack a smirk.

"Get your fucking lazy ass out of the truck before I kick it out," Jeremy said.

The shack had four bunks, a wood stove in the centre, and a kitchen. Jeremy lit a kerosene lamp. Tom unrolled his sleeping bag on the lower bunk opposite Jer's. The floors whined whenever one of them moved. Mice pitter-pattered through the rafters. The kerosene lamp on the stove hissed. Tom took off his shoes and lay down on the sleeping bag. The bunk's musty smell made his nose itch. Jer drank out of a mickey of vodka. He sat on his sleeping bag and leaned over, offering Tom a drink. Tom shook his head.

"We should call your mom," Jeremy said.

Tom couldn't think of anything he wanted to do less. Hi, Mom. I'm in hell. How are you? "Okay."

Jer rummaged through his knapsack and pulled out his cell. He shuffled around the cabin trying to get a signal and ended up on the porch. Tom could hear him laughing, chatting. Jer poked his head in the door and gave Tom a look. Tom pushed himself off the bunk and went to take the phone from Jer.

"Hi, honey bunny," his mom said, her voice choppy with static.

"Hi, Mom," he said. The two coolers glowed in the light coming out of the shack.

"You sound tired."

"Long trip," Tom said.

"Are you car sick? Oh, dear. I told Jeremy you were too weak to go fishing. I told him. You can't go straight from the hospital to the wilderness and –"

"I'm fine, Mom. Just tired, that's all."

"Oh! Tom, do you want one of the bedrooms that faces north or south?"

"I don't care."

"The south ones face Pender. But they're farther away from the living room. Maybe we should wait and see. I wish that man'd move out of Jer's condo faster. I'm tired of the hotel. Honestly, how long does it take to move one old man into a nursing home?"

Tom massaged his temples. "Okay."

"I should let you get your sleep," she said. "Love you."

"Love you, too," he mumbled.

"Hugs and squishies! Have fun!"

"Bye," Tom said.

"Catch lots of fish!" She seemed to be picking up enthusiasm as the phone call drew to an end.

"Bye, Mom."

"Kisses!"

An endless period of smacking sounds, like deranged dolphin sonar, and then dial tone. Tom handed the phone back to Jer.

"She'd be easy to get rid of," Jeremy said. "Give her enough money for a really big bender and then beat her to death and dump the body in an alley."

The back of his neck prickled – not from the threat, but the casualness of it, the comfortable way Jer said it, as if he'd thought about it, considered his options and knew exactly what he wanted for dinner or which socks he was going to wear.

"I'm doing everything you say," Tom said.

"We're going to have a long day tomorrow," Jeremy said. "Get some rest."

He could hear Jeremy breathing, but Tom couldn't tell if his cousin was asleep or not. Tom raised his hand and held it in front of his face. He couldn't see it. His own breathing sounded like an overheated dog panting.

Trees scratched the window. Just a few days ago, he'd been so bored, he thought he was going to die if he stayed in the hospital another minute. Tom wished he was back. He wished Paulina was lying with him, thrashing around and hogging the blankets. He wondered what she was doing right now. He wished he could talk to her. She had a way of cutting through the bullshit that made things clear when his brain was fogged. He tried to imagine what she'd say about this: lying awake in the dark knowing that in the morning you were going to bury the rotting bodies Jeremy had dismembered to fit inside the coolers.

"People aren't that tough," Jeremy had said. "It's like de-boning a chicken. All you need is a little elbow grease and a decent carving knife."

Left to ferment in an abandoned house, the bodies in the coolers had sloshed and rattled when Jeremy and Tom carried them to the truck. Tom didn't think he was going to make it through tomorrow. Couldn't imagine it. But Jeremy. Jeremy wanted him to clean up his mess. And Tom wanted to keep breathing. He didn't want to be a problem that Jeremy would have to solve with kitchen utensils.

A trickle of a stream ran behind the shack. (Sunshine almost always) A John Denver song from the radio alarm looped in Tom's head. (Makes me high) They used a dolly to bring the coolers down the path to the edge of the stream. Long grass slithered against their dark green hip waders. The thick rubber gloves made Tom clumsy as they manhandled the dolly into position. Jeremy opened the drainage plugs on the coolers. Brown sludge oozed into the stream, heavy trails that sank to the bottom. The sweet stench of rancid meat had a metallic undertone. Flies whined in the cool morning air.

Jeremy unlocked the first cooler. Deflated clothes covered humps of bones. How long did it take a body to liquefy? Something that burned his nose hairs and smelled vaguely like his mother's home perm solution had been used to speed things up. Jeremy snapped a pair of tongs like castanets before he pulled the sopping

218

clothes out of the cooler and dropped them into an open garbage bag at his feet. He held up a black balaclava, paused, and then smiled at Tom as if he was posing for a picture, as if he'd caught a fish he was particularly proud of.

While Jeremy burned the clothes in the wood stove, Tom pounded the bones into fragments. They'd placed them in a thick sack and Tom wailed on them with a sledgehammer. The sun was high. Jeremy kept feeding wood in the fire. The heat in the shack was ferocious. Tom shed his gloves, shirt, hip waders – everything down to his shorts. He paused, dizzy. He caught Jeremy staring at him. Sometimes his cousin stared too hard. Tom used to think it was the coke, because he'd seen Jeremy stare at a rug or tree bark with the same intensity, like he had X-ray vision and you harboured a bomb he was going to have to diffuse. Tom lifted the sledgehammer and pretended not to notice. Jeremy snapped back to the present and fed more clothes in the fire.

Tom thought of Paulie to get through the rest of the after-noon. Little things, dumb things they'd talked about or done. A few days ago, they'd had a long, meandering chocolate discussion in front of a hospital vending machine, trying to decide what candy bar to get. She didn't like cream-filled chocolates, but she could stand the nutty ones. She liked caramel, but not chocolate-covered caramel, which she said was overkill. They'd ended up with a bag of Doritos and Tom had fallen asleep on them and squashed them into crumbs.

"Is that my fault? You put them away. You have to find them your-self." The woman rolled her eyes, smiling lopsidedly, half-turned and leaning against the pay phone under the Carnegie stairwell, inviting Tom to participate in her telephone fight with a guy who was currently screaming through the receiver. "Well, then, you're going to be late. Baby, I'm not a fucking psychic. I can't make your keys fucking levitate to you so don't yell at me. Stop yelling."

Tom heard the people in line behind him shuffling impatiently, clearing their throats loudly, hinting at Not Psychic to hang up.

Not Psychic turned away from all of them. "Baby, I can't do anything. I can't."

After waiting in line for so long, Tom realized he was going to have to make a phone call or look like a total doorknob. He didn't have anyone to call. Jeremy wouldn't take his calls since the blow-up with Chrissy, and his family was staying out of it. Tom could phone the Kingsway Motor Inn. See if his mom was home yet or still hiding out with the rehab boyfriend. He didn't really want to talk to his mom. He was tired of the pointed, hurt silences and the unsubtle hints she wanted Tom to see a shrink. Maybe she was trying to help. Maybe it wasn't punishment for having secrets that made her nervous. He wondered what she would do if she knew everything.

Someone pelted Not Psychic with an apple core. She glared behind her, her eyes shifting, studying them as she continued to argue with her boyfriend. But she finally took the hint and wound down, saying she'd be home with pizza slices.

Tom pulled a matchbook out of his pocket. The motel clerk patched him through to his room and the phone rang and rang and then was sent back to the front desk.

"You want to leave a message?" the clerk said, sighing, and from his tone, obviously hoping the answer would be no.

"I'm staying in room 220 with my mother," Tom said. "Did she leave a message for me?"

"No," the clerk said.

"Oh, okay," Tom said. "Thanks."

"Yeah," the clerk said, hanging up.

Paulina was gone. Tom waited by the desk, wanting to leave but also wanting to see her. He waited and waited because he had nothing better to do and nowhere better to go. He considered asking the other volunteers when her next shift would be, but then he thought better of it. He scribbled a note for her. Tom, here. Just checking in to say thanks for bringing me to VGH, for hanging out. His phone number, in case she didn't run away, screaming.

"Does she know you?" the guy taking Paulie's place said.

Tom nodded. "We went to high school together. We were in band."

"What kind of band? Speed metal? Punk?"

"High-school band," Tom said. "She was a flutist."

"Man," the guy said. "You think you know someone."

▓

The Kingsway Motor Inn was two stories high. Age had stripped the stairs of paint, revealing grey, grease-stained concrete that was black in the middle where everyone walked. A waist-high iron railing rusted all along the edge of the covered walkway. Dotted with the grey skeletons of plants, terra cotta planters now served as neglected ashtrays.

They had moved into the corner room on the far side of the motel the night they left Jeremy's condo. Tom knocked on the door, just in case. She didn't like to be surprised. The room was empty. His mother used to leave him notes telling him not to worry, that she was out with friends. He never thought he'd miss being called honey bunny, sweetie, doll face.

As it touched the horizon, the sun broke through the rain clouds, flared orange, and then faded. Tom leaned against the railing. He almost convinced himself he wasn't watching for her. He brought a chair onto the walkway. Put his feet up on the railing. He smoked a joint, waiting for the soothing effect to kick in, for the blunt.

She hadn't even left the phone number of the rehab boyfriend. He had no way to reach her. He resented the rising panic he felt, the pictures in his head of her body in an alley, washed in rain, lifeless eyes turned to the sky.

He wasn't a kid. He could leave. He could get up and walk out, and she could take her passive-aggressive bullshit and eat it. Because that's all it was. Bullshit. He wouldn't do what she wanted so she didn't want anything to do with him.

Let her cool down, he'd told Jer.

Jer with his head lowered, beer in one hand, sullen and silent.

His mother and her sudden need for space: days and days of not seeing her, worrying the way she wanted him to worry.

Jeremy was entirely capable of making their lives history, a sentence on D72 of the newspaper tucked in between the robbery gone awry and the car crash that held up traffic and killed a family of four. And she wanted to press assault charges.

It's not fair, she'd say. He shouldn't get away with it. You're letting him get away with it.

He went back in the room, shut the lights off one by one, ignoring a growing sense of urgency. He left the hallway light on. He pulled his covers back, and shoved the extra pillows into position so that it looked like someone was sleeping in his bed. He heard voices outside in the parking lot, a woman's pealing laughter, a man's grumbling chuckle. He had frozen without realizing what he was doing. He took the cushions from the grungy plaid loveseat and made a bed in the hallway closet. He lay down. He carefully pulled the closet door shut.

His breathing sounded loud to him. If he fell asleep and someone came in, they would be able to hear him breathing. One part of his brain was saying, this is stupid. Go sleep on the nice bed. Another part of his brain was saying, go get a knife. Put it under your pillow.

They'd come a long way down from the condo. In the bathroom, he watched a line of ants trooping back and forth from under the sink to a crack in the flowered shower tiles. Tom splashed water on his face, trying to get into a semi-normal headspace. He heard a tentative knock on a door.

"It's okay," Tom said. "I'm decent."

After a long pause, the knocking came again, a little louder, more urgent. She'd probably forgotten or lost her keys. Tom wiped his face. He hoped she was going to talk to him tonight. He loathed her silent treatments, her offended sulks. Sobriety had made her unexpectedly judgmental, and she made it clear she found him unworthy.

"Hi," Paulina said, cramming her hands into her pockets.

The world was suddenly soundless. Traffic streaked behind her, tracers of light reflected off the wet pavement. Rain, backlit by the streetlights, sparks falling. Paulie's hair frayed loose from her bun, a wispy crown around her solemn face. Her eyes black in the dim light of the covered walkway.

"Hi," Tom said.

The pedestal fan by the window blew in the dusty smell of car exhaust from the traffic clogging the street in front of Paulie's house. The heat coming through the ceiling from the roof made the air sticky. Tom and Paulie had lazy morning sex, with long pauses when they stopped to go to the bathroom or eat the wrinkled oranges they scavenged from the bottom of Paulie's cocktail fridge. Afterward, they lay on their sides, resting their foreheads together.

The woman next door talked on the phone, complaining about her haircut, the parking-lot attendant who made her late for work, the shiftless co-workers who dropped their work on her desk before they took off early for the long weekend. The sprawling house had been divided into seven bachelor suites and everyone seemed to be home today. TVs and stereos played different shows and music and the sounds garbled. Outside, someone mowed their lawn. In the distance, fire trucks honked, blaring their sirens.

Paulie raised her head, propped it up with her hand and stared at him, letting her fingers wander around his face, tracing his eyebrows, his nose, his cheek. She tilted her head back and squinted. "Fuck. That can't be the right time."

She scrambled out of bed and tore open a drawer. She jumped into a pair of underwear and then pulled on a bra.

"What's up?" Tom said.

"I'm late for anger management," Paulie said.

"Oh," Tom said. He pushed himself up, yawning.

"Relax, hang out," Paulie said, flapping open a folded pair of jeans. "I'll drive you back to the motel after."

"No rush," Tom said.

"You should phone her before she calls in the army."

"We're barely talking. She's probably relieved."

"So you're going to stay the night again?"

Tom shrugged. "I can stay or go."

"I need to get out tonight. The walls are closing in."

"There's fireworks," Tom said.

"Fireworks? Jesus fucking Christ, Tom, I'm not four. I need grown-up fun."

"Give fireworks a chance."

Paulie gave him a quick peck before she was out the door.

He put an arm over his eyes to block out the light. If his mom wasn't going to tell him where she was spending her nights, he didn't see why he should. Let her wonder. The guilt crept in. That logic ranked right up there with sticking out his tongue and going nyah-nyah, especially after his disappearing act last year. He listened to the background noise for a few minutes longer, and then he pushed himself out of bed and hunted through his pants for the phone number of the motel.

"Kingsway Motor Inn," the clerk said.

"220, please," Tom said, feeling his shoulders tighten in anticipation of a fight.

"Just a sec," the clerk said.

Tom could hear a voice in the background complaining about the quality of the TV reception. The phone clicked and then rang again.

"What?" a guy said.

Great. She'd brought a date back. "Hi. Is my mom there?"

"Who the fuck is this?"

"Tom Bauer. Christa's son."

"I don't know who the fuck you're talking about."

"Chrissy. Chris. Look, tell her if she doesn't want to talk to me, that's fine."

"You got the wrong room."

Tom listened to the dial tone, wondering if his mom had told the guy not to tell him she was there. Tom had run blocking duty for her too many times not to know that trick. He phoned the motel again.

"Kingsway –"

"Christa Bauer, please," Tom said.

"Give me a minute," the clerk said. Tom could hear the slow click of hunt-and-peck typing and then a long pause. "She checked out last night."

"That can't be right," Tom said. "I'm staying with her."

"I've got her signature on the credit-card receipt. She checked out."

"Did she leave any messages? I'm her son. Tom Bauer."

"Nope. Nothing."

"Are you sure? Can you check again? Try Tommy Bauer. Or Thomas."

"Uh . . . I'm sure. She didn't leave anything. Sorry, man."

She checked out. She hadn't left a phone number. Instead of wondering and worrying about where he was, she'd taken the opportunity to sneak off. Like all her dumped boyfriends, Tom hadn't seen it coming. She was saying, you think you're leaving me? Ha. Not if I leave you first.

◼◻◼

The lobby had vaulted ceilings like a church. Two room-sized tapestries faced each other on the taupe walls. A uniformed man looked up from the concierge's desk and offered them a warm smile. Tom's mother squeezed his hand, biting her lip.

"Good afternoon, Mr. Rieger," the concierge said.

"Good afternoon, Bert," Jeremy said.

The elevator doors chimed pleasantly and opened to a hushed hallway with two doors made of burled wood. Theirs was on the left. Jeremy put the card in the lock and flung the door open with a flourish.

"Ta-da!" he said. "Welcome to your new digs."

Stark and storm grey from the lofty ceilings to the buffed streaked-marble floor, the entranceway opened to a living room as wide as their old apartment. A wall of glass on one side had a view of Stanley Park and the harbour between the office buildings. A large-screen TV and its speakers took up the other wall. On the other side, twin gunmetal staircases led up to two loft rooms that looked down on the living room like it was a courtyard.

"What do you think, Aunt Chrissy?" Jeremy said to Tom's mother.

"It's like a dream," she said. "It's like a fairy tale."

◼◻◼

His mom couldn't relax in the condo. She put a blanket down before she would sit on the sofa, ate over the sink, and wiped her fingerprints off the many glass surfaces. She agonized over whether or not to tip the man who delivered their groceries, sometimes giving him too much, sometimes not giving him anything. She wasn't sure how to treat the concierge, and would rush by him, avoiding eye contact. She washed her underwear in the bathroom sink rather than give them to complete strangers at the laundry service that picked their clothes up every Monday and Thursday.

"It's so quiet here," she said one night, curled into the corner of the sofa. "It's like we're the only people on Earth."

"It's soundproofed," Jeremy said. "You're not supposed to hear anything."

"Oh, I'm not complaining. You get used to hearing people in other apartments. I kind of miss it. Do you remember the Baker twins? Oh, my, were they a handful. All that guitar playing and drumming and screaming."

"You miss your noisy neighbours," Jeremy said. "Is that what you're telling me?"

"No, no, not at all. But you get used to people sounds."

"People sounds."

"Arguing, laughing, babies crying, people vacuuming, TVs blaring. Ordinary sounds. Oh, listen to me. I do sound like I'm complaining, don't I?"

Tom woke the next morning and his mother was gone. She'd left a Post-it note on the TV, "Mommy's night out! See you at breakfast! Don't wait up! Hugs! I love you, Tommy!"

Two days later, when she still wasn't back, he went looking for her. She liked to end an evening dancing at The Balmoral. She told him it always gave her a kick to think she was in the same hotel that the Queen herself had once been in. Tom was pretty sure Queen Vic wouldn't be sitting around getting wasted with her drinking buddies.

"Tommy!" she said. "Honey bunny, come sit beside me."

"Mom, I think we should go home. It's not safe down here. You're going to get –"

"Oh, don't be a fusspot. My friends will take care of me, right?" A chorus of agreement from the people around the table.

"Another round for my friends!" she shouted at the waitress.

Six rounds later, he tried to pull her up.

Her friends pulled him off, told him to go home, stop trying to spoil the party.

Tom sat with them into the evening, listening to his mother getting drunker. Her drinking buddies nodded their heads to agree with her as she rambled. The bar filled, and she was surrounded by people bumming drinks. She used to be the one looking for free booze, but now she sat tall, smiled at him whenever she decided someone was worthy of her generosity.

Tom started home after the bars closed. His mom was going to a boozecan. She'd invited him along, but he was tired of watching her play queen bee. She'd come home when she ran out of money, which might be a few days because Jeremy was giving her a monthly allowance larger than anything she'd ever earned at a job.

He stopped at The Raging Insomniac, a twenty-four-hour Internet café. He bought some pot off a guy, and then played *Doom* on-line until his wrists hurt. He squinted against the early morning light as he smoked up in the alley.

Jeremy had passed out on the couch, sitting with his head thrown back, mouth open. His slacks had a tear on the bottom. His jacket hung over the coffee table. The subwoofers on the surround sound for the TV rattled with distortion as zombies cornered a buxom, vocal victim. Tom decided he'd put on headphones or dig up some earplugs. Jer was like a ninety-year-old. He'd wake up the second the TV was shut off or made even a degree quieter.

"Howdy, stranger," Jeremy said, opening one eye.

Tom paused, hesitating at the hallway entrance.

"Watch this part," Jer said, sitting forward and pumping the volume even louder.

The zombies attacked in a frenzy of cheesy effects, wet smacks of flesh being chomped and torn.

"This is all pre-CGI," Jer said. "All the gigs are homemade. Pig guts and chicken skin. Cool, huh?"

"Yeah," Tom said.

Jeremy sucked in a loud breath. "I smell cheap hooch. How's your mom?"

He could feel a hot flush burning up from his neck and knew his face was going bright red.

Jeremy grinned. "Did Tommy miss his mommy?"

"Shut up."

"She ditched you, huh?"

"I'm going to bed."

"Grab yourself some dignity!" Jeremy yelled cheerfully after him. "You don't have to go running after her like some dumb dog."

||||

With September coming up fast, Tom found a school six blocks from the condo. Even better, they had self-paced classes where he could come and go as he pleased. He took assessment tests and passed Grade Ten in a matter of weeks. Grade Eleven was more of the same. He discovered that when he was in school or studying, he dropped off Jer's radar. Ironically, now that he had the freedom to skip as many classes as he wanted and blow off homework any time, his attendance and grades had never been better.

The self-paced classes were held in a maze of portables, exiled from the nearby main high school. The tables inside looked like they'd been filched from church basements, and the plastic chairs were duct-taped where they'd cracked. The computers were a mish-mash of donations, some of them as new as last year, some of them still using punch cards.

From his corner table, he would watch the other self-paced students. The only thing he missed about his old school was goofing around with Mike – endless hours of playing *Doom* or *Quake* or *Streetfighter*, getting stoned, watching dumb movies, and discussing why they were dumb. Complaining about school. Avoiding Mike's aunt, Patricia, and Tom's mom.

But he'd decided on no civilians. No more Willy Bakers. Mike might want to help and end up steamrolled if Jeremy blew his top.

Which was all good and noble, but when he admitted it to himself, he didn't want anyone to know how agonizingly strange his life had become. It was one thing to live it, and another thing to deal with people knowing about it.

║▓║

As the months passed, no matter how drunk his mother was, no matter how high Jeremy got, they wouldn't get tanked together. They would feel free to drink or snort in front of him, but they could never bring themselves to do it in front of each other. Sometimes, they would cross paths in the living room or in the kitchen, and they would play sober. Both of them would be swaying and

eyeball-rolling high, seriously discussing the weather or the outra-
geous price of winter produce.

▌▌▌

Paulie stomped back from anger management. She broke out the
cleaning supplies without saying hello. She slammed the pail into
the sink and filled it and dropped it so it sloshed. She scoured the
floor, frowning.

"You okay?" Tom said.

"Perfect," Paulie said.

"You didn't have to do that," Tom said. "Your floor's pretty
spotless."

Paulie ignored him. When she was finished, she closed her
eyes and breathed deeply three times.

"You want to get something to eat?" she said.

"Sure."

They caught the bus to the Granville Island Market and ate a
late lunch on the dock. Tom threw crusts from his sandwich to the
seagulls hovering hopefully around their bench. Paulie laughed
when two fat seagulls bumped heads going for the same crust.

"Kits Beach has a great view of the fireworks," Tom said.

Paulie rolled her eyes.

"It's free," Tom said.

Paulie turned shy when he held her hand, and they didn't talk
as they strolled out of Granville Market and followed the sidewalk past the marina, past the bridge to Kitsilano Beach. A group
of seniors in matching T-shirts rested on the benches. Little kids
screamed away from the waves and then ran back into the water
for more. Sailboats tilted away from the wind. The beach volley-
ball courts were noisy with the shouting from the bronzed
bikini-and-Speedo crowd while the basketball courts were all

232

teenage boys with their baseball caps backward, skinny kids in satin shorts.

Tom bought a Rainbow Rocket Pop for himself and a Creamsicle Dream for Paulie from a shirtless bicycle vendor wearing a white sombrero trimmed with fuzzy red balls. Paulie's tongue went radioactive orange. He asked what colour his was and then stuck his tongue out.

"Could you grow up, please?" Paulie said, her face screwing up in annoyance. "This is why I don't want to be seen in public with you."

"Hey, Paulie," Tom said. "Guess what?"

"What?"

"I love you."

Paulie glared at him. "Sometimes I want to strangle you."

Tom laughed.

"I'm serious," she said. "I want you to take me serious."

"I do," Tom said.

"Don't patronize me."

"I'm not," Tom said.

She punched his arm, hard, but she didn't let go of his hand.

▚

As Tom brushed his teeth, one of Jeremy's friends opened the bathroom door and stared at him. The man was pale with eyes so pinned you couldn't tell he had pupils. He swayed out of rhythm to the music. Tom hated being sober when everyone else was tripping.

"There's another bathroom beside the kitchen," Tom said. He rinsed and spat, wiped the toothpaste from the corner of his mouth with his T-shirt.

"Are you a narc?" Pinned said.

Tom laughed.

The man's eyes went big. "Are you wired? Are you recording this?"

"I'm Jeremy's cousin. Jeremy. Your host. I live here."

Tom pushed past him and started down the hallway. The man followed close behind.

"I know you're following me," Pinned said.

"No one's following you, you freak." Tom didn't see Jeremy, and everyone else ignored him and Pinned. Jeremy had a rotating series of friends in their mid- to late-twenties who had sprung from another species altogether, one with no sags or bumps or wrinkles or inappropriate body or facial hair. Unless they were going for the Goth or Betty Paige look, they were glowingly tanned, like someone had taken oil and a rag and buffed them to a high gloss. Tonight, Jeremy sat on the couch surrounded by people. The coffee table in front of him was littered with pizza boxes, empty beer bottles, and hand mirrors dusted with coke and snot-covered straws and rolled-up bills. The party was too loud and crowded to fight through. Tom decided to retreat to the Insomniac.

His bedroom was technically off-limits for Jeremy's friends. But Tom wasn't surprised to find a man and two women in his bed. The man was naked and bent over, a striped, orange McDonald's straw sticking out of his anus. One of the women was literally blowing coke up his ass and the other was hysterical about the whole thing.

"Do you mind?" the guy said as Tom walked in and grabbed his knapsack.

"It's my room," Tom said, slinging his knapsack across his shoulder. "You're on my bed."

"Get us a refill, luvvie," said the blow-woman, holding up a bowl.

Things to do tomorrow: buy better lock for door, burn sheets and mattress, Tom thought, turning and leaving.

▓

Kids screamed instructions or trash talk at each other as they played on-line games, the espresso maker hissed, and the skull-pounding Industrial CD thudded in the background at The Raging Insomniac. Teenagers coming off the party circuit screamed with delight as they savoured details of their latest outing. The staff argued about who was going to clean the bathrooms and then about who was going to change the toner in the copy machine by the door.

Tom sat at one of the computers in the back, surfing the Internet for anything he could find on Rusty Letourneau. There were a lot of Letourneaus, and it took him a few tries to find the man he'd killed. Rusty's real first name was Robert. His face, smooth and unbroken, stared back at him from a mug shot. He had wavy, black hair and a receding forehead that had formed a deep V. His eyes were not as blue in the mug shot as they were in Tom's dreams. His nose bulged at the tip. He had missed an arraignment hearing. He had a failure to appear charge on top of assault with a weapon and attempted robbery. Crime Stoppers offered two thousand dollars for information leading to an arrest. Letourneau was born in June and would have been twenty-four. He'd beaten a gas attendant with a crowbar when he found out the till only had eight dollars. Stills from the gas-station security cameras showed Letourneau bent over the counter, wailing on a clerk. Tom printed the mug shot.

He found pictures of Robert's father, Jack Letourneau, on www.gangwars.com. Sunglasses covered Jack's eyes as he bent his head over a casket, hands clasped in front of him. Tom wrote down the name of his chapter and then hunted until he found an address. He couldn't find the name of Robert's mother.

▌▐

The condo was quiet when he woke. Tom heard footsteps coming close to the laundry room. He stiffened. The door swung open and light from the hallway made him squint. Jeremy waited.

"It's getting to the point where I'm afraid to start the dishwasher without checking if you're sleeping there," Jeremy said.

Tom swallowed, trying to breathe as quietly as he could.

Jeremy opened the dryer. "I know you're in here," Jeremy crossed the room and opened the closet. "I heard you shouting."

Tom cringed as Jeremy's feet approached the wheeled laundry hampers. Jer shoved them aside and lifted off the sheets Tom had covered himself in. Tom stood sheepishly.

"There was a guy in my room," Tom said. "And some girls."

"You never sleep in your bed. You're under it, you're under a table, you're in a cupboard. And you just keep getting weirder." Jeremy pulled a crumpled-up piece of paper out of his back pocket. He unfolded it and held it in front of Tom's face.

Tom had hidden the mug shot under his mattress. He snatched it back.

Jeremy grabbed Tom in a headlock. "What are we going to do with you, hey?" Jeremy noogied him. "You suicidal retard. What were you planning to do? Confess?"

"I wouldn't say who I was," Tom said.

"You didn't bump his fender, Tom. You can't leave a note on his windshield saying hi, there! Sorry I killed your kid."

"Let go." Tom yanked at Jeremy's arms and Jeremy tightened his grip.

"You're wasting your God-given talent for guilt on Rusty."

"Jeremy, let go." Tom tried pulling out of the headlock and kicking.

"Let's be logical. Did you go out and hunt Rusty down and plan to kill him?"

"No."

"What was he doing in your apartment?"

Tom stopped fighting.

"Did he come to sell you Girl Guide cookies? Was he holding a Bible and asking you if you found God?"

"Jeremy. If my kid was missing –"

"You dumb-ass," Jeremy said. "They don't think he's missing. They think he jumped bail."

"That's not the point."

"No, the point is if you tell Daddy Letourneau anything, he is going to kill you. Slowly. Painfully."

"I want to do something."

"Saint Tommy, martyr of the freaks," Jeremy said. He let him go, and Tom tried to walk away. Jeremy shoved him into the wall. He stood in front of Tom with his arms crossed. "I'm serious. Drop this."

Tom stared at his shoes.

Jer gripped Tom's arm above the elbow and led him down the hallway to the kitchen. A tall, muscle-bound man with hair shaved down to his scalp poured himself a coffee. He was wearing navy sweats, a navy rain jacket, and so-white-they-must-be-new sneakers.

"Hiding in the fucking laundry room," Jer said. "It's embarrassing to be related to you, Tom. What do you think I should do with him, Firebug?"

"You're wasting your time trying to impress those whiny free-loaders," Firebug said, turning around. "You could get three houses for what you paid for this."

"You have no vision," Jeremy said. "Branch out, my friend. I can cut you in on some sweet deals."

"Counting is your responsibility. Yours," Firebug said. "Not some drooling, snot-nosed fuck-for-brains."

"He means you," Jer said.

Tom wished Jer would let go of his arm.

"Tommy-boy knows how to keep his mouth shut," Jer said.

"It's your funeral," Firebug said.

"Come on," Jer said, leading him up the stairs to his bedroom. He picked up a duffle from the floor and zipped it open. "Every once in a while, some moron pays us with party packs." He dumped the contents onto the bed. A riot of five, ten, and twenty-dollar bills swirled and fluttered as Jer shook them loose. Change spilled on the sheets, on the carpet, over their shoes. "I think they had a bake sale to pay this guy's debt."

Tom stared at the money pile. Jer's watch beeped.

"Make yourself useful. Separate and stack the bills into their denominations. I don't want to deal with the coins. Keep that. We'll call it your count fee."

"That's a lot of money," Tom said.

"Want to know where it came from?" Jer said.

"No," Tom said.

"Smart boy."

||||||

"Don't try tackling the whole quadratic equation at once, Tom," Dude said, his tone the aggressively patient one people used when they were talking to morons. "Work in sections. All you're

238

working with are binomials. You can handle binomials, can't you?"

Tom fingered the edges of his red-marked practice mid-term. Dude was a volunteer tutor in his mid-twenties with a shoulder-length shaggy haircut and some kind of facial smudge in the shape of a teardrop under his lip and a line of hair framing his jaw.

"Tom?" Dude said.

"I'm listening," Tom said.

The tutor didn't sigh, but he wore a stoic expression, as if he was a friend who was going to give you a ride home after a party even though he was really tired. Dude repeated the lesson slowly. Dude had a funny name, something vegetable-y, rutabaga or radicchio-sounding. Tom had taken to calling him Dude at first because he could never remember Dude's name, and then because it pushed Dude's buttons. Dude was supposed to be helping him prep, but Tom loathed the practice exercises.

"Maybe this would work better if you could tell me what part you're having trouble with?" Dude said.

Busted. Dude had been talking, but all it sounded like was wacka, wacka, wacka, carry the two, wacka, wacka. "Maybe it would."

Dude went squinty as a no-name cowboy in a dusty, lawless town at high noon.

"Try," Dude said, "to focus. All righty?"

"Did you just say 'all righty'?"

Dude lost his patient smile. "Maybe we should call it a day."

When Dude walked away, Tom rubbed his eyes with the heels of his palm. He felt heavy, sluggish, and unsure of what to do with the rest of the day. The clouds were low and dull, the rain steady as a pulse.

Tom was wearing his headphones, the Walkman turned up loud and all the lights in his room turned on. He rummaged through the opened books on his bed, sending paper drifting down to the floor. He caught movement and froze as Jeremy opened the door. Tom put his headphones around his neck.

"I said knock, knock," Jeremy said. He hesitated.

Behind him stood a tall, slender woman in a blue dress that looked like the hem had been caught in a blender and shredded. She put one hand on her hip as she strolled in behind Jeremy, and Tom half-expected her to do a catwalk swivel. Typical of Jer's women, she was flawlessly lovely. But they usually had less attitude and were much younger. Sometimes they lasted a week, the longest had lasted a month.

"This is Lilia," Jeremy said.

"Hi," Tom said, not getting up.

Lilia didn't bother to look over. She picked up a snow globe his mother had given him for Christmas, examined it, and put it down, wiping her fingers on her thigh.

Charming, Tom thought.

"Does he live here?" Lilia said.

"Yes," Tom said. "I do."

"Lilia's going to help me cheer you up."

"This room is hideous," Lilia said.

"Then be glad it's not yours," Tom said. "And get out."

"I refuse to work in here," Lilia said.

"We'll go into the living room," Jeremy said, yanking Tom up. "Come on, upsy-daisy. Let's get you laid."

▥

When her face came close, Lilia went slightly cross-eyed, not a woman who closed her eyes when she kissed. Her mouth tasted like cinnamon gum. Tom couldn't stop glancing at Jer, at the big-screen TV that showed him and Lilia together on the couch.

"Don't look at the camera," Jer said.

Lilia had a Hitler moustache over her clitoris; a black rectangular thatch, red goosebumps on the curve of her pubis, the skin swollen and angry. She had four scars running across her stomach, long and shiny smooth. She grabbed his wrist when he tried to touch them.

"Don't," she said.

Tom saw his hand on the screen, saw the camera focus in tight on Lilia's scars. Jer leaned forward, his face obscured by the camera's light.

"Let him touch you," Jer said.

Lilia paused for a coke break and Jer said nothing, waiting. The camera never left her scars, traced them lovingly as she breathed.

Under the fluorescent gas-station lighting, Paulie glowed in tiny cut-offs and a sloppy tank with an old grease stain above the left boob. Tom kissed the hollow of her collarbone, an unexpected sweet spot that she liked touched. She smelled musky with sweat and talcum-y with melting perfumed deodorant, something flowery and old-fashioned, tea roses. She pushed his head away.

"Focus," she said.

Tom unfolded the black and yellow rubber dinghy they'd found in a second-hand store. The connector was worn so Tom had to hold the air hose to it. The dinghy inflated resentfully, the bow drooped and the sides sagged. A few feet away, a pasty man in Bermuda shorts tapped his fingers on the flat inner tube he was holding. Bermuda Man glared at them like they were the cause of all his miseries.

Paulie carried two mismatched oars. Tom flipped the dinghy up and wore it like a hat, balancing it on his head and holding the frayed ropes that lined its sides. The people streaming to the beach flowed around them. All of the good viewing spots had been staked out earlier that day. Twilight brought out the mosquitoes, and Tom wished he'd brought repellent. He followed Paulie, who carefully picked her way through the people sitting on the sand. All the radios were tuned to the same station.

"Sit down!" someone yelled at them.

"Bite me," Paulie said.

"We're just passing through!" Tom yelled back. "Just passing through! Sorry, passing through."

Paulie gasped when she dipped her toes in the water. "Holy fuck, that's cold."

Tom waded into the ocean, gritting his teeth against the shock of brain-freeze cold shooting through his skin and making him shiver. He let the dinghy drop. It hit the water with a smack and bobbed in the waves. Tom held it steady. "Hop in."

Paulie slogged through the surge and threw the oars in the dinghy. Her thighs squeaked against the rubber as she straddled the side. Tom snapped a mental picture, knowing that someday he was going to masturbate to this. Paulie fell in the dinghy and scrambled up, indignant. She held on to the ropes along the sides. Tom pushed off, tried to hop in, and missed, belly-flopping. Paulie laughed so hard she snorted. He dog-paddled to the dinghy, hung on to the rope, and stuck one leg over the side, but couldn't manage to pull himself in. Paulie stopped laughing long enough to grab him by the knapsack and haul him up.

Paulie sat sideways as Tom struggled with the oars. One was longer than the other, and they listed to the left, going in a wide circle until Tom figured out how to compensate. Paulie leaned back and lay across the dinghy with her legs over the side. The bottom filled with water. Tom lifted his oars and put them inside. He took off his knapsack and pulled out a glow stick. He snapped it and then shook it until it glowed pink. He leaned over and lifted Paulie's hair. She watched him skeptically as he snapped it in place around her neck.

"So that the other boats will see us," Tom explained. "So we don't get run over."

"Ah," Paulie said.

Tom took out a green glow stick and Paulie helped him snap it in place.

"Just so you know," Paulie said dryly. "This doesn't mean anything."

Tom lay beside her. She stuck her hand under his armpit, wiggled it. Her fingers were icy. He pulled out an aluminum emergency blanket. She unfolded it and spread it over them. He took out a bottle of Pepsi and twisted it open before he handed it to Paulie. Police helicopters circled across the bay. A flotilla of boats in the distance blasted their horns and then went silent.

Classical music rang out from the radios on the shore. Everyone turned expectantly in the same direction, toward English Bay. The first fireworks were gold comets streaking up with glittering tails. They burst open, thousands of tiny green streamers, a forest of neon weeping willows. The fireworks reflected off the blanket, lighting up Paulie's face.

"Oh," Paulie said, with mock awe as each firecracker went off. "Ah."

3. The wicked are estranged from the womb: they go astray as soon as they be born, speaking lies.

Tom and Paulie took a long, slow walk along the Stanley Park seawall promenade. They reached Third Beach, a small stretch of sand past Siwash Rock. The wind made the trees sway like belligerent drunks. They walked down the sand. Tom slipped off his windbreaker and gave it to Paulie to sit on. Rain slid down his neck, soaked his shorts and shoes, chilling him. Paulie leaned against him. He wished she would say something.

The waves rolled up the beach in leaden humps and then flattened before slinking backward. Anchored in the Burrard Inlet, three tankers pointed in different directions as if they'd just had a fight and were refusing to look at each other. The peaks of the North Shore Mountains crawled with fat, white slugs of mist. A German shepherd bounded past. Its owner, a man wearing a yellow raincoat, swung a red leash. Seagulls shot upward out of the sand, squalling as the dog barked at them.

Paulie frowned. "Do you know where the bones are?"

Tom nodded.

"We should move them. That'll be one less thing for Jer to hold over your head," Paulie said. She frowned. "How much have you told your mother?"

Tom broke out a doobie and lit up, sheltering his lighter from the wind. "Nothing about Rusty."

"Nothing? Then what's she bent out of shape over?"

Tom exhaled. "It's lame."

"Lame?"

Tom hunched into himself.

Paulie nudged him. "We're only as sick as our secrets."

"What kind of name is Firebug?" Lilia said.

They stopped at a red light.

"I don't mind him," Lilia said, with a small twitch of her head she indicated the back seat where Tom was sitting. "But really, Jeremy. Firebug?"

"You're a beautiful woman. He's a sad, horny guy who just got divorced. Again."

"He's a repulsive bore," Lilia said.

"He was trying to impress you."

"We're here."

Jeremy pulled the Ferrari to the curb in front of Laurent's in South Granville. The window display had a row of headless mannequins in tuxes. Jeremy reached over and opened the door for Lilia. "We'll find parking and meet you."

They kissed. Lilia stepped out and pushed her seat down so Tom could get out. Jeremy snapped it back up.

"Isn't he coming?" Lilia said.

"We're right behind you," Jeremy said. Lilia closed the door. They drove to a nearby parkade. They parked on the lowest level, in a corner with no other cars around.

"What's up?" Tom said.

Jeremy stepped out and flipped his seat down. "Don't make a scene. We're helping out a friend of Lil's. He makes suits."

Tom didn't move.

Jeremy poked his head in, suspiciously cheerful. "I'm not going to force you."

Tom waited for the rest.

Jeremy stroked his chin, miming deep thought. "Hmm. How long do you think it would take you to polish all the marble in the condo with a toothbrush?"

Tom calculated his chances of making it past Jeremy. No matter what he tried, it would end the same way, but going along with it now meant he could save himself some bruises and the humiliation of being dragged around like a stubborn toddler. Tom clambered out. Jeremy slammed the door shut and keyed the alarm.

"You're an asshole," Tom said.

"Relax," Jeremy said. "You don't have to wear any of this crap."

◫

His mom picked up on the first ring. "Where are you?"

"Jer's getting fitted for some suits at –" Tom said.

"You're shopping!" Her voice a strangled squeak. "Shopping!"

"It was Jer's idea, not mine."

"I have the cake here! I spent all afternoon decorating! I already started dinner!"

"But it was Jer's idea, Mom."

"Why didn't you stop him!"

Tom rubbed the gunk off his eyes.

His mother sighed. "I'm sorry. Sorry."

"We're coming home later. You can surprise him then."

"But I won't be here! I'll be on the ferry!"

"He won't die if he gets a party next weekend."

Lengthy, offended silence. His mom lived in a world where everybody cared about spending their birthdays with family. Even twenty-four-year-old cokeheads should eat cake and hug and get teary-eyed over sappy cards and cheap gifts. She'd had it all planned, had phoned him for weeks with the details, had gotten a special day pass from Twelve Oaks to be with Jer on his big day and now everything was capital "R" Ruined. She had written a climactic Thank You speech, and in her world, Jeremy was going to be moved by it, *Touched by an Angel* by it, chest-thumping glad he'd been letting them leech off him for a year.

"Did you get him a card?" his mom said.

"Mom."

"Damn it, I asked you to do one little thing, and you act like I want you to climb Everest! Did you get him a present?"

"No. Mom, God, he's not –"

"People weren't exactly lining up to help us, in case you didn't notice. You could show a little gratitude now and then, Tommy. The least you can do is get him a card."

"A card then," Tom said, with no intention of following through.

The Thank You cards in the Hallmark store were either baby-animals saccharine or glad-handing businesslike. They didn't have a series designed especially for thanking your drug-demented cousin for covering up your first homicide, so he settled for a blank card with a sailboat.

Tom sat in the mall's food court with a notepad and a tub of New York Fries fries, trying to think of something appropriate to put in the card. *Thanks, bud. I'd be a pathetic virgin today if you hadn't made your girlfriend sleep with me. By all means, keep the video, Tom.* Not quite the folksy tone he wanted. *I'm grateful you didn't crack my skull open after I stole your Jag. No disrespect was intended. I thought it would get you out of my life, you big, fat fucking control freak.* Maybe a little too sour.

The card was dumb, but if he wanted to save himself grief, he had to give Jer something. Maybe his mom was right. Maybe he should give him a cake. A host gift, so to speak. A fuck-off forever cake, chocolate with booze and tranks and pot baked in to get everyone in a mellow mood when he announced he'd finished high school and wanted his own place.

A nearby joke shop had a pump that squirted unconvincing blood and the butcher didn't find his request for pig guts as odd as Tom had thought he would. Chicken skin was harder to come by. Tom had to buy a large roaster.

Tom set up the camera in the dining room. He went back to the kitchen and contemplated the chicken. He'd never skinned anything before. His chicken came in KFC buckets.

"What's going on?" Jer said.

"Hi," Tom said, surprised. Jer wasn't usually a morning person. "You're home early."

Jer cracked the lid of the ice-cream bucket filled with glistening pig guts that Tom had left on the counter. "Breakfast?"

Tom carefully withdrew his knife, so the skin wouldn't tear. "Birthday present."

248

Jer made a face.

"Surprise," Tom said. "It's a homemade zombie movie."

※

The kitchen table was covered with black garbage bags, which were stuck to Tom's back. Jeremy lowered a jagged knife to Tom's chest, pausing. Tom regretted the blood capsule he'd inserted between his cheek and gums. Jeremy only had eyes for his torso. Jer pressed the knife into the chicken skin covering Tom's chest. They hadn't been able to figure out how to make the blood ooze out like a real wound, so the cut Jeremy made at the top of Tom's chest was not very convincing.

Once the knife opened up Tom's fake guts, though, the pump they'd hidden spurted an impressive fountain of coloured corn syrup, splashing Jer's face and body. Tom bit down on the capsule and, after a few seconds, his mouth foamed red spit. He convulsed on the table, moaning. Jer pressed his fingers into the open skin and pulled out a length of gut. Jer's expression, rapt, engrossed. He was flushed. His hands shook.

Tom had a hard time not laughing. If he'd known this was all it took to make Jer happy, the last year would have been much, much easier. Tom had been planning to holler, but Jer looked annoyed if Tom distracted him from the real show, his fake guts spilling onto the counter.

Neither of them heard the front door open. By the time they realized Tom's mother was watching them, she had already turned, running out the door. The foil bouquet of Happy Birthday balloons drifted upward and bounced against the ceiling. Tom scrambled off the table. She wasn't supposed to arrive until tomorrow.

"Mom!" he yelled. "Mom! It's okay!"

"Fucking get washed up," Jer said.

While he was in one of the bathrooms, his mom came back with three security guards. One of them escorted Tom to the lobby, despite Tom's explanations. He sat on the bench near the concierge's desk. She came downstairs with the other two security guards. In the taxi, she wouldn't look at him.

"Where're we going?" Tom said.

"You should have told me," she said. "You should have told me he was . . . he was . . . sick."

▐▌▌▐

Tom left Paulie's place at midnight, driving a Rent-a-Wreck car to Jer's condo. He parked nearby, looking up at the twenty-seventh floor. The lights were on. Hopefully, no one was home.

Tom slung his knapsack over his shoulder. He'd been afraid the concierge or security would challenge him, he hadn't been living there for a while, but he seemed to barely register. He heard music coming from the condo, and paused, card key in hand. Jer might have left the stereo on when he went out or he might be passed out with the stereo on. Tom slipped his key in the door.

He stood in the entranceway, surprised at the crush of people inside. You couldn't hear the music above the roaring waves of conversation. The dress code for the evening was power suits for the men and plunging cleavage for the women. Firebug sat morosely on the sofa, staring at a boxing match flashing between the crush of bodies.

"Firebug!" Tom yelled. "Where's Jer?"

Firebug shrugged.

Jer's bedroom was empty.

"Jer?" Tom said.

Jeremy kept an ashtray on his nightstand, a little silver dome that held the stink of old smokes to an area around the king-sized bed with dark brown posts and a scratchy tan duvet. He tended to leave his lights on. His reading material ran from dry to drier: eye-glazing reports, adjective-heavy company brochures.

Tom found Jeremy's videotape collection tumbled together in heaps at the back of the closet. He hadn't even bothered to put them back in his wall safe. Tom quickly packed the tapes inside his knapsack, taking the tapes on top figuring they'd be the recent ones. He considered the remaining tapes littering the floor. If Jer had been taping him for as long as Paulie said, even the older ones might have embarrassing sections on them. Tom brought the tapes down to his rental car and dumped them in the trunk. He went back upstairs and took a second load of tapes. On his third trip, he noticed Firebug leaning against the entranceway wall, arms crossed over his chest, head lowered. They studied each other. Tom waited for Firebug to ask what he was doing. Firebug glanced at the bulging knapsack and then at Tom. He seemed to be waiting for Tom to say something. Tom could feel Firebug watching him as he walked out the front door and into the hallway.

He poured the tapes in the trunk. They'd soon find out if Jeremy noticed his homemade porn was MIA. If Tom left now, he was guaranteed to leave without a scene. But since he was staying with Paulie, she'd suffer the same things he did if Jer went ballistic. Better to face him while he was feeling good and surrounded by witnesses. Tom headed back to the condo and waited by the elevator, checking his watch every few minutes. He gave up and started up the stairs. Near the top, he met people from the party concentrating seriously on making it down the stairs in a hurry. Maybe there was a fight going on. Or maybe Jer had broken out the karaoke machine.

By the time he reached the twenty-seventh floor, the last crush of people had pushed their way in the elevator and the doors were chiming shut. The condo was open. The floors and tables were littered with liquor bottles and dusty hand mirrors. The Gypsy Kings played in the background. Tom heard someone moving in the kitchen, but when he got there, he didn't see anyone. On the counter by the sink, Tom recognized Jer's briefcase, shiny and expensive-looking metal. He shook his head as he snapped the case shut on the stacks of hundred-dollar bills and the three keys of coke. Jer was getting seriously sloppy. Tom swung the briefcase off the counter.

"Jer?" Tom said. He heard someone moving behind the butcher's block. "Jer?"

The call he'd made to the 911 operator was later used as evidence. Tom's voice, unsteady and breathless: "He looks bad, he looks real –"

"Shut up!" Jeremy yelled in the background. "Shut up!"

"I'm sorry, I don't understand," the 911 operator said, her voice low and soothing. "You'll have to repeat that. What is your cousin's condition?"

"He did some bad blow. He's crawling around and he's throwing up blood and he's got blood coming out of his ears and his nose. There's blood all over, it's all over."

"Shut up!"

"Did he inhale, smoke, or inject the cocaine?"

"I think he snorted it. It's still on the counter."

"What room are you in?"

"We're in the kitchen and there's blood everywhere. Jeremy! Jeremy!"

"Calm down, Tom. The ambulance is almost there."

"Jeremy! Wake up!"

Jeremy curled up on his kitchen floor. Tom shakily felt for a pulse and didn't find one.

"He's not breathing," Tom said. "He's not breathing and he has no pulse."

"Tom, you're going to have to perform CPR," the 911 operator said.

"He's got stuff in his mouth."

"Is it vomit? Turn him onto his side and clear out the vomit before you begin mouth-to-mouth."

"He's on his side." Tom stuck his fingers in Jeremy's mouth and fished out chunks. The sweaty, bloody cordless phone slipped out from between his neck and his head, squirted out like a banana from its skin and slid across the floor. "Shit!"

He turned Jeremy onto his back, and Jeremy's arm flopped, hit the marble with a smack. He could hear the operator's voice, tinny and distant, but was too busy feeling for Jeremy's sternum to pick up the phone. He pushed, hoping it wasn't too hard. He couldn't remember how many times he was supposed to do compressions. He couldn't remember how to give mouth-to-mouth. There was a mnemonic, something about airways, AIR, something like that. You had to tilt the head back. Or forward. He needed to talk to the operator and had decided to reach for the phone when the paramedics jogged efficiently through the kitchen door. They shoved him aside when he was too stunned to move.

▐▌

Tom had no idea where the spleen was or what it did, but the doctors and nurses he caught in the hallways assured him that it was an organ Jeremy could live without.

253

"He's going to live?" Tom said.

"Are you a relative?" one of the nurses said.

"Yes. Can I see him?"

"Not right now. Please sit down. Please take a seat, and someone will come out and talk to you."

"But everyone's been saying that and no one's done it."

"Have you contacted Mr. Rieger's family?" she said. "The phone is right over there."

He phoned Paulie first, explained why he wouldn't be home that night. The phone line crackled as he waited for her to speak. He thought she'd yell. She sighed.

"I can't believe you saved him," she said, and then hung up.

When he phoned Aunt Faith, he did not give details. He picked up the phone in the Emergency room and called her collect.

"It's late," she said, and then, joking, "It must be bad news."

"I'm sorry," Tom said. "It is."

"Is it Christa?" she said, her voice shrill with hope or alarm. He preferred to think alarm.

"I'm afraid it's Jeremy."

The ICU rooms were clustered around the central nurses' station. Jeremy's room was divided in two sections by a glass wall. The outer room had charts, signs, tables, equipment. Tom stood stupidly by the bed, waiting for Jeremy to wake up, until a nurse booted him out to do tests. Tom went back to the waiting room.

In the morning, his cousin was awake and deep in conversation with a man in a suit, so Tom thought things couldn't be that bad if Jer was already talking to a lawyer. But Jeremy stared so long when Tom walked in the room that he thought maybe Jeremy wasn't actually seeing him.

"Get out," Jeremy said.

When Tom didn't move, Jeremy picked up a bedpan and threw it at him.

"Get out! Get the fuck out! Are you deaf? Get out!"

"Well, what did you expect?" Paulie said. "A parade?"

"No," Tom said.

Paulie opened the oven door and lifted the cake pan out. The chocolate cake peaked at the centre like a volcanic mountain, cracked and burnt.

"Damn. Martha made it look easy." She turned the cake onto the cooling rack, and it broke apart to reveal oozing, uncooked insides. "We'll call it your I-saved-Jeremy's-worthless-ass cake."

Tom laughed. "That's about the size of it."

"He's going to blame you," Paulie said. "That's the way his little brain works. If Tom hadn't called the fucking ambulance, he's going to tell himself, I wouldn't be up on possession charges."

"He was dying, Paulie. He did die."

"Is he thanking you? Is he showering you with gratitude for helping him when everyone else buggered off?"

"What was I supposed to do?"

"Well, this'll learn you," she said, poking at the cooling cake. "Did you get the tapes?"

"Yeah," Tom said. "They're in the rental car."

"I'm glad something went right. Hand me the garbage, will you, hon? I don't want to look at this stupid cake any more. Martha I ain't."

4th BLOOD

Mel rolled her old-fashioned baby walker close to the bars. Her mouth was smeared with yellow icing from her Big Bird cookie, the walker and the cookie distractions provided by Firebug. She bounced in the canvas seat that held her upright and banged her free fist against the pink plastic tray that formed an O around her waist. The rusty metal legs holding up the tray were attached to wheels that squeaked as Mel manoeuvred, her bare feet paddling the painted concrete floor like Fred Flintstone in his caveman car. She paused, looking back over her shoulder, eyebrows rising hopefully. She wanted to be chased.

"No can do, babe," Tom said, raising his cuffed hands. The duct tape had left a sticky residue that clicked as he talked. "I'll watch you though."

Mel gnawed off Big Bird's shoulders. She paddled over to Paulie, who stood with her arms crossed, talking to Firebug and Leo like she was talking to a neighbour through the fence. Mel bumped into Paulie's leg, and Paulie absently reached down and

259

patted Mel's head. Mel buzzed around the room, laughing her hiccuping gurgle as she rammed her walker into the bed, the sink, the toilet.

▥

Firebug knelt and dropped Tom on the bed. The basement had no windows, just recessed fluorescent tubes in mesh cages above them. Paulie stayed near the bars, hip jutting out to hold Mel. Leo stood against the far wall, aiming his revolver at them. Mel screamed her outrage, reaching for the walker that Leo was holding.

"Neil will be watching you on the monitors," Firebug said as he stood. "Behave."

He slammed the cell door behind him. Leo went up first and Firebug followed. Neither of them looked back. The trap door shut. Firebug would come back and deal with them if there was nothing on the tapes. That was their only hope of getting out of the basement.

▥

Paulie made soup in the microwave by the sink. Instant noodles, shrimp flavour. He could tell by the spices. Mel cried by the mattress. She had a juicy diaper. Tom lifted her onto the bed.

"Don't," Paulie said. "I'll change her."

"I've got her," Tom said. His voice was hoarse from screaming. It sounded scratchy and thin, like he'd been drinking whiskey straight and chain-smoking. "Shh, baby, shh. It's okay. You're okay."

Tom rubbed her stomach until she calmed down. He felt as raw-eyed as he had the first sleepless week she was home from the hospital. The pain was still distant but the patch seemed to be

bunker with a weaning baby and an epileptic having rebound seizures, she still scrubbed the sheets clean and wrung them out in the sink and hung them over the microwave to dry.

III

Tom tested each of the bars. None were loose. The bars were thick, solid and painted the same colour as the floor, pastel green, a colour beloved of old hospitals and mental wards. Tom wrapped his feet in dirty wash rags and kicked the lock until his legs went rubbery. It didn't do any good, but he felt better and it amused Mel.

Tom stood on tiptoe on the toilet. He experimentally punched the ceiling to see if it would give. It was solid concrete. After cradling his fist against his stomach for a few minutes, he wrapped his hands in an old baby shirt and shook the wire mesh around the fluorescent tubes, hoping for a loose screw. Mel got into the spirit of things and banged the walls. Paulie made them tea.

On one side of the room, the cell had a metal sink, a metal toilet, and a microwave on top of a cocktail fridge. On the other side, it had a queen-sized foam mattress on the floor, a set of sheets, a wool blanket, two plastic milk crates with a pillowcase thrown over for a nightstand, a garbage pail, and a metal enamel wash basin.

Firebug had also left a file box filled with baby clothes, a box of diapers, a case of baby food, three cans of liquid baby formula. Their grub was a short list of eight eggs, four bananas, ten packages of instant noodles, a box of sugar cubes, and a tin of Red Rose tea. The cutlery was plastic. They had three Styrofoam cups. Paulie gave him the bathrobe.

"We need MacGyver," Tom said.

"Told you," Paulie said. "I've tried all that."

"Yeah, well." Tom sighed.

"Mmm," Paulie said, trying to tempt Mel to drink the formula out of a baby jar she'd cleaned. "Tasty milk."

Mel shoved her face in the mattress and turned it away.

"I think this used to be a daycare or something," Paulie said, eyeballing the mural with its happy bunnies.

"Yeah," Tom said.

"The baby clothes smell pretty musty and the walker must be twenty years old."

Tom considered the water rings dried varying shades of brown on the floor's light green paint near the bars. "Maybe a play room."

Paulie stroked Mel's hair. "That makes more sense."

"Jazz phoned," Tom said. "She said she'd check up on us if you didn't call her back. She'd be worried."

"Firebug brought Mel down here. I watched her on the security monitor. He said he'd shut off the lights and leave her in the dark unless I did what he said. So he gave me a cell phone. And I called Jazz. And told her you'd gone paranoid. Ripped up the apartment. That I was hiding from you."

They were sunk. If no one realized they were missing, no one was looking for them.

"Leo's on the security camera at work," Tom said. "They screwed up there. That might help."

Paulie's silence said she didn't think so, but didn't want to say it out loud.

▌▐▌▌

Just before dinner, he had his second seizure. When he woke up from it, he curled up beside the toilet, retching and shaking. He didn't know what drugs he'd been given, but on top of the pain and the lack of sleep and the sudden absence of his regular epilepsy meds, it felt like he was just getting off a three-week bender.

Paulie made noodles and eggs for supper. Tom stuck to plain tea. She mopped his forehead with a rag still pink from wiping the dried blood from his chest.

"It gets better," Paulie said.

"It gets better," Tom repeated, willing himself to believe it.

IIƎIII

The lights flickered. Trembling and miserable and too nauseous to lie down, Tom sat beside the mattress, holding Paulie's hand. Mel fisted her hand in Paulie's hair. The basement went dark for three or four heartbeats and then lit up again. Paulie shifted. She had been waking on and off since she lay down with Mel. He squeezed her hand and she went still again. Tom let go of the breath he had been holding.

When the power went, they would still have water. But they would run out of food in less than a week. Tom wondered if Firebug had paid the electric bill. If they had a few weeks or a few days or a few hours before the basement went permanently dark.

They hung off the light's protective wire mesh, kicking and tugging. The screws were rusted to the metal frame so they were hoping to pull them loose from the concrete. Tom's end squeaked. He slipped first, dizzy. Paulie swung her legs up and tried to get her toes hooked in the mesh. She slipped, landed on him, and they both lay on the floor, winded. Mel shook the empty ice-cream bucket Paulie had filled with the lids from the empty baby food jars.

"One more time," Paulie said.

The first screw came loose on their eighteenth try. It was six inches long and as fat as Mel's thumb. They paused. Tom couldn't tell if he was having an aura or an anxiety attack, and was relieved it was only a precursor. He woke to find Paulie playing patty-cake with Mel.

The next screw came loose on their twenty-fourth try. Their fingers went red and puffy. When the third screw came loose, a

266

row of screws popped and the mesh bent toward the floor until they rested their feet on the ground. Paulie stood on the toilet. Tom carefully broke one of the baby jars in the sink and handed Paulie the strongest, sharpest-looking edge. Paulie scraped the concrete behind the lights where the wires went up through the floor. A splatter of bits rained on the floor.

"It's soft," she said.

Tom whooped. Paulie sat on the toilet and rocked, hugging herself. Mel got scared and wailed. Tom and Paulie laughed. Tom picked Mel up and swung her around. Mel bawled until he gave her to Paulie.

Paulie cooked the eggs before they unplugged the cocktail fridge. Tom lifted the microwave off the top of the fridge and put it on the floor near the wall. He pushed the fridge under their chosen dig site. Paulie held the fridge still while Tom climbed onto it. He'd wrapped his hands to protect him from the heat of the light and the glass. The falling concrete made him sneeze. He used a broken baby jar to dig about six inches deep before he had to stop and lie down. Paulie jumped on the fridge and attacked the concrete. He picked up Mel, rolled in the bed with her, kissing her face until she covered it with her hands.

They took a break when they hit hardwood. Paulie wolfed down three eggs and two packages of soup. Tom couldn't manage anything except the broth. Mel ate his noodles and demolished two jars of apple sauce. Tom pushed his eggs toward Mel. She wasn't interested in them either.

"If we widen the hole," Paulie said, "we can stand on the fridge and punch through with the microwave. If we take out the glass and the door, it should still be heavy enough."

"My lady of destruction," Tom said, leaning in to kiss her.

Mel rolled her empty jar across the floor, studying it.

Paulie looked up, thoughtful. "If you stand on my shoulders, you'd probably fit through the hole better."

Tom said nothing, sipping his broth.

"Because of my big, nursing boobs," Paulie amended. "Not because you're, um . . . you know."

"You're going up first," Tom said.

▌▌▌

Tom pushed her butt up. Paulie's legs scissored as she grunted and squirmed her way through the hole in the ceiling. Mel screamed. She bobbed furiously. Her face went dark, dark red. When Paulie finally pulled herself through, Tom jumped down and scooped Mel up.

"Yay, Mommy, yay!" Tom said.

Mel cried harder. Tom braced his feet on the slippery top of the fridge and hoped Mel wouldn't move too much.

"What's the matter?" Tom said.

"Just a minute!" Paulie shouted back. She came back to the hole, out of breath. She reached her arms down as Tom lifted Mel. Mel squealed, excitedly giving frog kicks.

Tom passed Paulie the bucket filled with unopened formula tins and baby food jars and the packages of noodles and the eggs. He handed her two packages of diapers and the wipes.

"Mel, honey, stay close," Paulie said.

They linked forearms and Paulie leaned back. He caught the edge of the hardwood and wormed his way through, with Paulie grabbing him under the pits and hauling. One of the straps on her sundress flapped loose. Her hair was dusty and wild.

Near the bathroom door, a pair of sneaker-clad feet stuck out from under a sheet. Where the outline of the head was, the sheet was soaked red. Mel scooted toward the baby walker that had been abandoned beside the body.

"It's Neil," Paulie said. "Single shot to the back of the head."

"Damn," Tom said, shivering.

"Sharing didn't seem to be one of Leo's strong points," Paulie said. "And half sounds way better than a third."

"Let's go," Tom said.

"Check for a phone first," Paulie said. "Food. Weapons. Where the fuck are we anyway?"

Paulie picked up Mel and they went back to the master bedroom and turned on the security monitors. The blue truck and the black Land Rover were gone. It was still daylight, but the sun was slipping down the sky to the mountains. Early evening. The logging road was empty, as were the front and back yards. Tom pointed to the road.

"Firebug drove us in from this direction," he said.

"Me and Mel are going to the kitchen to hunt for weapons and food," Paulie said. "Pat Neil down for keys, his piece, a cell phone, anything. Take his clothes and his shoes."

"Gotcha," Tom said.

When they left the room, Tom pulled the sheet off. Neil was face down, his left hand rigid near his ear. Tom's skin prickled. He didn't want to touch the body. But he didn't want to look any more squeamish than he had to in front of Paulie.

"Sorry, Neil," he said.

The hole in the back of Neil's head was tidy, but his face was a crater of mashed flesh and bone. The shirt was splattered but salvageable. The pants were too big and the belt didn't have a small enough loop. The sneakers were too small. Paulie could use them. He'd use the socks. Neil had a holster, but it was empty, as were his pockets. A white shadow around his wrist showed where his watch had been. He'd been picked clean. He made a quick recon of the house – no one was home.

"Anything?" Paulie said as walked into the kitchen. She had tied her hair back in a high ponytail.

"Nada," Tom said, holding up the pants. He plopped the sneakers on the butcher's block beside Mel who was gnawing on a hunk of cheese. Paulie's face was greasy from the fried chicken she was scarfing. She held up a wing. He shook his head.

"Still queasy," he said.

"You should eat," she said.

"Here," he said, pushing the sneakers toward her, "they're too small."

Paulie threw one on the floor and jammed her foot in. Tom picked up the bread knife from the counter and poked a hole in the belt. He threaded the metal tongue through and tested the pants. They stayed up, but the pants sagged and the hems hid his feet. The pants were woollen which was fine while they were in an air-conditioned bunker but once they got outside, they were going to be in the middle of a heat wave. He sawed off the pants around his knees before he tucked the bread knife in his belt. He caught Paulie grinning at him.

"Don't say anything," Tom said.

‖‖

Paulie filled two white plastic grocery bags with their food, Mel's diapers and wipes. Tom went outside and stood on the porch, dazed. She stood beside him, taking deep breaths. She shielded her eyes as she surveyed the area.

"I think you're right," Paulie said. "We should go that way. Look how thick that smog is."

The sun dipped closer to the trees. They might not make it very far before nightfall, but by unspoken agreement, neither of them wanted to stay anywhere near the house.

▐▐▐

They limped up the first hill. Mel had a death grip on Paulie, so Tom slung the grocery bags over his wrists. The giddy, heady sensation of being free of the house gave way to the realization that they were lost and far from being home free. The adrenalin that had been sustaining him seeped away as they walked slower, the pains of the last few days catching up with them.

Tom thought he was sweating, until Paulie made a face. He looked down. A red circle soaked his shirt over the nipple and smaller spots dotted his torso.

"The mosquitoes are going to love me," Tom said.

"Are you okay?" Paulie said.

"I'm fine," Tom said.

"Do you want to use the sneakers?"

"I said I'm fine."

Mel wanted to walk. Paulie let her down and finger-walked her a few steps. Mel found the ditch at the side of the road interesting and strained toward it. Paulie steered her back on the road. Tom walked along the smoother tire treads. The road wobbled. He blinked sweat from his eyes. He wanted to flop down like Mel and hold his hands up for Paulie to carry him.

▐▐▐

271

As the sun dipped closer to the trees, their shadows stretched behind them. Tom stopped, recognizing the clearing that Firebug had first brought him to. The tire tracks from the truck were still visible in the dirt and there was a trail of flattened grass and bent bushes where Firebug had lugged the equipment back and forth.

"What is it?" Paulie said.

"Nothing," Tom said.

Tom's teeth chattered. His skin goose-pimpled even though he was sweating. His ankles had disappeared. Tom bent over and poked the skin of his feet. His finger left a dent mark. His thighs felt scalded. Birds sang as the sky went milky blue. Tom wondered how much time that meant before they were in darkness.

"It's going to get really dark in an hour or two," Paulie said. "We should get moving."

Tom pulled at his shirt. Blood had glued it to his skin.

"God," Paulie said. "They're getting worse. I didn't think they could get worse."

The burns had bruised deep purple like ink splatters on his torso. They were crusted with puss. He couldn't remember breaking his ribs, but they cramped when he took deep breaths or bent too far. His nipple had puffed up and split so it looked like a drooling, fat lip.

"Paulie," Tom said. "Firebug and Leo could be looking for us right now. If you don't leave, we're all up shit creek."

"I'm not leaving you here."

"It hurts to breathe," Tom said. "It hurts to blink. I'm not going to make it to the highway."

"We need to get you to a hospital. Two seizures the day before. Three this morning. Tom –"

"Go. Get help. You'll move faster without me."

272

"No, we don't split up."

"I'll be fine."

Paulie's attention shifted to something behind Tom. He turned, and saw a dust cloud billowing along the logging road. Very faintly, they could hear an engine.

"It's coming this way," Paulie said.

"Here," Tom said, handing the bread knife to Paulie. "Take Mel and hide. I'll stand behind this tree. If they look friendly, I'll flag them down. If not, I'll stay hidden and when they're gone, you run like hell to the highway."

Tom stayed behind the tree. A black van driving slowly down a logging road with its lights off couldn't be good. He remembered the black van that had been in the parking lot of Lucky Lou's. As it cruised closer, the engine dominated the darkening forest, drowning out the birdsong Tom hadn't been aware of until it was gone. The noise of the engine and the forest's darkness must have frightened Mel, because at that moment, she began to wail.

The driver cut the engine a few feet from Tom. Mel's crying became muffled but was too loud to miss. All the van's doors opened. The driver was young, tall and weedy, dressed in shorts and a blue T-shirt. The man who exited from the passenger's side was bald, older, and chunky, his gut straining the seams of his muscle shirt. Jeremy Rieger stepped out of the side door, his grey sweatsuit glowing against the dark trees. They drew their weapons as if on a signal. The two men kept going toward Mel's crying, but Jer stayed by the van.

"Nice night for a walk," Jer said.

Mel's crying suddenly stopped, and Tom could hear Paulie whispering a song to her. He knew that when they reached Paulie and

273

Mel, that would be the end. He couldn't make himself move.

"How old is Mel, Tom?" Jer said. "Almost a year?"

Tom strained to hear what was happening. He could hear the men making their way further back.

Mel started to cry again as Paulie carried her toward the road. Tom stepped away from the tree, and Jer turned, flicking the safety off his gun.

"So close," Jer said. "But no cigar."

▌▌▌

The back of the van had the coppery tang of fresh blood. The window was open and the radio was off. As Tom's eyes adjusted to the dark, he could see two metal dog cages glittering. Firebug was still alive, hands cuffed behind his back, gag stretching his mouth open. He hit the cage with his feet. Leo lay in the second dog cage, unnaturally still. He had a dark hole in the middle of his forehead.

"All in all," Jer said. "You did pretty good. You lasted longer than Firebug. Big fucking mouth on that backstabbing whiner." Jeremy made his voice high and squeaky. "You ripped me off, Rieger! You're going to pay! Dumb fuck. It's the fucking stock market, not a gas station."

Tom turned to study his cousin. Jer grinned. The door of the van squealed open, and the light showed him Paulie and Mel in the passenger's seat.

"We should turn him in," Tom said.

"That's loser talk," Jer said.

Tom became aware of his breathing, how shallow his breaths were getting, how it felt like he was breathing through a straw.

"I've met a lot of big talkers," Jer said, "who piss their pants and cry when things get bad. But you, Tom. You got everybody fooled. I know you. I know what you can do. You're a stone-cold killer."

"I can't," Tom said.

"Push comes to shove," Jer said. "You push back."

Jer reached under the passenger's seat and pulled out Betty, Firebug's pistol. He twirled it like a cowboy and held it, grip facing Tom, an offering.

"I can't," Tom said.

Jeremy spun the pistol again and then held it in front of Tom's face. "Other people walked away from me when I needed them. You understand loyalty, and that's why you're not in the ground, Tom."

Tom couldn't take his eyes from the barrel.

"Is this the life you really want?" Jer said. "A job a monkey could do with brains left over to fart. Bills you can't pay. Kids you can't feed. A girlfriend one card short of a full deck. Playing Mother Theresa to schitzy freaks in the skids."

Tom raised his eyes, gauging the distance between them.

"There's my killer-diller," Jer said. "Not far from the surface, is he?"

"You've been following me," Tom said.

"I've had you followed," Jer said.

"Did you know where we were all this time?"

Jer shrugged. "I heard. I still have to report back in the evenings." He raised an ironic eyebrow. "I've got a weekend pass to help Aunt Chrissy look for you. I think your mom's read one too many Agatha Christies. She just expects the cops to haul me off because she has a bunch of bad transcripts. She thinks I don't know she's hired another rinky-dink PI to –"

"You knew where we were. You didn't help us," Tom said. "Why?"

"Why did you move the bodies? Why did you take the tapes?"

Tom flinched.

"Exactly. You don't trust me. And I have to say, Tom, after all we've been through, I'm hurt," Jer said, not sounding hurt. Sounding smug and cheerful now that he was holding all the cards again.

"I don't want to kill Firebug," Tom said.

"You reap what you sow," Jer said.

Tom didn't know what that meant, if it was a message intended for Firebug or for him.

"Mel and Paulie don't go anywhere until you clean up your mess." Jer offered him the pistol again.

The weight of the gun was strangely comforting. Tom hugged it to his chest. "They go home."

"We all go home. We never speak of this again," Jer said. "And everyone lives happily ever after."

<hr />

The hefty man opened the back doors of the van and the cage shrieked as it was dragged along the van's floor. Paulie nursed Mel in the passenger's side of the van, guarded by the skinny man. Leo lay on his side, his eyes locked at a point directly in front of him.

"Little men with big mouths and greedy girlfriends," Jer said. "But hey, who am I to judge? A girl needs her stash, and Leo's not exactly boyfriend of the year."

They followed the long parallel drag marks leading off up the slight incline. Flies buzzed around bright red splotches that matted the bent grass. A small plane throbbed overhead, a yellow button of colour low to the horizon. Firebug's pistol was heavy and slick in Tom's sweating hands.

"Ready?" Jeremy said.

We never took any home videos of Mel, Tom thought. Lack of time, lack of money, lack of energy, but now she was almost one, and they had no movies of her. (Crows caw nearby in a tree unseen by the camcorder. The sun beats down at them from a steep angle. Firebug kneels. His hands are cuffed behind his back. His bare feet are nailed in place with spikes. Yellowed grass sprays between his feet.)

They had a scattering of pictures, snapshots of her at other kids' birthdays, Christmas, New Year's Eve. He kept Mel's newborn picture – grumpy and blotchy and swaddled in hospital blankets – in his wallet and people made forced "ooooh" sounds. He'd made a mental note to go get a new picture of her so people could see her in all her jowly-cheeked, fuzzy-haired glory. (Jeremy takes Firebug's face in his hand, helpfully draws a large red X on his forehead with a Magic Marker.) They had a set of pictures, the Deluxe Package, waiting for them in Wal-Mart, and were saving up to pay for it so they could give everyone a Mel picture at her first birthday party. Paulie was going overboard: a magician, for Pete's sake. A tarot card reader. A psychic juggler. All volunteers, Paulie's friends, people who balanced their chakras and ate raw food to counterbalance years of using. (Firebug refuses to play for the camera, is stubbornly mute as the camcorder light picks up his sweat and mean, glittery-eyed stare.) They had a park picked out, and Paulie had asked Jazz to go early in the morning to claim the barbeque pit. Paulie had a menu. Paulie had found a Cinderella cake pan in the Sally Ann and was watching the Food Network for pointers on decorating the birthday cake, high baroque, curlicues and gilding. Late nights after exhausted days staying up to carefully print the invitations with a calligraphy pen, blue ink and ribbon, pink paper, decoupage and vellum. (Point and shoot. Point and shoot. Point and shoot. It's almost idiot-proof.) I was born last, Paulie said, after three brothers. I never got any birthday parties. She overcompensates with Mel, but Tom enjoys it, a taste of normal. (The tape is short. Tom walks into the frame. He presses Betty against Firebug's forehead to muffle the sound. The unseen crows aren't disturbed and continue to argue in the background. The recording stops.)

NOTES FROM THE AUTHOR

1. Made the Whole Thing Up

I prefer the older, bloodier versions of fairy tales. Set in Vancouver and surrounds, *Blood Sports* is an homage to the original *Hansel and Gretel*, the version where Hansel uses a finger bone from a previous victim to convince the witch he's still too skinny to eat.

For those who are curious, this story is not autobiographical or based on anyone that I know. Although I borrowed shamelessly from the stylistic conventions of social realism, this is a dark fantasy.

2. Couches I Have Slept On

Many thanks to the following for their financial support:

The Canada Council for the Arts, the B.C. Council for the Arts, the Markin-Flanagan Writer-in-Residence Programme at the University of Calgary, the Banff Centre for the Arts, Yukon

Archives & Education Writer-in-Residence Programme in the Whitehorse Public Library, and, last but never least, my parents, John and Winnie Robinson.

3. Patience Is a Virtue

My creative process involves copious drafts and partial drafts. Sometimes, deadlines notwithstanding, I abandon entire manuscripts and submit a new first draft altogether. Many thanks to my agent, Denise Bukowski, and my editors, Ellen Seligman and Jennifer Lambert of McClelland & Stewart. You are all extremely virtuous.

Eden Robinson
Kitamaat Village, B.C.
2005